ALPHA

DARK WATERS
BOOK 3

J.L. DRAKE

CAST OF CHARACTERS

- **Daniel:** Cole's father, first generation Blackstone. Married to **Sue,** Cole's mother.
- **Edison:** Cole's grandfather. Married to **Meg,** Cole's grandmother.
- **Abigail "Abby":** Mark's adopted mother, Cole's childhood nanny, house aide. Sister to **June.**
- **Dr. Reid Roberts:** House psychologist. Dating Abby.
- **General Frank Brandon:** Blackstone contact for the Army. First generation Blackstone member.
- **Zack:** First generation Blackstone member.

FAMILIES

- **Cole:** Owner of the Shadows safe house. Leader of the Blackstone special ops team. Married to **Savannah**. They have two kids, **Olivia** and **Easton**.
- **John:** Blackstone member. Married to **Sloane.**
- **Mike:** Blackstone member. Married to **Catalina.** Daughter **Gabriella.**
- **Keith:** Member of Blackstone. Married to **Lexi.** They have two kids, **Brandon and Reagan.**
- **Mark:** Blackstone member. Married to **Mia.** They have a set of twins, **Liam** and **Ethan,** and a daughter **Tabby.**
- **Paul:** Blackstone member. Deceased.
- **Dell:** North Rock member. Dusk Safehouse in North Carolina.

- **Davie:** North Rock member. Dusk Safehouse in North Carolina.
- **Steve Chamness:** North Rock member. Dusk Safehouse in North Carolina.
- **Denton Barlow:** The American. Deceased.

ANIMALS

- **Goats:** Friendly reminders of home.
- **Chickens:** Annoying and always in the way.
- **Scoot:** A-hole house cat.
- **Butters:** Mark and Mia's Husky.
- **Tripper:** John and Sloane's German shepherd.

~~To the hollow parts of our hearts, this is for you.~~

Screw it…

When you get to the end, if you're upset, please direct all negative emotions to Liz Clark and Jamie Johnson.

Any positive emotions, direct my way. I'll gladly accept it.

Happy Reading.

ONE

ERIC

"You're never gonna make it," she snarled from the back seat, and I stole a hasty glance at her pissy face in the rearview mirror. I needed to concentrate on the washed-out road in front of me and knew I didn't have much time. Normally, I'd be thrilled the rain had returned to cool off this Godforsaken country, but the thought of who I had in the back had me in more of a sweat than I cared to think about. I needed to get behind the protected gates of my house. The wipers beat across the windshield, and I squinted at the quickly forming river ahead of me. My phone rang, and I stuck it between my shoulder and my chin as I quickly put the car in reverse.

"Stick to the opposite shoulder, gun it, and get the fuck out of there," a voice screamed at me. One of Castillo's men, I assumed. I tossed the phone on the passenger seat, lined up my wheels on the shoulder, and gunned it. Water started to seep around my boots as my passenger shrieked, and I could feel the pressure of her feet as she propped them up out of the water.

"You're crazy!" she yelped.

She had no idea.

I shifted into four-wheel drive. A plume of water flew out behind me as I plowed along the edge of the steadily rising water. Finally, all four wheels were clear, but I never slowed down until I hit the city limits. I took the turns hard as I wove up the hill and finally took a deep breath as I drove through the wrought iron gates to my house.

I reached for my phone as my men approached the car, but I hopped out and held up a hand to stop them.

"I got her." I opened the door. "How do you wanna do this?" I immediately saw fight flicker in her eyes as she took me in. "You're highly outnumbered, so we can get you inside, cleaned up, and settled, or you can make a scene. Believe me, lady, you'll be the one who'll end up getting hurt. Your ass'll be inside one way or another. It's up to you how." I watched her weigh the odds. If I'd learned anything over the years about the kind of woman Blackstone attracted, I knew it wasn't going to be easy. These women were a tough lot, and if I gave her an inch, I knew she'd take advantage of it. I had to set the ground rules now.

When she didn't move, I reached for her hand. She'd been waiting for that and tried to headbutt me. I wasn't stupid and was ready for her. She wouldn't be the first woman who'd tried that one on me. What I didn't expect was as she fell, she twisted hard and caught me with her shoulder. I stepped back quickly and let her fall to the ground hard. Her knees hit first and then her hands. She spat like a cat and screamed obscenities. I was impressed by her repertoire, but I was done with her, and I was pissed when I heard a snicker from one of my soldiers.

"Done yet?" She tried to kick out, but I carefully stepped out of the way. Her feet were still tied, so she could only do so much. Rain beat down on her as she looked up at me in fury and her hair hung in strings over her face. I'd had enough, so I grabbed her and threw her over my shoulder and carried her kicking and screaming toward the house.

"Get your asses back inside," I yelled at the men as I went by them.

Alejandro gave a quick, low whistle as I entered the house and I glanced at him. He moved his gaze to a few men I hadn't met before. I wasn't a newbie in this business and immediately understood what I was up against. They sat at a table pretending not to notice me. Smoke from their cigarettes swirled thick above them as they played a card game.

I glared at them as I hauled the woman through the room and down the stairs. I dumped her on the bed in the cage and held her still with my foot. Leo, one of my men, had left the needle on the small table ready for me, and I grabbed it and gave it a flick.

"No, no!" She started to panic, but I grabbed her arm and injected the drug under her skin. Within seconds, she went limp, and I sat beside her on the bed to catch my breath.

"Little wildcat," Leo chuckled, "hope this cage holds up."

"Take off her shoes," I ordered as I ignored his comments about what she might look like underneath her clothes. "Socks too." I cut the ropes and examined the raw marks on her wrists and ankles. I rubbed cream into the red areas, then, satisfied, I decided to give her a second shot that contained pain meds. I knew the journey wouldn't have been easy, and the bruises on her arms and cheek told me she she'd put up a fight.

I didn't know who grabbed these women from the streets, and I didn't need to know, but it pissed me off when they were marked up. Time was money, and it took time to get them ready for sale. This particular woman concerned me more than usual, and I sure as hell wasn't going to be blamed if she was scarred up.

"What about her shirt?" He grinned at me.

"No." I shook my head. When she woke, I didn't want her to find herself undressed and think I was some kind of creep who did shit to her while she was drugged.

"Whatever. I'll just watch the reruns." He chuckled, and as I shot him a questioning look, he pointed at a camera in the corner of the room. I didn't react but swept my eyes around the room. I could see a few cameras had been installed while I was away.

Fucking Castillo.

I stood, about to rip them out of the wall, but stopped myself. Who was to say there weren't any more? Maybe this was a test, and if there were cameras, maybe there were mics around too.

Castillo: I need a proof of life.

Eric: I said no cameras.

Castillo: It's merely a precaution.

Eric: Bullshit.

I thought for a moment then took out my switch-blade and carved an oval on the wall then cut in my recently designed signature tag. I stepped back and snapped a quick photo of her with my mark in the background.

"Why'd you do that?" Leo came up behind me.

"Proof of life, *amigo*, and I feel like playin' the game this time."

"The game?" He looked puzzled.

"Who made the biggest score, who made the loudest noise. You know, like in the media. This," I snapped a few photos, making sure the light was perfect, "is for braggin' rights. You never heard of a tag?" When he shook his head, I pointed to the oval with my initials inside. "It shows she's held by me," I rubbed my finger over the engraving, "Eric Noah's possession. Braggin' rights."

"Kinda like a signature on artwork without sharing your name."

"Precisely, and if she isn't art in our world, I don't know what is." I laughed and sent the photo to Castillo and a few others then flipped on the TV to an American news channel.

"Impressive." He grinned and went to slap me on the back but thought better of it and backed off.

I dragged over a plastic tub and set it next to her bed. I pulled out some clothes, a water bottle, and a pair of flip flops.

"A tracksuit?" He looked at the black pants and over-sized hoodie with a raised eyebrow.

"Do you ever shut the fuck up?" I'd kept enough women here to know they were more comfortable in sweats. Something warm that didn't show their womanly shape. It was too tempting for the men around them, and I didn't need the hassle. My part of the operation was to keep them as clean and safe as possible until they were sold off to Chili, who could do whatever the hell he did with them.

"I'm just sayin' maybe something silky would be better." He reached out and fingered her shirt.

"Know your place," I warned him and batted his hand away. I wasn't sure I could trust him with a caged woman in the place. "You touch her, and I'll break your fingers, individually, with a hammer."

"Sure, sure, I hear you." He put his hands in the air. "I'm just sayin'."

"Well, don't." I pointed at the door, and he left with a quick glance back at her. My gut told me he shouldn't be allowed down there at all, not even with someone else. I had a reputation to uphold, and I wasn't about to let some punk kid ruin it for me.

The woman stirred just as I stepped out and locked the cage using a five-digit code. I didn't trust she couldn't pick a lock, and at least she couldn't see when I entered in the numbers. Only a few would know the code. One could never be too careful.

Her eyes fluttered open, and she shot straight up, then heaved over and gagged. I knew after the drugs she'd had, she might get sick. I could have warned her to take it slow, but I knew it would be pointless. Her feet hit the floor, and she tried to stand then fell forward on her hands and knees with a moan. She put a hand to her head and sat up.

"If you sit still and take small sips of water, it'll help with the side effects," I said calmly.

Her head whipped over to me, and her hair fell over one eye as she blinked her anger at me.

"Or maybe you don't drug me at all." She lowered her head and tried to fight it.

"Okay, look." I eased onto the table and felt a weariness come over me. This part of the process exhausted me. "Let's look at this from my point of view. You're here in a cage, and I'm here outside the cage. Clearly, I've done this before. I'm very good at it, by the way. I know what I'm talking about. So, if you just sit back and drink some water, maybe you'll see I'm just trying to make this easier on you."

"Screw you." She puffed and managed to stand for a moment then allowed herself to sink to the bed.

"Fine." I sighed deeply. "Clean clothes are there, water is there, and there's food on the table." I pointed. "If you're done trying to prove to me how tough you are, I'll leave you be. In the meantime," I stood, "smile for the cameras."

I waved over my head and as I walked out. I eyed the cameras to see how they were being used.

"Wait." She called me back. I almost kept going but thought about it and turned around, then as I walked toward the cage, I nudged a paintbrush forward a bit on the floor with the toe of my boot. "Can I get some sugar?"

"Sugar?" I pretended to entertain her odd request so I could take a moment to move the bucket that stood against the wall a bit closer to the cage. "Why would you want sugar?"

"I have low sugars, and I faint easily." I could see the lie but used it to my advantage as I pretended to think about it. I scuffed a mark in the dust with my heel.

"I'll see what I have." She nodded, and I headed back toward the stairs.

Pedro, one of Castillo's higher-ranked soldiers, watched me as I came toward him. He put his cards down on the table. I grabbed him by the hair and yanked his head back, and with the other hand I snatched the cigarette from his mouth and put in out on the side of his neck. He bucked straight up, but I used my weight to slam him back in the chair.

"Have some fucking respect in someone's home," I hissed and tossed him backward in his chair. He toppled onto his back then leapt to his feet where he was met with my gun in his face. "You're here to watch over this place, so fucking do it!"

I pulled out my phone and called Castillo.

"How's she settling in?" Castillo mused from wherever he was.

"If you insist on your dogs being here, they stay outside," I seethed inches from Pedro's face. "This is my house, and you hire me to do my job, now I have to have your pets and your cameras invading my space?" I shouted and knew I hovered the line of disrespect, but I didn't care. "We had a deal, and you broke it."

He went quiet, and I half expected him to walk through my front door with guns blazing.

"Eric," his tone changed to a quieter one, "the cameras are for us."

"I don't seem to have a link to the feed."

"I'm sending it now." A moment later, my phone vibrated, and I saw a link had been shared with me. "I know things are different with this one, but you must understand, Eric, one can never be too careful. She is, after all, a Blackstone bitch."

"Yeah, thanks for the heads up on that one, by the way." While I talked, I motioned with my gun to Alejandro, and he stepped forward and began to herd Pedro and his buddies outside. I gave him a nod as I moved to my office. "The bitch told me on our drive here."

"Interesting." He seemed amused. "Was she feisty?"

"A bit." I knew I'd better feed him the truth on that. I still wasn't sure what he could see and hear. I also knew he liked his women a bit wild, and I didn't want to stimulate his imagination. I used my fingerprint to open my Mac and clicked on the link. It brought me to the basement cameras.

"Hang on. I have a call coming through," he rasped, and I rolled my eyes as I was placed on hold. While I waited, I grabbed a pencil and sketched out the basement room in my notebook. Then I quickly made notes of all the blind spots the cameras couldn't see. Only half the bucket could be seen, the paintbrush was in full view, but the line next to the cage where my chair was tucked in the far back corner was completely hidden. Whoever installed the cameras didn't put much thought into where they were pointed. I turned up the volume, and it crackled a bit then cleared, and I could only hear some white noise. All of that told me it wasn't hardwired. The fact that it was more than likely wi-fi connected worked in my favor. The phone in my ear went live as Castillo clicked back on.

"I have some guests arriving soon. I have to go."

"Wait, what's her name? Which Blackstone member is her husband? How can I sell her with no information?"

"You're not selling her." He chuckled. "We'll pump her for information then dispose of the bitch."

TWO

IVY

The sound of people talking brought me back. I was in a heap on the floor of my office. I desperately tried to clear the fog that held me captive.
Was he gone?
I strained to listen, too scared to move. Silence. My teeth started to chatter as pain made its way through my consciousness. I felt it build as I lay there.
"Oww." I started to cry but instantly went quiet when I heard a noise. I was simply too terrified to move as I stayed where I had been left, by him.
"You know what I'm capable of, Dr. Knight." His threat came back to me in one horrific flash, and I blinked as the memory of it all overwhelmed me. I remembered how I watched him as he went through

my purse then held up my ID. I knew it had my home address on it. "You open your mouth, and I'll kill you." I'd never forget the look on his face.

Stop.

I forced my eyes open to take in the room. I saw my chair, the one my mother had so proudly given me when I moved into this office. It now lay on its side with two broken legs. My lovely glass office table was shattered, and the desk looked like a tornado had hit it straight on.

With all my might, I sat upright. My head pounded, and I gently touched it. My fingers felt around a large, tender goose egg, and when I looked at my hand, it was covered in blood.

I brushed the wet hair from my eyes and carefully toed off my heel. I tried not to make any noise as I used the wall to help me stand. I forced through the vertigo and eyed the closed door to my personal bathroom. Slowly, with shaky knees, I moved across the room, took a deep breath, and pulled the door open. It was heavy and creaked on its hinges, and I felt my heart beat my rib cage with the force of a baseball bat.

As soon as I saw it was empty, I lunged across the room for my phone. My fingers were slick with blood as I madly tried to swipe the screen open. Finally, I took a second to wipe them clean on my shirt, and with a desperate swipe, I was awarded an open screen.

One, two, three…finally, on the fourth ring, he picked up.

"Ivy?"

"Uncle," I tried to make sense, "I, I don't know what happened, but he was here, and—"

"Who was there?" His voice turned serious. "Where are you?"

"I'm at my office. Reid, please…" Suddenly, my office door opened, and his murderous eyes found me.

"Noo!" I screamed.

I jolted awake and sucked in a lungful of air as I took in my surroundings.

"Welcome back." Mark studied me from the front seat. "Sounds like you were somewhere dark?"

"No," I sat up straight and ran a hand through my hair to catch my breath, "I'm good." I must have slipped off to sleep. I pulled my laptop up off the floor and tucked my paperwork back into my bag. I glanced at the time and saw Ty should have landed by now. He'd taken the redeye to New York, and I was concerned that he'd barely said anything to me before he left.

I unconsciously reached up and touched my head where the goose egg once resided. That night had been one of the scariest of my life, and until things were resolved, I knew I'd continue to be in this tailspin of flashbacks.

"I used to have nightmares." My hand dropped away as Mark eased forward from the stoplight. "Every time I closed my eyes, there was my mother dead on our couch." He cleared his throat. "You want to know what I did to make them go away?"

"Let me guess. You saw a doctor?" I tried to curb my annoyance that he'd seen me at such a weak moment.

"Nope, I faced it." He looked at me in the mirror. "I know you're dealing with something. That's obvious. We've all seen Frank talking to you privately. But I also know it's none of my business."

"It's not like I'm trying to hide from it," I muttered. "It's just taking a long time for something to happen—at least for my part in it to happen." That was partly true.

"Oh, it's court related." He scrunched his face and nodded as he hit the nail on the head. "Savi's been there."

"So I've heard." I hated that I sounded rude, but I was not happy on this topic. Always having to be cryptic, the secret was growing old. I was trained to get people to open up and talk about their problems, and here I was having to dance around my own issues. I hated that I had to suppress it all. I felt like a hypocrite. It was totally unfair.

"Did Savi tell you what I did to help her get through that pissed off feeling you have right now?"

"No." I sighed heavily and caught his grin in the mirror.

Mark chuckled but held up a hand to end the conversation as he pulled into a parking space near the bus stop. We both could see Olivia happily chatting with her friends and their parents as they gathered in the parking lot. She was leaving for Girl Scout camp. I hopped out of the truck when I spotted the Logans as they watched from the edge of the group. I was glad they'd called us so we could catch Olivia before she left. We'd been on our way to run some errands when we got the call that they were here.

"Uncle Mark?" Olivia threw herself at him. "I thought I missed you."

"Me?" He beamed down at her. "Let my Livi leave without a hug? Please, child." She hugged him again then reached over and hugged me, too.

"Have a wonderful trip, sweetie." I'd barely planted a kiss on the top of her head before she raced off at the sight of another of her friends.

"Are we sure about this?" Savannah threw an uneasy look at Cole.

"You think I'd let her go if I wasn't?" He nodded to a woman, and when she bent over to grab a bag, I saw she was carrying her sidearm. "I hired two undercovers." He grinned.

"And Liv has no clue, right?" Savi eyed her husband. "Because we agreed she was going to have a normal run-of-the-mill kid trip."

"Ten bucks," Mark leaned in close to whisper, "Liv's already spotted them and knows their history."

"You think?" I eyed him then held out my hand to take the bet.

"Liv," he called, and she bounced over with her friend trailing behind, "you feelin' good about this trip?"

"Yes. Oh, Dad, thanks so much for letting me go." She beamed at her parents and wrapped Cole in a hug.

She trotted over, and I could tell she caught Mark's mischievous expression. She looked carefully at him then at me.

"Well, all set? Everything good with the trip?" Mark asked. She playfully rolled her eyes.

"Poor Ivy." She glared at him. "How much did he bet you?"

"Ten." I smirked. Lord, she was good. "Have you spotted them?"

"No, but I know they're here. Dad would never let me go anywhere without someone. I don't care." She shrugged. "I'm just excited to be going with all my friends!"

"And that's all you should be thinking about," I added.

"I gotta share something with you, Ivy." She looked very serious. "Anytime my uncle bets you on something, never take it."

"Hey," Mark playfully pushed her arm, "you can't tell her that. That's my thing."

"I thought eating was your thing." She giggled and turned to her friend. "Ivy, this is Milly and her dad, Callen." A tall man stepped forward and rested his hands on his daughter's shoulders.

"Dad, this is who I was telling you about." Milly grinned up at him. Callen was quite handsome, strong arms and jawbone, pleasant smile, green eyes, almost red hair.

"Ah, yes, the famous, Dr. Ivy Knight." He smiled at me. "I've heard a lot about you."

"I can assure you none of it's true," I joked and shook his hand. "Nice to meet you, Callen."

"Isn't she pretty?" Milly whispered, and I felt my cheeks warm. "Do it, Dad."

Oh, God. I looked at Mark, whose eyes were now slits as he studied Callen. I knew he was thinking of Ty. I made a show to roll my wrist and check the time, thankful I'd worn my watch. Sometimes the simplest things could give you that moment you needed.

"Please excuse me. I have a session in fifteen, and if we don't leave now, I'll be late. We just took a quick side trip to come and wish Olivia good luck on her trip." I turned to Olivia. "I hope you have a wonderful time. I can't wait to hear all about it when you get back."

"Deal." She hugged me again and danced over to her parents.

"Ivy," Callen ran a hand through his hair, "maybe we can go for coffee sometime?" He held out his card, and I took it, not wanting to be rude. "Or maybe ice cream." He smiled. "The girls have been filling me in on what you like."

"Oh, really?" I eyed Milly, who winked at me. "I'll remember that."

"Lovely meeting you." He steered Milly away, and I glanced at Mark. He looked unimpressed.

"What?"

"Don't what me," he scoffed and followed me back to the car. "You flirted with him."

"I wasn't flirting. I was being nice."

"To a guy, that's flirting."

"So, I have to be rude to someone," I opened the door and hopped in the back seat, "so I'm not sending mixed signals?"

"Yes." He started the engine.

"That's ridiculous."

"I didn't make the rules, Ivy. That's how it is." He pulled out into traffic.

"And men say women are complicated." I rolled my eyes and lifted the lid to my laptop.

"We're not complicated," he went on. "We're very simple creatures once you understand us."

"Oh, please enlighten me," I huffed.

"I've taught you so much already, but if I must." He took a deep breath, and I groaned dramatically. "Men need obvious clues, so when a woman looks them in the eye, answers their questions, smiles, takes their number," he looked in the mirror, "we think, 'Great. She likes me. We're on.'"

"So, you're saying by me being kind to Olivia's best friend's father, I have agreed to a date?"

"Yes."

"No."

"Yes, and because you took his number, you sealed the deal."

"I did not seal a deal!" I laughed. "Okay, tell me how I should have handled it, then."

"You should have said hi, backed up a step, and not made eye contact." He held up a finger to show he wasn't finished yet. "Then ignore him, and if he misreads your body language and still asks you out on a date, you say no, I'm dating Ty who just came back from a special ops mission in Afghanistan." He grinned. "Sprinkle a little fear around you as a barricade."

"You're insane!"

"Why?"

"I'm an outgoing person, Mark. I won't be someone I'm not." I stared at him in the mirror. "You're just protective of Ty."

"Yes, I am. That's how Blackstone works." He paused. "You should've brought up Ty. Just sayin'."

"Why do I need to bring up someone I'm casually seeing just to draw that line in the sand for someone I just met?" I huffed. "There's no ring on my finger, Mark. I can be kind and talk to whomever I want. I never said I was going to call him, and I have no plans on calling him."

"And yet you still took his number."

"Okay," I closed my eyes, tired of the argument, "truth?"

"When do you ever lie to me?" He quickly turned around with a look and made me chuckle. It was like arguing with a child.

"I really like Ty, but I also know he's got unfinished business with someone else." It was true.

I thought back over our night at Zack's. He'd draped his jacket around my shoulders, and I thought we'd made progress, then the next night he left my room when *she* called and never came back. I couldn't deny that sex with him was great, but neither of us knew if there was much more than that. I pulled myself back to Mark.

"Yeah, I mean, how can you get serious with a guy when he's got someone else on the side doing God knows what with? Why should I close the door on my life when he hasn't on his?"

"I didn't know that." His tone relaxed.

"I love that you're protective of your brothers, Mark, but I'm a good person and would never hurt or cheat on Ty. I've dated and was even engaged a few years back. I finally know what I want in a man and won't settle for less."

We sat in silence for a moment, and he tapped the wheel as he mulled over my words. He pulled into the UPS Store and parked by the door. We were here to pick up the first package I'd ordered from an online store that Savannah had put me on to. I was excited to see how well the clothes would fit. She'd explained how it brought her piece of mind to shop that way instead of having to go into the city. It got tiresome always having to watch your back. We always had to be escorted, and it was a waste of time and manpower. She was right; it certainly was a lot less stressful this way.

"I really feel like Dad should be here for this conversation." He rubbed his head.

I tapped my pen on my lap and grabbed the opportunity to change the topic. "Forgive me for not knowing all the dynamics of the house, but why do you call Daniel Dad? Wasn't it Abigail who adopted you?"

"Yeah, but he's just my dad." He shrugged.

"Then who is Sue?"

"Mom, or Sue." He popped a piece of gum in his mouth. "Abby is Abby or Mom, doesn't matter."

I laughed. "I'm confused."

"I see what you're doing here, by the way, so don't think you're off the hook about takin' that guy's number." He smiled, and I had to grin at the bright pink gum that showed between his teeth. "I'll enlighten you since I'm sure your doctor brain is spinning off its axis." I lifted a shoulder, as it in no way bothered me, but I liked the spotlight on him instead of me.

"I had a shitty mom, no real idea who my father was, and my brother—" He shook his head like the memory was too hard. "In school, all the kids had moms, dads, uncles, aunts, grandparents, but I had no extended family, at least none I knew of. So, the day I found the Logans, everything changed. I decided I wanted it all. I wanted a real family. As far as I was concerned, Abby adopted me, and I love her like no other, but I got two moms that day, and a dad, and a brother. Shit, I even got a dog." He smiled. "It might be confusing to some, but to me, it all makes sense."

"That's incredibly sweet, Mark."

"Oh, I know." He grabbed the keys. "My sweetness and this smile," he beamed wider, "it's all the Lopez charm."

"And you never changed your last name."

"Nope. That's the one thing I kept. Needed that to fuel my fight. Long story, but a reminder and some controlled anger never hurts anyone in this business."

"You really have your head on straight." I was impressed.

"I do." He reached for the door handle of the truck then hesitated and looked at me hard. "And I also know when I'm being used, so where were we?" I knew we were back on me again. "What are you looking for in a man?"

"Why? So you can give Ty an advantage?" I grinned, and he raised a brow at me and got out.

"Can't blame a guy for trying," he said as he opened the door for me, and I was blasted with the intense heat. We hurried inside. "Oh, and one more thing," he whispered. "Never let Ty come here." He pointed with his chin, and I saw her. She stood behind the counter in a red dress. Her fake boobs spilled over the top of the low neckline, and her JBF hair was so full of spray it looked like you could snap it off. "Yeah." He rolled his eyes and made a motion for me to follow him.

"Be sure to step back and not make eye contact," I whispered in his ear.

"Pfft." He threw a glare at my attempt to toss his own words back at him.

"Good morning, Mark."
"Christina." He shuddered.
Yikes.

THREE

Tstood in the back in full dress uniform where the trees offered dappled light to help me blend in. I stayed a distance away from the grieving family and friends. I had no wish to bring any attention to myself. I was thankful the temperature in Washington was cool with fall quickly approaching, and I was ready for its return.

My buddy Kit Moore spotted me and made a curious face as to why I hadn't gone to stand with the rest of them. I shook my head and looked away. I'd been asked to be a pallbearer by Brown's mother, but I'd respectfully declined her offer a few days back. I didn't feel I was worthy of such a role. After all, I hadn't returned her son to her. If she only knew.

I understood the need for a funeral and for closure,

but the knowledge that the six-foot-one casket was about to be laid to rest empty nearly tore me apart. A part of Brown was still out there, and that haunted me.

The gunshots rang out and I swallowed the knot that was lodged in my throat. With the sound of each shot, the guilt inside me grew. It was as if my friend was being shot over and over in my mind, and I could only stand there and try to bear it. I knew I needed to let it go, knew I needed to do it for my own sanity. I made myself a deal as I stood there. When I returned to Shadows, I'd double up my sessions with Doc Roberts. I knew I needed to shed this awful pain if I was ever going to be able to focus and move forward.

My eyes followed Moore as he hugged some of Brown's family members then made his way to the coffin. He reached out and squeezed the dog tags we'd ripped from our friend's neck as we ran to escape the Taliban. Frank had returned the belongings to his family shortly after we arrived back on US soil. I thought about the bottle of whiskey I'd brought home in my bag. I knew it was ours to savor. I had already broken the seal, but I waited to have a drink with Moore once he arrived. We'd save the last drink for our friend and be at peace with all this. I only hoped that day would come.

Mom approached and tentatively reached out to touch one of the medals on my uniform then looked up at me with tears in her eyes. I hunched my shoulders and leaned down as she put her arms around them and brought me into a hug.

"Why didn't you say anything?" A sob caught in her throat. I'd known this conversation was coming. "We spent that whole dinner with you in Montana, and you never mentioned it. Not even once."

"I wasn't ready." I kissed her cheek and looked over at Brown's parents. "I'm still not."

"I just wish you'd share more of what's in here." She pulled back and placed her hand on my chest. "I hope you at least talk to Kit. You boys have always been so close." She dabbed the corners of her eyes. I always found it odd when people used Moore's first name. To me, he was always Moore.

"Dad." Shelly came to my rescue. Thank God for sisters. She gave him a pointed look, and he gently moved Mom aside and gave me a hug.

"It's hard not to worry, son," he whispered. I made a mental note to try to communicate better with them. I couldn't understand why I seemed unable to share things with them. I knew I didn't want them to worry, but it was more than that. It was like I had a mental block when I was around them.

"Hey." Shelly moved close as Dad walked Mom to the car. She just stood and looked up at me for a moment. "Have you spoken to his parents yet?" We both looked over to Brown's mom where she stood with her husband. She held tight to his arm like an anchor.

"Only when I told her I didn't want to be a pallbearer." I felt horrible over that.

"Ouch." She winced.

"Yeah."

"What about Ivy?" That threw me for a loop, and I stared down at her in surprise. "I stayed behind at Zack's. She's really nice, Ty."

"Why am I only hearing about this now?" With that, she shot me a look, and I knew she had me. I never call.

"We can talk about Brown or Ivy. Your pick." She shrugged.

"She's good," I muttered and felt uneasy I hadn't known Ivy had talked with Shelly. I didn't share well, and this felt strange.

"Are you two dating?"

"I don't know." I really wasn't sure exactly what we were at this point.

"Okay." She nodded. "Well, all I'll say is this. Ivy seems a hell of a lot more stable than Demi."

"Agreed." I nodded and scanned the faces around me. I wished I could catch Moore's eye and get him to step in with my sister. He was the chatty one, not me.

"Then why haven't you cut Demi loose?"

"I tried."

"No, you didn't." She rolled her eyes. "She's like a golden retriever. Doesn't matter how many times you throw the ball, she'll keep coming back for more, until you shut the damn door on her. So do it. Tell her you've moved on to, I don't know, Ivy."

"Shelly," I warned. I didn't want to have this conversation here. I didn't want it at all.

"I'm just trying to prep you."

"Prep me for what?"

"For the fact that Demi's here, and I'm sure she'll want to spend the night with you."

"What?" I didn't need any more stress, and I could feel my anger build.

"She doesn't take *no* very easily, Ty."

"Fuck me."

"Look, Mom and Dad found a cute little spot to rent in Redstone. I tried to talk them out of it, but…they want more of you. They get me all the time." She chuckled then leaned in and hugged me. "I know you have a lot going on, but please do me a favor and make a little time for them." She waited for me to answer.

I gave a quick nod, and she got tight-lipped but seemed satisfied with that. She pulled her coat tight around her as she walked away.

I caught Moore's eye, and he said goodbye to someone and started toward me, but before he could reach me, Brown's mother suddenly appeared. Her face was that of a woman who was utterly broken inside. Her weathered eyes and worn-out stance told me I needed to make things right with her.

"Mrs. Brown," I cleared my throat, "I'm…" My words got tangled, and all I could see was my best friend looking back at me through her glossy gaze. "I'm so sorry I couldn't bring him home."

She went to open her mouth, but her husband appeared and took her arm. He stuck a finger in my face.

"I've been hearin' things, Ty." His chin quivered. "Is it

true you were there when our son died?" I nodded slowly. "That the man who shot him was under your command? Did you see what happened? Do you know the truth?"

"Yes." I nodded again.

"And?" he nearly shouted.

"It's my word against his." I swallowed.

"But you were the captain. Shouldn't that count for something?"

"He's got a buddy giving him an alibi." I clenched my fists.

"I heard you got a promotion." He glared at me in sudden fury, and I could see spit in the corner of his mouth. "I would hate to think you got promoted so you'd help cover up my son's death."

"Stop," his wife whispered and put a hand on his arm. He'd gone too far, and she knew it. His words cut deep. "They were friends. Roger, you know Ty would never—"

"Brown was my best friend." I cut her off and spoke through clenched teeth. "I tried everything to stop what happened. I gave my statement when I got back here, and he gave his. I'm trying to find a way to prove it, and I haven't given up. I won't."

"I don't care what you have to do." He stepped closer, and I raised my chin. "If that filth doesn't pay for what he did, I'll put a bullet in his skull myself." His body shook. "He was your brother. Do something, for Christ's sake!"

Our loud voices had begun to attract attention, and Mrs. Brown tugged her husband's arm.

"We need to go, Roger." She glanced at me. "Make this right, Ty. Only you can."

They turned and left me there. My fists vibrated at my sides as I stood there filled with remorse. I could only imagine what they thought now that they knew. They thought I'd stood there and let my friend be killed while I did nothing.

"Jesus," Moore muttered, "that was harsh."

"No," I shook my head, "they're not wrong. I was the only one there. I'm the only one who can make this right."

"Come on," Moore pointed with his head, "let's go get a drink. It's close. We can walk."

I nodded and walked with him. As we got close to the street, I saw Shelly, who waved me off. She'd gone to run interference for me with Demi. I gave a little wave and veered right. Moore caught on quickly and followed.

"I heard your mom talking to your dad about renting a place in Redstone." Moore tried to fill the silence and stop the loop that plagued both our heads.

"That's what I hear."

"That'll be nice," he mumbled. "It wouldn't hurt to have your family close."

"You sure about that?" I glanced at him.

"I am." He shook his head. "You've hidden yourself away in Afghanistan for nearly a decade, then you finally return to the States for good, and a few days into it, you disappear to the mountains."

"You act like I'm running."

"Are you?" I could feel his eyes burn into my head.

"No." I let out a puff of air as my emotions rose to the surface. "I just don't do family well."

"Does *Ivy* know that?" I wavered in my step, and he smirked. "Your sister. She tried to dig to find out what I knew."

Seriously?

"Why's my life so damn interesting to everyone?"

"Because it's a mystery to those who love you." He gave me a hip check as he grinned.

"Apparently." I held my hand up to stop a car as we entered a crosswalk. We made a beeline for the bar and waded through the crowd outside.

The bar was just getting busy when we got inside. We found a table in the back and nodded at a few others we'd seen at the funeral. One waved us to come over, but when I shook my head, his friend motioned at him to give us space.

A few beers in, and I finally relaxed a bit. A young woman strummed a guitar and sang quietly. I recognized an old Dean Martin song.

I wanted to change the subject so we could get off the topic of me.

"You sign the paperwork yet?"

"I sent them back over to Frank last night." Moore grinned around his bottle. "Sounds like I'll be there before you know it."

"Good." I rubbed my head, thankful I was about to have someone to watch my back.

"Now that I've signed everything, care to share a bit about the house? Or maybe about any lady interests?" He held my gaze for a moment, and I knew he and my fucking sister had a longer conversation than I had realized.

"Fuck." I muttered, and he laughed at my expense.

"What does Demi think of your new girlfriend?"

"She's not my girlfriend," I hesitated, "but she's something," I admitted. "As for Demi," I shrugged, "you know perfectly well we were just friends with benefits. It suited us both."

"Right, but apparently, she not only showed up for dinner in Montana with your family, but also it seems she's here. Nice job slipping past her, by the way." He lifted his beer mug and clicked mine.

"I didn't—" I paused and remembered who I was talking to. "It didn't feel great."

"Because you're not an ass." He took sympathy on me. "But in all seriousness, if you want to be with someone else, just tell Demi. Because she's obviously past the friends with benefits thing and has got you in her sights."

"I know." I rubbed my face again.

"So, tell me." His mood lightened, and I knew he was trying to keep the topic light for both of us. "Are there any hot chicks at the house?"

"They're all hot, but they're also all married with kids."

"You mean all but Ivy?" I rolled my eyes and tried not to let my mind go back to the funeral. "Give me something here, Ty. What's Ivy like?"

"Why do you care?" I smirked.

"I've known you since grade school, and I know your reputation with the ladies, my friend. I know you always date for a while then break up with them as soon as they want something more from you."

"That was high school."

"And when we joined the military," he reminded me, "you met Demi and hung on to her for sex and nothing more. Now here you are, living in the same house as a woman you're sleeping with. The writing's on the wall, so to speak. This isn't you. So, what makes her different?"

Her gorgeous face popped up in front of me, and I suddenly wished I had her in my arms, and not just under me to curb the pain I was carrying.

"I don't know," I lied. I wasn't about to try to explain it to him when I didn't know myself. "She just is."

"So, say I told you that she told Shelly she was meeting up with someone named Justin, you wouldn't mind? I mean, Ivy going on a date with someone else." My face fell, and he rolled his eyes and took a big swig of his beer. "Is this how it's gonna be?"

"You're an ass." I cleared my throat and felt the sudden anger fade away. "And you and Shelly are officially shut off from talkin' to one another."

"That'll never happen," he assured me. "But

remember I know you better than anyone else, so you better be nice, or I'll feed Ivy some information on you."

"Watch it, my friend, or I might be forced to find some exposed mountaintops," I teased, but I could see the darkness that comment brought him, to both of us.

"Those were some bad times, weren't they?"

"Yeah." I nodded, and the sadness we'd just forced away swept back in. "Once you're settled at the house, let's have a drink for us and Brown."

"I couldn't agree more." He laughed a little too heartily in an attempt to keep the mood light and finished off the rest of his beer. "This new chapter will be interesting for both of us."

"Can't wait to have you back, brother." We paid our tab and headed back outside.

I grabbed a cab and went with Moore to the airport. I found it hard to say goodbye, but I knew it would only be a short time until he joined me at Shadows. I was more than ready to focus on building my own team.

I tried to decide if I should stick around town for a bit or see if I could get an earlier flight. I decided on an earlier flight and went back to the hotel to grab my suitcase. I stood in the lobby and checked the time to see how far away my driver was.

"Ty?" Her voice made my shoulders tense, but I turned to her. Demi stood dressed to kill, and I tried not to react. "I forgot how sexy you look in your uniform." I moved toward her. I didn't want to be a jerk. She'd come all this way to support me, and I'd just ducked out on her.

"Would you like to get some coffee?" I could cancel the car.

"Coffee or a hotel room?" She smiled hopefully as she held up a hotel key card. I ran my tongue over my teeth then cleared my throat as my taxi pulled up out front.

"All right. Just let me cancel the taxi." I indicated the car out front. I jogged out and handed him a bill then waved him off. I hoped I wasn't making a mistake.

"Give me a sec." She smiled as she held up her phone. "I just need to take this. Won't be a sec." She threw me a kiss, and I sat back in a lobby chair to wait. As I questioned myself about what the hell I was doing, I slipped into a memory.

"Ooowee!" Brown wiggled his eyebrows at me as he elbowed Moore in the ribs. "Seems someone's got eyes for Beckett."

"Where?" Moore didn't miss a beat and craned his neck to see.

"Your three."

I followed their line of sight and saw a woman with long dark hair and seductive eyes. There was no doubt they were on me; I could feel the heat. Her breasts were on display, and she looked to be on the prowl.

"Not really my type," I muttered and looked down at my beer.

"No?" Brown smirked. "Yeah, hot as shit women aren't mine either," he mocked me.

"*Twenty she's a freak in the sheets and wins him over by the end of the night.*" *Moore slapped a twenty down.*

I gladly took the beer the waitress held out and downed more than half of it.

"*Oh, shit, here she comes,*" *Brown hissed.* "*Jesus, she's a tiger! Be ready, Beckett. This one's got some balls.*"

Fuck me. Fine, here we go. *I figured, what the hell. I hadn't had a woman in nearly thirteen months, so this could be a good break for me.*

I waited for her to sit, and she did, right on my lap. She pulled the beer out of my hand and took a sip while those eyes burned through me. She was just the kind of woman I needed right now. She seemed to want control. I wondered how hard it would be to get her to submit. This could be fun.

I let my mouth run to see how she'd handle it.

"*I don't date. I'm not lookin' for serious. My work's my only priority.*"

"*So, we're on the same page,*" *she purred.*

Okay. I took it farther.

"*I don't do romance. I like control in bed, and I won't call for anything but a hookup.*"

"*Should I give you my number now or later?*" *she challenged and pulled out a card from her cleavage. She stared me down as she tapped it with a long red nail.*

I suddenly felt bad. I was being a selfish prick, and

she didn't seem to care. I thought I'd give it one more go.

"Listen, I'm not lookin' for anyone. If you want me, it'd be just for sex, nothin' else."

"Just tell me when and where." She held up the card. "Demi."

Fuck. I took it.

"Ty," I gritted and downed my beer then stood. "Coming?"

"I hope so." She smirked, and I heard the gasps as my buddies reacted to that one.

"I'll take that." I slid the twenty from under Moore's hand. "Order me another beer in about twenty." I took Demi's hand and headed for my truck as Moore sputtered after me that he'd won.

I started the engine to warm the air, and before I could get a word out, she straddled me, and her tongue was in my mouth. At first, she naturally took control, but when I pinned her wrists and made her submit, she gave in. We were both looking for something and took it. No apologies. It was fast, straight to the point, and little to no romance. It was all I wanted.

When we were finished, she climbed off me, wiped herself with a tissue, and pulled down her skirt. Her cheeks were flushed. "I knew you'd be good."

"Are you sure you're okay with this?" I couldn't help but ask again. There was no way I could allow myself to get emotionally invested in anyone.

"Relax, Ty." She flipped down the visor and fixed her wild hair. "We all have needs, and you're serving mine just fine. So, we're good." She smiled at me. "How long you home for?"

"Three weeks."

"Where are you staying?"

"I have a place in town."

"Good. Me too." She grabbed a marker from the dash and scribbled her address on my forearm. "When you're not visiting family, call me, and I'll keep you company." She winked and hopped out, and I watched her walk back toward the bar with an over-the-top swing in her hips. I smiled and had to admit I was much more relaxed than I'd been only a few minutes earlier.

Little did I know Demi would develop feelings for me at a time when I'd just found what I wanted with someone else.

She put her phone in her purse and walked toward me with a smile as she waved her hotel key card.

"Just coffee." I stood and shook off the memory. Her face fell, but she recovered quickly and fell into step with me. We walked down the sidewalk toward a small bistro I'd spotted earlier.

We ordered and stood there until we were handed our coffees then took a seat by the window. My head spun with the day's events. The memory of Mrs. Brown's haunted face and her husband's words sat heavily like a nasty wound in the center of my chest. As usual, I fumbled around inside to come up with something to say but found nothing, and the silence hung between us.

"I thought I wasn't going to catch you," she finally said. Her smile soon faded when I didn't respond. "Are you okay?"

"Today was hard," I managed.

"Okay, I get that, but are *we* all right?"

I stared into my coffee. I wanted to get up and leave the bistro and never look back. Conversation had never come easily to me, and I really wanted to avoid this one.

"Ty," she reached out and covered my hand, "I'm sorry about your friend, but I can't help but feel you're pulling away from everyone who loves you."

Love? I felt my throat tighten. When did this happen? When had we ever been more than casual fuck buddies?

"Your mom was devastated when she found out about Brown. Why didn't you say anything when we were all at dinner?" I blinked a few times as I still struggled with just how I got here with Demi. Why was she talking to my mother so much? When had we crossed that line in the sand I thought we both had drawn years ago?

"I'm a private person, Demi," I tried to get my words out right, "and my head isn't on straight anymore."

"So you've said." She grinned as she leaned across the table to get closer to me. "And why do you think that is?"

"What?" I hated that she muddled my train of thought.

"Since you've been back, we haven't had any alone

time. We both know what you need when you get back from that hellhole. You need someone who will give in to those needs." Her mouth lifted at the corners, and her expression changed to a sexy, devious one. "Someone who isn't scared when you lose control and—"

I felt a vibration and pulled out my phone to see a text from Frank.

> Frank: I pulled a favor for you. Your flight leaves in one hour. I emailed you the details.

"Shit," I stood quickly, "I have to go."

"Ty," Demi reached across and caught my hand, "when can I see you again?"

"I don't know." I stopped myself. "Look, Demi. You know what I really want from you?"

"Anything." Her eyes looked desperate, and I felt like shit.

"I want you to find someone who makes you happy." I leaned in and kissed her head. "You deserve that, but that person isn't me."

"So, just like that, this is over?" Hurt flashed across her face.

"Look, I'll be honest. I met someone else." I twisted my wrist to glance at the time again and I heard her sniff.

"Well," she stood, "I hope she knows what she's in for, because your heart's black, Ty Beckett, and you have a history of hurting those who open up to you."

"I know."

"I want to meet her." My stomach sank with disbelief at her words. *No.*

"Demi, I never meant to hurt you, and you'll make someone happy someday, but that someone isn't me. You know, I've tried being honest about my feelings, and I'm sorry you crossed that line, but I never did." I held up my ticket. "This wasn't how I saw this happening, but please understand I've got to catch this flight."

She called out after me as I grabbed my suitcase and hurried out the door.

I caught a cab and rushed to the airport, glad I could skip the long line at check-in since I only had a carryon. The TSA were polite, I was sure thanks to my uniform, and whisked me through to the gate.

> Frank: When you get to the airport, call me.

I quickly tapped his name and listened for the call to connect.

"Hey, Ty, how was Brown's funeral?"

"Rough." I paused. "Look, Frank..." I hesitated, not sure how to ask the question. It was something I had to do, and I needed him to know how important it was to me. "I need permission to dig further into Hill. I need to do a lot more. This thing is eating me up. I have to do something."

There was a moment of silence as I heard a door shut.

"That's why I wanted you to call me. I've heard a few things—"

"Such as?" I was all ears, desperate for anything.

"Ty, before I fill you in, I need you back at Shadows. You're on the clock as of tomorrow morning, so don't miss your flight. Although I want you to keep me in the loop, this is something you chase on your own time. Got it?"

"Understood."

"I think the best way to handle this is to not draw too much attention to yourself. He knows you're not giving up, but you don't need him covering his ass more than he already is."

"All right." Something strange passed through me. "Is something going on over there I don't know about?"

"It's Sam, Hill's brother."

"I figured."

"How much do you know about him?"

"Enough to know he's shady as shit," I growled, thinking how crap ran in families.

"That he is. I did a little digging on him, talked to a few people I know over there who work in the courts. They've had their eyes on Sam for a while. Trouble is when you're on the side of the law, things can get over-looked. If you know what I mean. The guy's an asshole JAG lawyer. Seems he kicked up a hell of a shit storm with a judge a few years back. It's a long story, but he thinks he's God's gift. My buddy's seen him in action. He's like a bulldog and won't stop at anything to win, dirty or not. Must run in the family. Anyway, he's been heard making comments. Puttin' it out there that there've been wrongful accusations made about his brother. I think he might be setting the stage for something."

It really is all about who you know in this world.

"Thanks for that, Frank. I appreciate the insight."

"I'm texting you an address. It's a bar in Washington called The Rusty Nail."

"Yeah, I know it." A lot of the guys went there to blow off steam.

"Word is that the bartender might know something about what happened over there. I don't know much more than that, but it'll be a good place to start. We can talk more when you get back."

"Agreed. I'll look into it." I heard the call to board my flight and was about to tell him when he interrupted.

"Shit, I have to go, Beckett." I heard the click as he hung up. I guessed we were both in a hurry. I handed the agent my ID, and she waved for me to go on. I knew my rush to board would probably end up with the plane sitting on the tarmac for another twenty minutes, but the urge to do something had me trotting down the ramp to the plane. As I sat there impatiently waiting for our take-off, I thought over Frank's words. I only hoped that bartender knew something, and it wasn't going to be a dead end.

My head still spun as we taxied then took off for North Dakota.

We touched down a few hours later. I met Mark at arrivals, and we began the drive back to Shadows. I took a breath of relief when we drove over the border and was pleased to be back in the quiet of the mountains.

"All things considered, how was your trip?" he finally said when we were a few miles from the house. Mark was usually chatty, but I appreciated that he knew when silence was needed. I wasn't the first guy to use it as a coping mechanism.

"Rough."

"If it helps," he looked over at me, "it doesn't get easier." He went back to the road, and I appreciated the truth he gave me. I'd been impressed with how Blackstone honored their fallen. I'd listened and seen how they kept Paul close to their hearts, so he'd never be forgotten. Maybe I needed to do something like that, too.

"How's everything at the house?" I could use a distraction now that my mind was exhausted.

"Good. Ivy got hit on by a parent from Livi's school." He didn't hesitate to throw that out there. I could feel his eyes on me.

"Really?" I shifted in my seat and refused to meet his gaze. I suddenly felt incredibly protective. I was pleased at the thought that Blackstone had my back, though. "Anything I should be concerned about?"

"She's loyal," he nodded, "but she's a catch, and Redstone's a small town. It won't take long for word to spread there's a single woman in town."

"She's not single."

"Then you better make that known sooner rather than

later." He pulled off the road, and we headed toward the first checkpoint.

We didn't talk much after that, and soon the house was in sight. I was surprised at the feeling that filled me. I was home.

After I unpacked and showered, I made a beeline toward the dining room. I was suddenly ravenous. Everyone was gathered around the brightly colored dinner table. John had told me about how Savannah loved her seasons, and that the fall and winter were her favorite ones. The serving dishes and decorations were either dark green, orange, or red. Little orange pumpkins were wedged among a driftwood type centerpiece, and the scent of cinnamon lingered in the air. I felt like I was back at my mom's about to eat Thanksgiving dinner. My stomach grumbled at the thought of turkey.

"This looks amazing, Savi." I caught John's eye, and he shrugged with a grin.

"Thank you." Savannah looked pointedly at Ivy's empty chair. "How was your trip?"

I didn't share why I'd left. Only the guys knew, so I kept it light. "It was nice to see my family." I looked away as I wondered where Ivy was.

"I heard your buddy Moore will be joining us soon." Mike handed me a bowl of baby potatoes. "We're looking forward to meeting him."

"He's a good soldier, and he'll be a great asset." I aimed my comment more at Cole. "He's had my back longer than anyone. I trust him."

"His file is impressive," Cole agreed.

"My apologies," Ivy stood at the entrance of the room and seemed worn out from her day, "but my phone call ran long."

"Not a problem." Savannah beamed. "Please come and eat."

"Doc Roberts is still working. He said he'd eat something later." Savannah nodded as Ivy moved her gaze to mine. She took her seat across from Mark and me.

"Welcome back." She smiled.

"Thanks."

"Hey, Keith," Mike leaned forward, "any chance you could ask Liza to find me that knife I showed you the other night? I think it'll fit perfectly in that leather pouch I got."

"Yeah, sure. I'll send ya her number. You can talk to her yourself."

"My, my, so many numbers being passed around today," Mark muttered and looked at Ivy. Ivy's eyes widened. *Wait, did she get that guy's number?*

"Meaning?" John asked.

"Mark, are you startin' shit?" Mia glared at him. "So help me God, if you meddle in something that isn't meant for you, I'll scalp you in your sleep."

Savannah laughed and lifted a glass to Mia at her comment. The women in the house were wonderfully ruthless, and it made life here so entertaining. I looked over at Mark to see how he took her comment.

"Do you see the abuse?" Mark pointed his fork at his

wife, and a few of us smirked. "Everyone picks on poor, innocent Mark."

"There's nothing innocent about you," Mia scoffed.

"If I may," Abigail stood at the far end of the table, "I actually have something to share. I'm sure some of you have noticed I haven't been myself lately. I've had some tests run—"

"You had what? When?" Mark's face fell, and he whipped around to look at Mia. "Did you know—" He looked back at Abigail. "Did she know about this?"

"Just listen." Mia patted his arm.

"As I said, I had some tests run," Abigail tsked at Mark, "and I'm pleased to share it's nothing more than low blood pressure. I might feel a little funny for the next week while I adjust to the medication, but I'll be back to my old self in no time. So, there's no need for anyone to worry."

"That's wonderful news, Abby." Daniel looked around the table then tilted his head at Mark. "Yes, son, I knew, but I promised. If there was something you needed to know, you'd have been the first to be filled in."

"You mean fourth to know." Mark leaned back in his chair. "You and Cole knew, Doc Roberts knew, and oh, yeah, apparently, my wife knew. But you know who didn't know? Me, her son."

"Oh, Mark, you're a bit extreme sometimes." Savannah egged him on. "You're at nine, and you need to be like at three."

"Excuse me?" He rose from his chair. "The only thing

that's a nine right here is this face." He waved his hands around his face, which brought laughter around the table.

"Uncle Mike?" Cole's son tugged at the sleeve of Mike's shirt. I heard a little snort come from Savannah and looked over. She wore a dark smirk.

"What's up, little man?" He fist-bumped him.

"Can I tell you a secret?"

"Of course."

Easton hit his arm and screamed, "Suck it, sucker. You're it!"

John leapt from the table, and Mike tore off after him, knowing that was John's play with Easton.

"That's my boy." Cole laughed and pushed his chair out from the table as Easton climbed up on his lap.

"John's in the lead," Savannah explained. "Well, out of the Blackstone team. It's all on the scoreboard in the barn."

"Good to know," Ivy cut in. "I have a session with him tomorrow." I chuckled at her dark side; it popped up every once in a while.

"See how well you fit in here, Ivy?" Savannah laughed.

"Good evening, everyone." Dr. Roberts drew the fun his way, but it quickly fizzled out as we took in his worn-out expression. Even his tie was loose at the neck, which in itself was odd, as the doc always looked impeccable. "Forgive me for interrupting, but Ivy, I need a word with you."

"I was just about to eat. Can it wait?"

"No, I'm afraid this can't."

Her face paled, then she set her napkin next to her untouched plate and excused herself.

The table stayed quiet as we all wondered what was going on.

"Cole," Mia spoke up, "in celebration of Kit Moore coming to the house, maybe we could have a bit of a party out back. It's getting cooler, and there won't be much more time to use the lake."

"Yeah! Can we, Daddy?" Easton squealed.

"I like that." Cole nodded at Mia then at Savannah, who clearly had a part in it.

"Ty, anything in particular that Moore likes?" Mia pulled out her phone and waited like she was about to take notes.

"Um, food." I shrugged, the girls rolled their eyes, and the guys shook their heads. "What?"

"Take it from me." Cole chuckled. "Give details now or regret it later."

"They're relentless." John ducked as Sloane went to swat him as he came back in the room.

"Umm," I searched my worn-out memory, "IPAs, whiskey, country music, any kind of food, really, no allergies to anything. He always says he hates pickles, but he secretly loves them, and he likes long walks on the beach," I said, deadpan.

"Long walks on the beach?" Savannah raised an eyebrow.

"That's what his Tinder says."

"He has a Tinder account?" Cat covered her mouth.

"He does, thanks to me." I leaned back in my chair.

"Give me more." Mark waved for me to go on.

"You have Furbies and tag. I gave Moore a Tinder account." The table broke out in laughter.

"What did he do to you to get that kind of response?" Mia typed away after the noise died down. "I mean, it must've been big."

"Yeah, that one I take to the grave." I picked up my plate, stood, and snatched another roll. As I headed to the kitchen, they all shouted that it wasn't fair I wasn't sharing the entire story.

After we cleaned up, I caught Cole on his way back to his office.

"Hey, Cole, can I steal a minute?"

"Sure." We stood in the hall not far from Doc's office. "Is this a closed-door minute?"

"No," but I did lower my voice, "Frank gave me a lead on Hill. Some bartender in Washington has information about my last tour and Brown. I'd like permission to chase that lead on my free time."

"I'm good with that." He nodded. "Just keep me in the loop and let me know if you need anything. I'd like to help where I can." I was a bit surprised by his offer, and it must have shown on my face. "Your problems are Shadows problems now, Ty. That's how it works here. If it was any one of our Blackstone brothers who was killed by a fellow soldier, nothing would stop us. Heads would roll until we got to the bottom of it."

"Copy that." I held out my hand and he shook it.

"Ty, have you thought of approaching any of the men who came home with you? Any who might have had encounters with Hill before?"

"I've made some calls, but the usual response is a click on the end of the line."

"In person is best." Cole pressed his lips together as he thought. "Maybe after you speak to that bartender, you should see if you can round up some of the men, approach them head-on."

"Wouldn't hurt." I nodded.

"We also both know someone who's good at worming their way into people's heads." He moved his gaze from mine to Ivy's door.

"I thought of that, but isn't it risky for her to leave Shadows?" I felt uneasy about the idea.

"You're right, but if you did it in Washington, Frank's there. Eagle Eye is stationed there, too, so you'd have backup if needed. Should be safe. Plus, she's going there soon anyway, so if we're not on a mission, maybe you could take the time. Besides, it could work out better for me. I'd prefer not to send one of my Dusk guys to Washington to watch over Ivy. I've pulled them enough as it is. She's more comfortable with you, anyway."

"Yeah, of course. I really appreciate the suggestion."

"Any time." We both looked up as Doc stepped out of Ivy's office then disappeared into his own behind us without a word. I threw Cole a look.

"I know I'm not supposed to ask, but is everything okay?"

"I'm thinking not."

"Cole?" Savannah appeared at the end of the hall and gave me a wave, but her smile didn't reach her eyes. "I need to speak with you."

"Sure, be there in a sec."

"No," she took a step closer, "I need you now."

Something passed between them, and he hurried off to follow her into his office. I hoped everything was all right with Olivia at camp.

FOUR

"I can't believe you right now!" I tried to contain my anger. I caught my reflection in the window and ran my fingers through my hair and absently caught it up in a clip. I looked worn out and frazzled. It was near two a.m. in Montana, and Bronson Fitzpatrick was the last person I thought I'd be having a conversation with at any time, let alone the wee hours of the morning in my office.

"Hey, come on, hun, like you wouldn't have stopped and heard them out if they brought up my name?"

"Yes, Bronson, I would have, but the moment they started asking personal questions about you, I would have walked away not listened and not given out details about you and your family."

"I guess that's where we're different." He sighed, and I

closed my eyes, taking a moment to gather myself. "I would never intentionally hurt you, Ivy." His voice pleaded for forgiveness.

"I know," I nodded like he could see me, "just tell me exactly what you said so I can get ahead of the storm."

"I was coming back from the gym," he started. "Two men approached me in front of that little bakery. You know the one you and I used to go to."

"I remember it." I rolled my eyes at his obvious attempt to remind me of our past. "Did they say who they were? The press?"

"No. They weren't with the press. They said they'd been hired by someone."

"Who?"

"I don't know. I'm on my way home from visiting a friend. The information's at my office. I have it written down." He sounded frustrated with my questions, but I also got the feeling he wanted me to ask who the friend was.

"Just tell me what you told them, Bronson."

"They wanted to know where you're staying." He paused. "Where are you staying? Because I know you're not at your place."

"Are you checking up on me?"

"I'm worried about you, Ivy."

"I'm fine. I'm staying at a friend's place."

"And which friend is that?"

"You don't get to ask me those questions anymore." I wanted to lash out at him again but thought better of it and swallowed hard. "I'm proud of the way things ended with us, Bronson. Let's keep it that way."

"I believe you wanted to end things more than I did, Ivy," he huffed.

"We weren't a good match, and you know it. Don't make things up that weren't there." I clenched my teeth. I didn't want him to put me off track. "Then what happened?"

"They wanted to know if I was in contact with you. Of course, I said no, but I don't think they believed me. They asked me about your clients, too. One of them even asked if I knew if any of them were more than just clients."

"What the hell does that mean?"

"I don't know. You tell me," he shot back, his voice dripping with sarcasm.

"Surely, you're not questioning my professionalism?" I felt like I barely knew this man anymore.

"Look, I don't know what the hell happened with you, but did you screw one of your clients?"

"Did you seriously just ask me that?"

"I did."

"No, Bronson, of course I didn't. But thanks for the confidence…or lack of it." *Unbelievable.*

"When are you back in the city?" He changed topics, and I fought to keep up as my mind spun.

"I don't know. I've got a lot going on here."

"I want to see you."

"Why?" Up until now, we had been fine not being in each other's lives anymore.

"Do I really need a reason to want to see the woman I almost married?"

"Look, we've had no contact in a long while, and I think it's best we stay away from each other."

"And your reasoning for that is…?"

"Because we're not who we once were, and I don't want you getting hurt." I meant that. Bronson was a good guy, just not good for me. "I have to go. Thanks for letting me know about this, and if you'd get those names to me, I'd really appreciate it."

"Yeah." He obviously wasn't happy. "Bye." He hung up, and I tossed my phone on the table behind the couch.

I covered my face with my hands and let out a strangled scream into a handy cushion. How did I get here?

"I thought I heard you in here." Ty made me jump with a yelp.

"Lord, you scared me." I pressed the cushion hard against my beating heart. "How was your trip?"

"Shitty. I'd ask how your day went, but I can see it wasn't great either."

"Shitty, too." I nodded and unclipped my hair and ran my hands through it to ease the anger. I caught his hungry expression and suddenly felt the mood in the room shift. Clearly, we both needed a release.

In two strides, he pulled me into him and slammed his lips to mine. I met him with equal enthusiasm, running my hands up his chest, shoulders, neck, and into his hair.

He reached down and flung the cushion I held toward the couch then tugged my skirt up over my hips and sat me on a long table against the wall. He stood between my legs and undid my blouse as I undid his belt, button, and zipper, all in a matter of seconds. I freed him then gripped him and pumped a little to drive him wild.

He bent down and kissed my breast then nipped at my nipple through my lacy bra. I pulled his head so he could do the same to the other. Once he was finished, he stood, wrapped an arm around my waist, and tugged me toward the end of the table with such force it told me he'd taken control. With hooded eyes, he massaged my lower back while his free hand pumped his shaft, and signs of his arousal appeared at the tip. It was incredibly sexy to watch his thumb coat the head then nudge it between my legs. We both watched as he slowly slipped himself inside me while my walls stretched to take all of him in.

Yes, this was what I needed. To feel something. I was wound so tight I could burst.

I dragged my gaze up his flat stomach, flexed arms, and strained neck to his lips. They parted, and he looked down at me. I saw he was trying to control himself.

"Good?" he whispered, and I was thrown by the knowledge he was worried I might not be okay. I gave a tight, very positive nod, and he dove down and caught my lips and devoured my mouth. His hips flicked and rolled, and all I could do was balance and hold on to him.

Noises escaped deep down in my throat as he rubbed all the right places. His tongue was forceful and dictated the kiss to match his thrust.

My nails dug into his back, and I sank my teeth into his shoulder, which intensified his hold on me.

"I heard you got hit on today," he muttered between licks.

Really, Mark. I rolled my eyes. I really didn't want to have that conversation right now.

"I met one of Livi's friends, and her father asked me out."

"And?"

"And I'm on a date with him right now." My voice dripped with sarcasm. He glared at me as his nails dragged across my sensitive skin. "I'm not looking for anyone else, Ty."

"Mm," he mused as his expression darkened, and I felt a feverish heat burst through me. Ty had a way of being alpha with one simple look, and that was it.

Then he suddenly ripped away from me with a growl.

I found myself spun around and placed with the arm of the couch against my lower back. My head and shoulders dropped to the cushion as he held my legs and towered over me. He gathered my legs in his arms and held them straight up against his chest as he thrust over and over. Every muscle in his body was taut as a bowstring. I felt my climax grow deep in the bottom of my belly, my skin prickled, and my head lightened. I clawed at the cushions, desperate for something to cling to.

Something drew his eyes to the table next to me, and he looked down at it with an intense expression. For a split second, he slowed his rhythm but seemed to shake whatever it was off, and he looked away and kept going. He lowered my legs a bit and circled his hips while I fought to keep my screams at bay. The office was much more exposed than the bedroom upstairs.

"Ty." I bowed my back and knew I only had a minute or two before I was going to come. "I—I'm…" He thumbed my bud, and I let go. A million and one emotions tore through me, and I vaguely remembered him grinding himself to his own release.

When my vision cleared, I let a happy smile stretch lazily over my lips as I took in the man above me. But instead of a smile, his expression told me he was bothered by something. He helped me to my feet, and I quickly rearranged my clothes as I wondered what was up.

"You missed a text." He handed me my phone, and I felt my stomach drop. I clicked on the screen and read the words.

Bronson: Hearing your voice today makes me realize I still love you.

I tossed my phone on the table and tucked my blouse back into place. Ty was watching me, and I could tell by the way his jaw ticked his mind was probably working overtime.

"That's my ex-fiancé." I didn't need to explain, but I chose to as I considered he'd seen that message while he was deep inside me. "That's who I was on the phone with before you came in."

"And he's still in love with you." It wasn't a question, more of a statement.

"Even if he was, which I don't think he really is," I finger combed my hair and looked about for my clip, "we're not compatible. We tried it and failed."

"Do you still love him?" He folded his arms, and I couldn't help but admire how sexy he looked when he was unsure. I didn't think it was a position he often found himself in.

"I wouldn't be having sex with you if I was." His brows narrowed, and I stepped forward, closing the gap between us, but I made sure not to touch him. "Doesn't feel that great, does it?" I hiked up an eyebrow, and his face fell slightly.

"What?"

"I'm unsure where you stand with—"

Suddenly, an ear-pricing siren blew through our phone speakers, sending the fear of God through both of us. Every tablet, computer, intercom, smart watch, any technology screamed for our immediate attention. We both scrambled to grab our lit-up phones as they danced wildly on the table. It could mean only one thing. As we looked at our screens, we froze.

Cole: Code Red.

Ty's gaze flew to mine. He quickly fixed the collar of my shirt, grabbed my hand, and tugged me toward the door. We raced together down the stairs.

Everyone knew to gather in the living room. Two small red lights I'd never noticed before flickered on and off above the door. The vibe in the room was high, and we all knew something bad had happened or was about to happen. Mia called me over to sit next to her at the back of the room while Ty joined the rest of the Blackstone team near the fireplace.

"Abigail?" Cole waited for her to look at her phone.

"You're clear." She pressed a button and the lights turned off.

I glanced at Mia, confused.

"We need to make sure there's someone watching the kids," she explained.

"Any idea what's going on?" I tried to keep the worry from my voice. Cole looked serious, and Savannah looked all business. Something was seriously wrong.

"No idea. Code Red has only ever been talked about in our orientation sessions. It makes sense to know what to do in an emergency, but," she shrugged, "from what I understand, Code Red has never been used before." Mia strained to see across the room. "However, the fact that my father is here with two men I don't know makes me more nervous than anything else."

"That sound," I held up my phone, "was terrifying."

"I think that's the point."

"I need everyone's attention." Cole stepped up on the

hearth so we could all see him. "You're here because this involves all of you in some way." He looked around then took a deep breath, and that was when I spotted Daniel next to Keith. Their expressions were grim. "Earlier this evening, we found out that Lexi's gone missing." Mia's head swung over to Savannah, and something passed between them. "The security team I had in place advised that she went to a night club and gave them the slip. They spent twenty-four hours doing a grid search and watched her apartment, but she never returned. The team exhausted their search but turned up nothing, so they contacted us."

Jesus, Mark was right. Cole did have people watching her. I wonder if she'd spotted them, and if so, why she'd skip out on them.

Cat moved to Keith's side but didn't touch him. I knew Cat and Lexi had been close, and this was no doubt a huge hit for her as well.

"Frank, will you come up and explain what you know?" Cole looked at Frank, who nodded then stepped up and took Cole's spot.

"I'll keep this brief. Both Agent Ortega and Agent Lodge were sent to watch over Lexi for the first few months in Canada while she got settled. Everything seemed to be going fine until a few days ago when she was spotted hanging out at a local pub with a few old friends from the Almas Perdidas." Worried looks were exchanged, and Mia leaned into me.

"They were a bike gang she got herself wrapped up in

years ago. It's a long story, but most of them were taken out by the Devil's Reach. The Almas Perdidas are ruthless. Keith helped her escape them back then, and he went through hell doing it. He's going to be devastated to know she's back in with them. As if he doesn't have enough on his plate." She shook her head.

"Oh, no." I couldn't imagine what must have been going on in Keith's head at that moment.

Mike spoke up. "Any chance she's with them? Maybe they got a new clubhouse?"

"No. Latest intel is she left the bar alone a few hours before it closed. She walked down Barrington Street then disappeared. They finally got hold of some street footage in the area, and she can be seen getting into a dark blue van. The plates are registered to a local auto shop. The owner confirmed it's his company truck. Apparently, he's pretty loose with it, and often his employees or their family members borrow it. We're working on that, but nothing so far. By that, I mean the truck hasn't been found."

I scanned the room and saw worried faces, but no tears were visible. These were strong people and action oriented. They wanted facts before emotion.

"What about POL?" Mark cleared his throat and glanced quickly at Keith as he said it.

"Proof of life, right?" I whispered to Mia to make sure I hadn't missed something. Sometimes Shadows used different acronyms than I was used to.

"Yes, proof of life," she answered. "If the Cartels got

hold of someone, that's normally the next step. Given that Lexi is," she paused, "was Keith's wife, she'd be extremely valuable to them." I appreciated her candid explanation.

"Got it. Jesus." I shook my head at the severity of the situation.

"We've heard nothing yet." Frank looked grimly at Keith.

"Cole says," Mia quietly went on, "we're more valuable than even the guys are because Blackstone will do anything to get us back. I'm sure the cartels would know that. That being said, take away what poor Lexi might be going through for a moment." She grimaced. "If they do have her and get her to talk, just think what that could mean for all of us."

"She wouldn't do that, right?"

Mia looked around the room, and I followed her gaze. Various quiet conversations were going on. Savi and Cole had their heads together, and Frank spoke to Keith. She kept her voice low as she spoke.

"No, she'd never want to, but the Cartel are ruthless creatures, and you never know what they'll do to make her. Just ask Savi." I felt a cold chill wash over me. "This is bad, Ivy, for so many reasons." We both looked up as Cole spoke loudly.

"As of this moment, all Blackstone, Eagle Eye, and Dusk members are on standby. Beckett," he turned to address Ty, "I need you to catch Moore up to speed as soon as he gets here."

"Understood."

"Copy that." John spoke for the others and moved over to stand next to Keith.

Cole started to bark out orders to everyone, and in a matter of minutes the house was in full swing.

The women came together, and we all slipped outside to talk. We wanted our own chance to talk things out among ourselves. We followed Savannah down to the dock house; it had been turned into a hangout of sorts. Couches and a few chairs were huddled in the little room, and a small lamp provided some light and Mia lit some candles. We all found a spot, and there were a few moments of quiet as we all digested everything. My brain spun like a dreidel. I felt like I needed to speak.

"I want to say how sorry I am to hear about Lexi. I've only met her a few times, but this is some next level of crazy. And as unsympathetic as this may sound, I need you to walk me through this, ladies." I leaned my tired arms on my thighs. "I need to be as helpful as I can. Help me understand so I can help all of you."

"Okay, yeah," Mia looked around, and I was pleased they saw my question for what it was and got right to it. "If the Cartel took her, then it could be any day or even any moment now, we'd get proof of life. It's a waiting game, and they hold all the power."

"Got it." I nodded.

"I also think it's fair to say she might've gone back to her old gang," Mia added. "I've had a really hard time getting through to her this past year. Who knows where her head is."

"I understand that."

"Lexi has no regard for safety." Savannah shifted uncomfortably, and I could see this wasn't easy for them. After all, she was one of them, so I could only imagine just how unsettling it was. "I hate to say it, but she's drawn to trouble."

"That's true." Mia cleared her throat. "Cat, you're closest to her. Did you see any signs?"

"No." Catalina brushed a tear from her eye. "I mean, she was pulling away, but when is Lexi not?" She looked at me. "Lexi has cycles of being on and off again, but the fact that she slipped out on her security is something I can't understand."

"However, to circle back to the Cartel, if they took her, there's always the possibility they already killed her, and any POL is fake," Savannah whispered. "I just need you to know that the guys' heads'll go there."

"Yes, they will." Mia reached over and rubbed Savannah's shoulder. "Right now, my dad is probably calling his informants in Mexico to lean on them to find out something. We'd only have a small window of time to get her back."

"I hate to pull the *I come from a Cartel family* card," Catalina said, and I pulled in my chin and eyed her. I was unaware that she had any ties to the Cartel. "Can we just get real here for a moment?"

"I know." Savannah nodded, and I looked at Catalina to go on.

"We're gold to the Cartel, and so are our kids. There's

nothing we can offer to get her back. If they have her, Lexi's fate is already sealed." She swiped at a tear with the back of her hand. "They never got over losing you, Savannah. The American made that quite clear. I mean that's what put a giant target on Blackstone years ago, the fact that they were the ones who rescued you. And you weren't even married to Cole then. Now they've got Lexi, I don't know." She looked down and picked at a bit of dog hair on her knee.

"Wow," I sighed into my hands.

"Ivy," Sloane came to sit next to me, "all of what was said here tonight is true, but Blackstone has pulled off the impossible countless times before."

"That's true." Catalina nodded, her eyes hopeful again.

"Right now, the best we can do is to act as normal as we can with the kids and be supportive with the guys. However, don't forget all the things we've done in the past to help them. Keep trying to think of any details or ideas you can that might help. We also need to crawl into the guys' heads and remind them who they are and what they've done in the past. They can do this. They just need you to remind them of that. Which means," Sloane looked around, "it's time to share our stories with Ivy."

"I'll start." Savannah licked her lips and took an uneasy breath. "The day after my twenty-seventh birthday…"

———

The following afternoon, I felt like a zombie. I was running on three hours of restless sleep. Ty and the rest of the guys spent their time downstairs in the conference room. Frank had June and Abigail making arrangements for the kids to be taken to Washington in case both safehouse locations had been compromised.

"Any word from Bronson?" My uncle carried a steaming cup of coffee into my office and set it on the coaster next to me.

"Thanks, and no. The fact that he dropped his little 'I still love you' bombshell and nothing else means he'll expect me to call him back."

"So, call him."

"I have a meeting with Keith in five. I will when I'm finished."

"Ivy," he sat down across from me, "Cole needs you now more than ever, and he trusts you, so you need to handle this whole Lexi situation with Keith. It could get really ugly. Blackstone needs him, and you're their best bet to get him in the right headspace."

"I know that." I blew over the top of the mug. "I won't push too much."

"Or maybe you should." He gave me a pointed look. "Blackstone works best under pressure. I believe Keith would respond better to you if you didn't tiptoe around him. It's your specialty, anyway. Leave the warm hugs for the wives while you get in his head and fuel him for this fight." A smile broke across my lips, and he frowned at my reaction. "What?"

"Sloane told me the same thing last night. The girls told me their stories about how they each ended up here. It's neat to hear how much they listen and take your advice."

"That's nice to hear." He cleared his throat. "Did they really share their stories?"

"Yeah." I set my coffee down. "I loved that they let me in. Each one of them was wonderful about it. Wow, though. They sure went through a lot." I paused. "My situation's got nothing on them."

"I disagree." He leaned closer. "Ivy, you're just too close to your story, and it isn't over yet by any stretch of the imagination. Don't belittle your situation, please, because the truth is it's a dangerous one. The situation is obviously picking up speed. Ben Oliver isn't someone you can hide from forever. You need to get the names of those PIs Bronson was talking about, and soon. We need to find out what's going on and who hired them."

I suddenly felt cold. He was right. Ben had already proven he had no problem shedding blood and was clearly unbalanced. I knew he'd stop at nothing to keep me quiet.

He looked at his watch. "Keith is late for your session. I've got to go, but please call Bronson."

"I will."

I gave Keith another ten minutes then went downstairs. I stood outside the sliding glass door that led into the conference room, the glass was frosted. I knew I was about to interrupt an important session, but I knocked twice anyway. John slid the door open, and I saw the screens go blank, and the folders rustled as they were turned over.

"Keith," I stepped by John and gave Ty a quick glance, "you're late."

"Sorry, Ivy," Frank said. "We've got a lot going on."

"Understood, but I was told I had a mandatory meeting with Keith. It was also stressed that it was not to be rescheduled." I glanced at Cole, who looked down at his watch then over at Keith. The guys all stared at me, but no one spoke.

"I'll rebook for tomorrow," Keith mumbled.

"That's up to your team leader." I felt the air get sucked out of the room as the guys all shifted with discomfort, and Keith glanced over at Cole who'd suddenly become interested in his phone. "I can just sit right here," I swung the chair around next to John and looked at them all, "until a decision is made." I looked again at Cole.

"She's like one of the wives," Mark hissed under his breath.

"Then you know I'm not going anywhere," I assured him.

"Keith, I know you want to be here right now, but Doc Ivy's right. You need to go, brother," Cole told Keith with a serious expression.

"Fine." Keith didn't argue as he slid his file over to Mike and stood.

"I apologize for the interruption," I said to Cole, who tried to hide his amusement. "I won't keep him long."

Keith walked ahead of me with his head down until we got to my office where he stepped aside to let me go in first. No one could fault the men in this house for their manners. It was endearing, actually.

He sat down on the couch, and I settled in the chair. I scooped up the cat and placed him gently on the armrest. I looked at my skirt and realized black wasn't a good color for me when I considered my new furry companion.

"I'll make you a deal." I took charge of the session. "I'll cut your time in half and let you get back to the others if you give it to me straight. Where's your head right now?"

"Dark," he mumbled, and when I didn't speak, he knew I wanted more. "And seriously confused." Good. I'd hoped for that.

"Confused on how you should be feeling?"

"Exactly."

"Makes sense. I mean, this just pours gasoline on some nasty wounds she's already inflicted." I wanted to piss him off. I knew he'd have to get angry before he'd let me in. I needed to know all of it, what lay beneath the pain. So, I gave it to him. "She confessed she doesn't care about the kids. Said she doesn't feel anything for them."

"Yeah." His voice held very little emotion.

"She broke the house rules, resented you, fell out of love with you, left you and your kids to fend for yourselves, and now is hanging out with the same people you got her away from with the help of the Devil's Reach."

"She ripped out parts of me I didn't even know existed." His face grew red as the pain tore through his center.

"And now she might have been yanked off the streets by the very people you're all at war with. That's a lot to digest."

"I, ah," he stood and turned away from me, "I need to hurt something."

"I get that. It's so you can feel something other than emotional pain." I made sure he knew I followed his train of thought.

"Yeah," he huffed as the veins in his arms popped.

"That's fair. There's a boxing ring downstairs. Why don't you go kick the shit out of your sparring partner?"

"Tempting." He gave a dark smile, but it quickly faded.

"You know, it's okay to feel a hundred different emotions at once." I stepped carefully into the true feeling he was experiencing. "You can hate Lexi while still caring deeply for her safety."

"Good, because it sure as hell is confusing." He looked so earnest, I wanted to hug him, but I knew that wasn't what he needed.

"She broke your heart, Keith. She left your kids without a mother, then she was reckless with her newfound freedom. Or at least it seems that way. If she was snatched up by the Cartels, it was her own fault. I'd be pissed, too! If it wasn't the Cartel and she just took off, it's not only dangerous but stupid because it could lead to the same end."

"Pissed doesn't even begin to describe it."

"What does?"

"I hate her," he seethed. "I hate her so much for hurting our kids, for tearing me apart!" he yelled. "I fought hard for her—for us, and look where it got me! I don't deserve this, and my kids sure as hell don't either. All I ever wanted was to fight those pieces of shit in the south and be able to come back to my family. I wanted something positive to focus on, to fight for. Because if I don't have that, then what the hell am I doing all this for?" The last word got caught in his throat as he whirled around and punched a hole straight through the office wall.

I set my iPad down slowly and moved to where he stood. Careful not to get too close, I leaned my back against the wall next to him and looked up at his heaving chest. He looked down and rubbed his fist.

"I don't even know if I can do this, Doc," he whispered, keeping his eyes on the damaged plaster. "I'm not even sure I want to find her." Then he broke, because he'd just admitted one of his truths. Silent tears rolled down his cheeks as his chin fought to hold back the cry that so desperately wanted to come out. I could almost see the pain as it battled against his strength. "Fuck," he swallowed down a sob, "what the hell does that say about me, Doc?"

"It says you're human." I rested a hand on his shoulder, offering him a careful touch to ground him.

"What now?" He closed his eyes as more tears flowed.

"Now, you take a moment for yourself and let that ugly shit you're holding inside come out. Then you get back downstairs and you do your job. If Blackstone could find Savannah, you can find Lexi." His gaze shifted to me. "You can hate her, but you know at the end of the day your children still need their mother alive. She's still a part of them." I knew there was still a part of Keith that cared for her, too, but fueling the fight for his kids was the best way to get him through this right now.

"Yeah," he let out an unsteady breath, "I have to do it for them."

"Then," I paused to get his attention and to give him something more to fight for, "when you're ready, and I mean after all this is done, you can go your separate ways and no guilt will rest on your conscience. You can be free to focus on what makes you and the kids happy."

He just reached over and squeezed my arm and gave me a tight smile. I saw something shift in his expression, and the skin around his eyes relaxed a little. I knew he'd heard me.

"Thank you, Ivy."

"Anytime, Keith, seriously." I cocked my head toward the door for him to leave, and with a deep breath, he gathered himself and left.

Once I was alone, I let myself carry his pain for a few moments. We were taught to connect to a patient then let feeling go. But given this situation, I knew I needed to stay connected, and as I didn't have any emotional connection to Lexi herself, I used Keith for that. I closed my eyes and felt the pain as if I were him.

Later that evening, I joined the ladies in a game of poker in one of the spare rooms downstairs. It was nice to get the scoop on what had happened in the house while I was in my office.

Apparently, Frank's informants had gone quiet over the last while and were only now beginning to surface.

"What does Cole think?" Mia tossed down a card, and Catalina handed her another.

"He hasn't said too much." Savannah looked up at us. "He's processing a lot."

"I heard Mike on the phone as I came in earlier. He spoke with someone named Trigger." I moved my ace of hearts to sit next to the queen in my hand and noticed everyone had gone quiet. When I looked up, they were all looking at me. "What did I say?"

"Are you sure?" Catalina glanced at Sloane then back at me.

"Yeah. I was coming inside from my run, and he was in the kitchen on his phone."

"What did he say?" She lowered her cards.

"He asked for a favor." I frowned, not following. "Who is this person?"

"Remember, I told you about the Devil's Reach, the guy you haven't met yet, helping out Keith? Trigger is the president of that motorcycle gang."

"So, he knows a gang member? So what? I went to

school with some Stripe Backs. It doesn't mean I'm a bad person, does it?"

"Of course not. Not all bikers are criminals. Well, I guess it really depends on how you want to look at it," Sloane cut in, and I knew she was referring to the law.

"But if Mike called Trigger," Catalina explained, "that probably means they're asking him for some help."

"Which means they know something." Savannah rubbed her forehead. "And it also means Cole allowed it."

"Wow." Catalina leaned back in her chair. "Who's next? The Capris," she joked darkly and looked at me. "It's a crazy story I'll leave for another time, but they're the head of the Italian mob."

"Geez," I huffed. They sure had some interesting contacts.

"Word of advice," Catalina lifted her cards to her face like she was ready to play, "if you ever get the chance to meet Trigger, maybe not mention you know any Stripe Backs."

"Good to know." My phone rang, and I saw it was Bronson. Finally. "I'm sorry, ladies, but I have to take this." I glanced at Sloane to let her know it was about my own situation.

"You're up, Savi." Sloane pulled the attention off me.

FIVE

Cole called me into his office and gave me a crash course on everything I needed to know about how they planned to deal with the situation. Every now and then he'd stop and ask for my input or if I would do anything different. At first, I thought he was trying to understand how my head worked, but I quickly realized that he was drawing from my own experience to see if there was anything he could use to make his plan better.

I really respected the way Cole was as leader. He never used his rank to show he was superior. He made you feel equal and, most of all, heard. I sat back and soaked up the way he did things and what he offered so I could apply it to my team. Now I understood why the Logans had the reputation they did. They were well known in the military as well as outside it. I was damn proud to be part of what they'd built here.

"Logan," Mike held up a hand and pointed to his phone, "Trig says he's heard one of the Coppolas has been seen with the Castillos. Do I have your permission to contact Elio?"

"Yes."

"Copy that."

"Italian mafia families." Cole answered my upspoken question. "We're crossing over into the gray area, Beckett. I hope you're okay with that."

"I've spent a lot of time in the gray. Don't worry about where my head is on that."

"Good." I could see Cole didn't like to blur the lines of good and bad, but sometimes you had to do what was necessary. "Let's call it for now." He stood and gathered the files on the table. "Until we get something firm, we're not making a move."

"I don't know what kind of magical power Ivy has," Mark came in and leaned against the table, "but she screwed Keith's head back on right."

"Yeah?" Cole looked over at him.

"He's ready to leave when we are." I smiled to myself. Ivy had no idea just how good she was at her job. "Girl got some balls, bustin' into the meeting the way she did."

"Reminded me of Savi." Cole chuckled as he turned off the computer monitors.

"Reminds me of all of 'em." Mark looked at me. "How's it going with her, anyway? You get a chance to talk to her about that other guy?" I glanced at Cole, unsure how he felt on the topic.

"I'm not blind, Beckett." Cole made a face. "Just don't get messy, and we won't have a problem."

"Understood." I looked at Mark. "It's going."

"That's all I get?"

"Yup." He followed me out of the room.

"Why?"

"Because you're ruled by the women in this house, and they crack you wide open like a walnut after a few drinks."

"I'm insulted."

"No," Cole rolled his eyes as he looked back at us, "he nailed you."

"Just because the ladies prefer my company over yours at an evening gathering does not mean I spill secrets."

"No, you spill gossip." Cole tossed back. "I know you can keep secrets."

I veered away from the bickering brothers when I spotted Ivy outside.

"Beckett," Keith stepped out from the living room, "got a moment?"

"Yeah, what's up?"

"Besides Moore, do you have any other guys you went to combat with we can call on for support? Ones you trust?"

"I have a few I'd put my name behind." His face slipped for moment, and I couldn't help but feel my chest tighten in sympathy.

"How quickly can you get them here?"

"I have a few buddies who've taken jobs here in town as law enforcement. Frank knows them, too. Maybe mention it to him, see what he thinks." The fact that Cole never mentioned this to me made me wonder what else Keith might be thinking. "I have a few other friends I could reach out to. A couple are from Mexico. If you want, I can get in contact with them, see if they've heard anything."

"I'd appreciate that a lot."

"You got it." I slapped his shoulder. "We'll do everything in our power to get her back. You have my word."

"Thanks." He spotted Cole and headed in that direction.

I slipped out the front door and walked up to Ivy, who held her phone to her ear. She had her back to me as I approached.

"I do appreciate you." She paused. "Yes, I remember that." There was a lightness to her voice, which made me curious to know who she was speaking with. "Thanks for letting me know, and when I'm back in town, I'll give you a call." She nodded like the person on the other end could see her. "Dinner sounds nice. All right, then. Bye." She hung up, and her shoulders sagged as she turned around. She suddenly jumped as she spotted me. "Do you know you have a habit of doing that?"

I slowly folded my arms, and she leaned her head to the side with a frown. I loved the way she could look attractive no matter what time of day it was. I wasn't used to being so caught up by a female. It was uncharted territory for me.

"Is there a problem?"

"Who were you talking to?" I also hated how possessive I sounded. Her mouth twisted, and she matched my stance.

"Why do you want to know?"

"You were really wound last night, and today you seem," I thought for a moment, "better."

"That's not the word I'd use to describe that call." She lifted her brows. "Did you ever consider just why I might seem a little *less* wound?" She dropped one eyebrow, and I felt my pants tighten below my belt. "Not that it's any of your business, Ty," she came closer, "but it was Bronson. He had information, and I played flirty to get it."

I ran my tongue along my teeth while I absorbed her words. "I see." My tone bordered on jealously, and I tried to drop it. I didn't like it any more than she did. She rolled her eyes as she began to move past me. "When do you go to Washington next?"

"Ah," I'd thrown her off balance at my change in subject, "I think I need to be there sometime next week."

"Okay."

"Why? Do you have to approve my trips now?" Her chin rose, and I stepped closer.

"No," I shook my head, "I'm just making sure that it meets up with my plans."

"Your plans?" Her brows pitched.

"I got the green light to investigate some leads on

Hill. Cole asked me to escort you to Washington, so I'm trying to sync our trips."

"Oh."

"You can't go alone, Ivy."

"I know. I guess I just figured Doc would take me."

"Why Doc?"

"Because he's—" She stopped herself. "Let's just hope you aren't going to end up in Mexico just when I have to leave."

"Yes, let's really hope that won't happen at all." I linked my fingers through hers and gently pulled her close to me. Her free hand landed on my chest, and I instantly felt grounded.

"I don't like Bronson."

"I don't like Demi," she shot back.

"I told her at the coffee shop that she and I weren't anything." Her blink was obvious.

"You had coffee with her?" Slowly, her hand slipped away from me. "Was she in New York with you?"

"She went with my family to the funeral."

"I see." She stepped back, and I stepped forward to close the gap between us again.

"What?"

"You just got jealous because of my phone call, but you went on a trip with your just new ex." She put her hand on her chest. "Surely you can see why my back would be up. Were you even going to tell me she was there?"

"Why would I?" I frowned. Her head pulled back,

and she laughed and shook her head. I closed my eyes for a second as I realized I'd sounded like a dick. "I didn't mean it like that."

"It's fine." She plastered on a smile and looked over my shoulder. "Hey, Doc." I turned and greeted Doc Roberts.

"Hey, Ty. Ivy, did you get it?"

"I did, yes."

"Wonderful." He gave me a pleasant smile, and I wondered how much Doc knew about Ivy's situation. I sensed he was involved and couldn't get a handle on why. "How's Bronson doing?"

"He's fine. It was good to catch up. It's always nice to know where you stand with someone." She tossed me a look, and I felt her silent kick to my gut.

Doc looked at me and then looked at Ivy. I caught their exchange, but I wasn't about to leave. I knew I'd messed up and needed to make the situation right.

"It was who we thought it was," she said cryptically. Doc's face fell, but he recovered quickly.

"Oh, dear. I guess I should go make some calls." He gave a wave before he left, and I turned to face her.

"Ivy, I'm sorry. I didn't mean to come off the way I did."

"It's fine." She started to brush by me, but I snagged her arm.

"It's not, and I'm sorry." I bent down so we were eye level.

"Ty," she pulled her arm free, "our lives are incredibly

complicated right now. This was only supposed to be lust and nothing more. Let's keep our promise of just that."

"I'm not sure if I can," I blurted.

"Well, I'll tell you what. Until you know, maybe we should cool it with the sex."

"I disagree." I hated the idea of her not being mine to touch. "I know how much I crave you." I went with raw honesty, and she could take it whatever way she wanted. "I know how much I like being around you. It's why I reacted like an ass when I realized you were talking to your ex."

"Well, Ty, that sounds mighty close to something called a relationship." She put her hands on her hips, and her eyes bored into mine.

"Then let's have a relationship." I held her gaze.

"I don't think either of us is ready for that." She ran a hand down my arm as if it was the last time she was ever going to touch me. I flared with frustration. I wanted her to want this as much as I did, so I lashed out.

"You were ready to have a relationship with *Hill.* I mean, you dated him. You were ready to give him a chance." I knew I was dangerously close to her walking away.

"First, I had no idea that Carson was Hill. How could I?" She glared at me. "And second, it was just dating. I was putting myself out there to have a bit of fun."

"Have fun with me, then."

"We did, and now look where we are. We're both jealous when we shouldn't be."

"Because we both know we should be in a relation- ship, together." I cornered her with my words, and her mouth opened and closed again as I caught her in her own contradiction. "C'mon, let's try it, Ivy." I hooked her around the waist and tugged her closer to me. "I know it comes with a risk, but how will we ever know if we don't give it a shot? The idea of some other guy having you makes me want to tear his throat out. That's not just lust, Ivy. That's something more."

"I don't know." She cast her eyes about as though she searched for the right answer. "If we do this, Ty, you need to know that seeing your old sex buddy is not okay with me."

"Understood," I leaned down and inhaled her scent, "as long as you understand that there are times I might be possessive."

"I'd never have guessed." She dripped with sarcasm, but her smile lightened as she molded into my hold for a moment then pressed her hands against my chest and looked up at me. "Ty, if we start to slide south, we need to stop and reevaluate. You're here for your job, and I'm here for both a job and my safety." She caught herself on the last word. "You know I am," she admitted.

"Yet, another reason I want to keep you close." I devoured her mouth, full of relief and excited about where this might take us.

"I'm serious, Ty." She pulled away. "We have to make sure this relationship doesn't take us down a road where we can't ever be friends. There's too much at stake here for both of us."

"I hear you, and I get it." I kissed her again.

The sound of an engine pulled me away from her, and I smiled, knowing my brother was here to watch my six.

"Who's that?" She looked around me to where the SUV pulled up in front of the house.

"That's Moore, the second addition to my team."

"Oh, the famous best friend," she teased as we made our way over.

The door flew open, and Moore hopped out in our normal attire of t-shirt and fatigues. He dropped his duffle bag on the ground. When he spotted me, he leaned forward for a shake, then grabbed me in a what-the-hell hug. I could feel his excitement.

"That was a long-ass trip, brother." His voice was muffled against my shoulder. "But I'm here, and look at this place." He gave a whistle.

"I can promise you," I knew I could let my guard down a little, "it's well worth the journey."

"Fuck yeah, it is." He suddenly spotted Ivy, and a shit-eating grin spread across his face. "Sorry about my mouth, little lady." Moore held out a hand and she took it.

"I've heard way worse." She smiled. "I'm Ivy."

"Trust me, I've heard a lot about you."

"Is that so?" She glanced at me. "Like what, exactly?"

"Where to begin?" He wrapped his arm around her shoulders and walked her toward the house.

"Don't make me regret this," I muttered as I snagged his duffle bag from the ground and followed.

We headed inside, and I rolled my eyes at the bullshit he fed her. Of course she was wise to him but played along just to get a rise out of me.

Ivy gave him a quick tour and introduced a few people along the way. Though the house struggled with the Lexi situation, they made sure it didn't show as they welcomed our new housemate. After the tour, we went out back, and I indicated a seat for him, then Ivy and I sat next to him so we could all admire the lake.

"This sure wasn't what I expected." Moore let out his breath in a whoosh. "Let's just say it's an entirely different vista than the Taliban-infested mountains." He huffed a little laugh.

"Agreed." I still couldn't believe my life now. It boggled the mind.

"Do you miss it?" Ivy looked at the two of us.

"I was done with the place well before our last tour," Moore explained, "but this guy," he looked at me, "I think he could've done another lifetime there."

"Really?" She tilted her head to study me.

"Yeah," I agreed.

"What's better?" Moore asked, to my surprise. "Here or there?"

"It's very different." I shifted uneasily.

"If you were told you could go back, would you?" Ivy dug deeper into my head.

"Do you still have a bag packed in the closet?" Moore

grinned, knowing old habits died hard. "Beckett would go home like the rest of us because we had to, but he always kept his bag in his closet, ready to go again. He couldn't wait to get back onto Afghan soil. It's why he's ranked where he is. He's a born soldier."

"Careful." I sent him a quick warning in Dari, and he put his hands in the air as he realized he might have gone too far.

"What does that mean?" Ivy tried to repeat the word I used.

"It means you're beautiful." Moore quickly jumped in.

"Does it also mean you're full of shit?" she shot back with a smirk and made him laugh as she stood. "I'll let you two catch up. I've got a meeting in a few minutes I can't miss. I'm pleased to have you here, Moore, and even better, I know this guy's real happy about it." She pretended to punch my shoulder.

"Well, I'm happy everyone's happy." Moore laughed at her, and Ivy joined in with a chuckle then she gave a little wave and headed toward the house.

"Sorry," Moore whispered.

"It's fine." I watched her bend down and pat Butters on the head as she whisked by him.

"She's gorgeous, Beckett," he murmured and drew my attention back to him. "Quite a step up from Demi, I gotta say."

I rolled my eyes and couldn't agree more.

"I have to ask, though," he leaned forward and rested his arms on his thighs, "do you?"

"Do I what?" I kept my eyes on Ivy as she disappeared into the house.

"Do you still have a bag packed?"

"Old habits." I shrugged.

"Right, but we aren't going back. So, why do you have it packed?"

"I-I don't really know. Maybe there's a part of me that hopes we will go back," I admitted. I wasn't sure if that was the whole truth.

"You'd leave her to go back?"

"No, but it's what I know."

"You're a runner, Beckett. You run from things, even things that make you happy."

"I may have a history of that." I nodded. "I've steered away from relationships, but I'll have you know," I pointed my beer at him, "just before you arrived, we put a title on us."

"Wow, really?" His face stretched in surprise. "That's big, buddy."

"Yeah, it is."

"But you know what's interesting?"

"What?"

"She can feel your nerves."

"You've known her for all of, what, ten minutes?" I rolled my eyes.

"The truth was in her reaction to you when you gave me that warning in Dari. She's intuitive." *That she was.* "You like her, right?"

"Yeah."

"Then don't give her a reason to be nervous."

"I have enough shrinks in my life, Moore. I don't need another." I chuckled, and he backed off, but he had a point.

I took some time to fill Moore in on everyone and what was happening as Cole had asked. I knew Frank had talked to him about most of the guys before he came, but he still hadn't met everyone in person, and it would take a little time to get him completely up to speed, especially with the situation we had on our hands with Lexi's disappearance.

"Beckett!" Mark's sharp tone had me on my feet in a flash.

"This is Mark Lopez," I said to Moore.

"Nice to meet you." Mark gave his hand a quick shake. "Sorry to drop you straight into the thick of it, but I'm sure Beckett's told you about our situation." As Moore nodded, Mark went on. "Well, that situation just got bigger."

"What do you know?" I braced myself as another siren suddenly pushed its way through our phones.

Code Blue.

"We just got proof of life," he yelled over the sound. I could see him flinch as he said it. "It's confirmed. Lexi's been taken by the Cartel."

SIX

ERIC

T tried to find a moment alone, but no matter what I did, someone was always watching. I felt claustrophobic and on edge. Alejandro mentioned his car had been followed. He thought he'd lost them and called Filippo to meet him at a local bar, then moments later some of Castillo's men suddenly showed up there. Our cars had to be bugged. I eyed my phone and figured it had been bugged as well. I tried to process what that meant. Why was Castillo so jumpy? Why wasn't he confident I'd keep the girl safe and do what he said? No matter how I looked at it, I knew something had changed.

Chili: I got my fourth girl. So, who the hell do you have? I thought we had an agreement.

I wanted to respond to Chili, let him know about just who I had, but I knew if Castillo found out I'd jumped the gun with my buyer, it could bring everything crashing down. Besides, the fool had said he wasn't going to sell her.

> Eric: We do have an agreement. You have my word. She's for Castillo. If I'd known, I would have told you. I'll be in touch when I can.

Hopefully, that would be enough for Chili to stand down and know something was up but was out of my control. Maybe he'd discover who she was without me having to tell him. I couldn't risk a text right now, not until I knew my phone wasn't being monitored.

Over the next few days, I watched the woman on the live feed. I learned her mannerisms, the way she ate, the way she angry cried, then got mad at herself. I studied her every move. She was feisty, I'd give her that. She actually made me smile when she used a broken tray and tried to beat Leo over the head with it. He was furious when he came cursing up the stairs with a bloody rag pressed against the cut above his eye. I was glad to see he knew better than to react and try to hit her because he knew he'd have to deal with me. He knew my weapon wouldn't be just a tray.

I noticed a few small things that showed me what she was made of, like she always ate, which was smart, as that would keep her strength up. She always asked for more water, also smart because it kept her mind sharp, and she used the handle of the fork to track her meals with small marks on the wall just above her bed. I was especially amused by that. Most woman just gave up and sobbed after the first day. They'd curl up in a ball and sink into their own mind. But not this girl. She had spirit. I wondered if she'd been in a bad situation before and had managed to get out of it. Maybe she'd learned a thing or two. Either that, or she'd had some kind of training. It was fascinating to watch.

"Here's everything we found." Alejandro dropped a file on my desk late one night. "She's got a history." He waited for me to scan the contents. "Lexi Keith," my brows rose at her last name, "late thirties, used to run with a street gang called the Almas Perdidas, dated the club president until a motorcycle gang called the Devil's Reach did a drive-by and killed most of them. Rumor has it, her husband, who was just dating her at the time, pulled a favor and asked the Devil's Reach to help take them out." That was interesting. I'd never had any encounters with the motorcycle gang itself, but I remembered I'd met an older guy, Allen something, who claimed he'd founded the club. He'd worked a couple deals with Castillo. He's a shady fucker, so I kept my distance.

"Anything else?"

"Yeah, actually." He glanced out the door then lowered onto the chair across from me. "We know Blackstone has a connection with The Devil's Reach, but guess who the Devil's Reach President is friends with?"

"Who?"

"Elio Capri. He's that big mob boss, the one who's been splashed all over the papers and magazines and shit. You must've caught the story. Wasn't all that long ago."

"Story?"

"Yeah, it was called The Quiet Mafia of Italy or something like that. There's a whole series about them. He and his wife did an interview."

He looked at me like I was crazy for not knowing.

"Yeah." He nodded slowly as he brought up something on his phone. "Castillo needs to be very careful. Read the article I just sent. It'll show what I'm sayin'. Why Elio Capri might be headed this way." I felt my phone buzz with an alert. "You can't tell me that's some loco coincidence." Alejandro raised his eyebrows at me.

"Mm." I let my gaze go to the window as I thought.

"Castillo might be getting messy." His words drew my eyes back to him. "He just pissed off a shit ton of high-powered people."

"Seems that way."

"A Blackstone wife is downstairs." He pointed down and pulled in his lips. "I'd bet money they'll call the Devil's Reach to get involved in this. Rosa Coppola might be locked up at Castillo's because she owes a debt, but don't think the Capris aren't lookin' for her." He shook his head and went on. "From what I heard from Grim Gates, who knows Elio's cousin, Vinni Capri, Elio's on a full-out manhunt for Rosa and her pal Tieri. All I'm saying is, that chick down there might help Rosa get out from under

Castillo, but she could bring us one messy load of shit." He stood as I held up my hand to stop him.

I needed a moment to think. I rubbed my chin as I leaned back in my chair and opened and closed my pocketknife as I ran through several scenarios. I thought about what play I'd have if this did indeed go south.

"How many of Castillo's men are still on the property?"

"Twelve, give or a take a few." Alejandro's brows went up as he tried to see where I was going with this.

"Any inside?"

"A few. I totally agree with you. They should stay the fuck outside. They don't listen." He motioned over his shoulder that some of them were in the next room.

"Filthy rats." If Castillo was about to pull me into the middle of a war, I needed to get ahead of it. I knew I couldn't get five feet without someone watching me, so I needed to deal with it the only way I could. I stood and tapped my finger against my lips while I thought. "Maybe these cameras can be useful after all. Pull the outside feed up on your phone. I'll get rid of the rats, then you make sure none of them come back in."

"Okay."

"In about," I checked the time, "at the top of the hour, kill the wi-fi."

"What're you thinking?"

"I want to know if the name Rosa Coppola means anything to her." I swung open the door and shook my head at Filippo, who opened his mouth like he was about to say something. He needed to know now wasn't a good time. "Keep the wi-fi off until I say otherwise. Watch that clock, Ale!" I barked over my shoulder. I blew through the living room, glared at Castillo's men, and ordered them outside. Once I knew they were gone, I went down the stairs and used the code to open the door. Then I carefully stood back out of the camera's view.

"What?" Lexi rose quickly from her bed, and her chin went up as she took a fighter stance at the sight of me. I ignored her and hid my smile at her attitude. I tapped my phone screen and glanced over at the computer and waited for it to blink red. A moment later, the camera feed went down, and I stepped inside the room. I tapped the tile on the wall as I stepped close to the cage.

"Lexi," I used her name, "I'm going to ask you something, and it could mean the difference of getting more food or not."

"Not interested."

"You should be."

"Why?" She put her back to the wall of the cage and gave me a bitchy face. "I know how this works."

"Enlighten me." I gave a soft shrug and tucked my hands in the pockets of my pants.

"I've seen your faces, I know your name, I know exactly what the house looks like, and you know who my husband is. Play your games, negotiate, starve me, screw with my head, whatever, because for me, this is just a waiting game until they come for me."

"Rosa Coppola." I watched her face carefully for any sign of recognition.

Nothing.

"Who?" She scrunched her face and stared at the ceiling. I glanced at the cameras to make sure they were still off.

"Devil's Reach." I tried again, and this time her face stretched into a smile.

"I'd pay good money to see you up against Trigger in his slaughter room." *Interesting.* "Maybe I'd be so lucky to use some of his medieval weapons on you."

I made one last comment and hoped it would spark the right reaction. "Where's the Blackstone safe house?"

She burst out laughing and flung herself against the bars close to me. I didn't react except to glance once more at the red light to ensure the cameras were still down. She quickly followed my line of sight and slit her eyes at the camera, but she didn't comment.

"Even if I did know," she hissed through her teeth, "it's the one thing I'd take to the grave." She pressed her face closer and lowered her voice. "And honestly, Eric," I kept my face expressionless, "do what you want to me, because when Blackstone gets their hands on you, you'll wish you never laid eyes on me."

"Rosa Coppola," I repeated, and I saw the lines between her eyes deepen as she studied me. She shook her head then and went back and sat down on her bed. With that, I turned away, tapped the tile on the wall, and closed the door behind me. My mind whirled as I walked back upstairs.

"Boss?" Alejandro handed me his phone and mouthed, "Castillo."

"Yeah?"

"What happened to the wi-fi?"

"Construction down the street," I grunted. I knew his guys would have seen them working on the house down the street. It was being gutted. The road was lined with workers all hours of the day. "They said it'll be back on any moment—" I nodded to Alejandro to turn it back on.

"It's on," he interrupted. "Have you spoken to the woman yet?" I rolled my eyes. We both knew he would have known if I had. He obviously had someone watching the cameras.

"No, but I plan to, tonight."

"Or you could just force it out of her. It would be fun to see what's under that sweatshirt." He chuckled, and I knew he was watching her now.

"Or I could do it the way you pay me to," I shot back.

"Watch your mouth."

"I never asked to babysit the bitch!" I saw Alejandro's eyes widen at my tone to Castillo. "As I pointed out before, you chose me for this job because I'm good at what I do. I can get her to talk, and when she does, you'll know it'll be accurate information and not a bunch of bullshit. But if you think you can crack the bitch, go for it. You take her. I don't want her here, anyway." I knew he wouldn't. Castillo gave orders; he never wanted to do the dirty work himself. Entitled prick.

"I want something by tomorrow night."

"I'll be in touch." I hung up and tossed the phone back to Alejandro.

"I can't believe the way you talk to him. Aren't you afraid he'll kill you?"

"No, and he's an idiot."

"Does she know who Rosa is?"

"No, she hasn't a clue." I headed for my office.

"Hey," he called after me, "you wanna go to church or something? I mean, it always helps to calm you down."

I considered it, but only for a second. I looked out the window at Castillo's men and wondered which one would try to sneak downstairs to play with the woman and which ones would follow us.

"Not today." I slammed the door shut.

———

"Excuse me for asking, boss, but I guess I just don't get it." Filippo watched me as I poured myself a stiff drink. I'd just finished trying to question Lexi for the second time and got nothing but sass and silence. "I mean, why don't you just go down there with a gasoline can and a blow torch and scare her into giving you the information."

"I could, but it wouldn't get me anywhere." I allowed Filippo to occupy my mind. He was, after all, trying to learn the ropes, so I answered his question. I glanced at my watch as I realized I still hadn't heard from my contact with an update on Talya. I'd heard she had information for me on a possible target Blackstone might go after. Grim was overheard talking about it over a card game. I knew he had a connection to the mob in Italy and had been seen in the past with Vinni Capri. It was a small world, and information was money. I had to shake my head when I thought about it. The smartest people got themselves caught because they forgot who was around when they shot their mouths off after a few drinks. Though, with Grim, I wouldn't put it past him. He might be testing the room for snitches.

I decided to answer Filippo. "She's not like any of the women we'd had here. This one's been trained for situations like this. We'll get nothin' but lies and bullshit out of her at this point. I doubt she'd give us anything we can use. Not yet, anyway."

"So, you're making her wait it out?"

"Time's hard to measure when there's no end in sight." I tapped the screen on my tablet to turn up the lights where she lay. I knew it would play harder on her head. "Living in a cage like some pet in a windowless basement will fuck her up more than having conversations with me. I'm her only human contact with the outside world. She'll see that eventually, so until then, we wait." My phone pinged with a message, and just as I read it, the door opened.

"Boss?" Alejandro craned his head in the doorway

then stepped back as he indicated he wanted me to see something.

I stepped outside the door to see two of Castillo's assholes walking through my living room. They disappeared downstairs like they owned the place.

"I was under orders and had to pass the code over." I wanted to punch his face in, but he was right to follow orders. "Should I stop them?"

"No," I sipped my drink and glanced at Castillo's text again and knew there was nothing I could do about it anyway. I shook my head at Alejandro as he started to move toward the door. We could hear her screams as they hauled her up the stairs and through the door. Her wrists and legs were taped, and the sack they had over her head hung half off as she fought them. I laughed, glad they were the ones who had to deal with her. Both of them were sweating, and one had a red mark from his eye to the edge of his mouth. They were much bigger than she was, but she was wild.

"Let me go!" she seethed as one of the guys yanked the sack down over her eyes again.

"Castillo says you're taking too long," one of the meatheads barked at me from where he stood. "He's takin' over." I could see he enjoyed his new power over me. His ridiculous cartoon dragon tattoo stretched over his fat neck as he grinned at me.

"Like I give a shit." I flicked my wrist for them to leave while I sipped my drink. He glared at me, disappointed, and pushed the screaming chick hard toward the door. I heard the car door slam a few times, then the sound of their tires as they spun across the yard.

"The fuck was that?" Alejandro studied me when I didn't respond. "Boss?"

"He'll get nowhere with her, anyway. Let him try." I shrugged, which probably made him wonder where the hell my head was.

"What if Chili comes by and wants to see her? I'm sure he's uneasy his fourth girl was a day late. We don't want to mess things up with our buyer."

"If that happens, we tell Chili the truth," I shrugged again, "that I had no idea what Castillo was up to. That I was under the same impression he was at the tunnel the other day. We tell him the girl's not here, that she's with Castillo, and to give me some time and we'll see if there's a deal we can make for him."

Of course, I wasn't going to let Alejandro know what I really thought. Castillo wanted Lexi dead, but not before he made Blackstone's life a living hell first. I knew she'd never talk, especially to Castillo. I figured I'd get her back here once he realized it. I just hoped he didn't mark her up too badly. I planned to sell her off to Chili for a cool four million if it was the last thing I did. She was going to be my ticket to the big league, and she sure as hell wasn't worth anything to me dead. Now, I just needed to change Castillo's mind.

"Eric," Alejandro came closer and stared me right in

the eye, "come on. Why don't you let me take you to church? It's been a while, and frankly, you're scaring the shit out of me right now." I pursed my lips and set my glass down. He was right; I did need it. I could use a clear head.

"You know what, I think that might be best." I grabbed my wallet, a wad of cash, and my phone, and we headed off to the house of God.

Alejandro and Filippo stayed outside with the truck. I went up the steps and took a deep breath in through my nose then let it out through my mouth and stepped inside. The church was quiet at this time of night. I disliked crowds, and despised children being there even more. Their loud whispers and complaints about how uncomfortable the pews were as they wiggled about always put me on edge. Leave them at home, for God's sake. They didn't want to be there, anyway. I needed to be alone with my thoughts.

I shoved a wad of cash into the collection box and lit some candles for a few friends. I drew the cross and kissed my fingers and felt the peace of the place seep into my head. Then it immediately disappeared as I felt someone watching me. I looked up to see the priest. He caught my eye and gave me a friendly smile from where he stood in the shadows near his office door. He took a few steps toward me.

"Welcome, my son." He kept his distance and gave me a small nod. "Shall we pra—" His words were cut off as he suddenly looked over my shoulder. I glanced behind me to see what had caught his attention.

"Boss." Alejandro's voice was urgent as he wiped the sweat from his forehead. He looked nervous for interrupting me in the one place he knew was my sanctuary. Because he knew better, I was instantly alert. "The girl escaped."

SEVEN

TY

"All right, listen up." Cole looked around the room. We were all gathered and had braced ourselves to hear what Cole would say about Lexi. "Before I lay it on you guys, let's welcome Moore to the house." He paused as murmurs and polite nods were tossed out to Moore. "I apologize for dropping you in the deep end." Cole grimaced at him.

"I'm here now. Use me." Moore was all business.

"Proof of life for Lexi came in an hour ago." The room went still, and a few stole a glance at our brother. Keith's knuckles were white as they gripped the leather on the armrests of his chair. "They're asking for two million for an even exchange."

"Which, of course, is bullshit," Mark shot from the back of the room.

"Agreed, but we're going along with it." Cole held his hand up. "As we speak, Dusk's team is getting the money together. Then we follow their instructions and meet their contact to make the transfer. At that point, Blackstone will follow the contact and see where it leads us. John." Cole looked at him.

"They'll be looking for a tracker." John leaned forward and looked down at his notes. "We know how they work. The money never leads to where the victim's being held. So, instead, while Dusk distracts the contact, Chamness will put a tracker on their vehicle. We'll need it if we lose visual."

"Frank forwarded the video of Lexi being taken to some people he knows. They have eyes on the border and are familiar with a lot of the Cartel's people." Cole pulled our attention back to him. "One male was identified as Julio Garay, who has ties to Denton Barlow." The room went so quiet you could hear a pin drop.

Moore looked at me with a puzzled expression as Cole's face twisted into something painful.

Daniel filled him in. "Barlow went after Logan's wife, Savannah."

"A few times." Mark added. "Fucker's dead now, though."

"Jesus." Moore shook his head and looked back at Logan.

"Dusk and Blackstone will check out the last known places Garay's been seen. We have forty-eight hours to find Lexi or at least some kind of clue as to where she's being held."

"What about the proof of life?" I spoke up. "Often, when we'd get photos of where our men had been taken, the captors didn't think of the shit in the background. Did you get any pics we can study? Look at the materials of the room, types of clothing, belongings, anything that might help us narrow down her location?"

"We're in the process of doing that," Cole looked at me, "but these guys aren't the Taliban. They're a lot more sophisticated. They'll often plant local products from other towns in the pics just to throw us off. There was one thing, though, that caught our eye." He tapped the remote, and part of the POL photo popped up. "They'll often tag their trophy victims, and Lexi would definitely be a big prize." He glanced sympathetically at Keith. "Whoever has her did exactly that." He pointed at the screen, and I studied the oval marking on the wall. "I'm not surprised. This photo will be circulated everywhere among their people, and they'll want to take credit. I just wish we could figure out who it was. We've put it out to all our contacts, and hopefully one of them will recognize the mark and we'll hear something that'll give us a lead."

"We got a hit." Daniel shot up from his seat, and Keith followed. Daniel typed something in the computer and brought up a map of Mexico. I glanced at Frank, who stared at his phone as though he was also waiting for something. I wondered just what kind of resources Washington really had when it came to this kind of exchange.

"My informant says he saw a woman matching Lexi's description two days ago, right here." He circled a street in Rosarito on the map. "We know this place well, guys. If he's tagging his photos, he might be tagging his territory too."

Cole tapped his fingers on the table and stared at his father, who gave him a nod.

"Change of plan, boys. We ship out in an hour."

In less than thirty, I was ready. My weapons were checked, and I was fully dressed in all my gear. I had time, so I walked back to the house, and as I stepped inside, I heard Cole talking in the kitchen. He was giving Savannah a CliffsNotes version of what happened. He told her that Daniel was with Mia doing the same thing. I turned toward the stairs to let them have their privacy. I fingered the rope bracelet Halim had given me. I decided to wear it for good luck. The wolf dangled at my wrist. It reminded me of the past and of all those we'd saved over the years in Afghanistan. It made me feel that those years were worthwhile. It meant a lot.

"Hi." Ivy tugged a sweater over her shoulders as she approached. "I heard you guys got a lead." She pulled the cuff of her sleeve, and I could see she was uncertain.

"We did." Her gaze took in my gear as I drew closer. "We leave in," I looked at my watch, "ten."

"I guess that's good." She chewed the inside of her cheek. "What's that?" She eyed the little charm.

"Just a reminder that not everyone is a bad guy." I smiled at her.

"That's true," she cleared her throat, "but please don't hesitate to shoot if you're not sure."

"I trust my gut and senses. I'll be all right." I wanted to reassure her, but my words just seemed to make her more edgy. "I don't want you going to Washington without me," I blurted, not caring about my filter anymore. "Can you stay 'til I get back?"

"You know I can't do that." She lowered her voice. "If Frank needs me there, I have to go."

"Lie and say you're not feeling well. Just buy me some time."

"Ty," her forehead creased slightly, "I'll be fine. Frank will be there."

"Beckett," Cole called as he came out the door, "let's move out."

"Copy that." I looked back at Ivy. Damn, I hated the timing on all this. I could see her nerves were on edge despite what she said. She stepped back when I didn't say anything.

"Be careful." She turned away, but I hooked her arm and swung her back to me then caught her lips with mine. I may not be able to control what would happen in Washington, but I could control this moment, and I needed to show her how important she was to me. She matched my intensity and gave me everything she had. Her hands squeezed the tops of my arms as if she didn't want to let go. I put one hand on her waist and held her to me, and the other went to the back of her head. I fingered her silky hair as my lips crushed hers. She tasted like candy, and I wanted more, but our time was up.

"Be here when I get back," I huffed. I kissed her deeply one last time and left. I wasn't good at goodbyes.

I rushed up the driveway, hopped in the SUV, and we drove up to the helicopter pad. The pilot had the engine on, and once we were all inside, he lifted off and we were on our way. I settled in and savored her taste still on my lips. In the past, I'd never have allowed thoughts of a woman to cloud my mind once I was in uniform and ready for a mission, but Ivy was always right there. I found myself needlessly thumbing the side of my jacket. I blinked back the idea of her soft skin inside it and swallowed hard as I adjusted my position. Moore caught my eye and threw me a quick smirk then turned back to his chat with John. I hated that he knew me so well.

Twice, Cole went over the plan and then over the back-up plan. He was thorough and left nothing to chance. Everything went silent, then each of us were lost in our own thoughts. I saw Moore looking at something, but before I could ask, Mark tapped me on the arm. He fished around in his pocket then pulled up something on his phone. It was a video of Ivy inside the chopper.

"I thought a little lady luck for your arrival date was smart." Mark's voice broke over the radio. "Once you decide on your team's name, you can add it." I fought a big fat grin as I watched Ivy lean forward on all fours to blow the flakes away. The video panned out from her tight ass, and I could see she'd etched the year on the helicopter wall. It was incredibly sexy, and now I wished I wasn't sitting in the belly of the chopper but alone with her in a room. "Make her be the reason you come home." He took the phone, and I felt Moore hit my leg as if to agree with Mark.

I leaned back and allowed myself to daydream about Ivy as we flew toward the unknown. It was a long trip. We made a stop and switched aircraft, then as we all settled ourselves for another flight, we used the time to get some sleep. Who knew when we'd get to shut our eyes again. All too soon, the sound of the engine changed, and everything became real again. All thoughts of anything except the mission disappeared as I did my mental checklist.

The rope hissed through my hands as one by one we descended onto enemy soil. The moment our boots touched the ground, we swung our weapons up, bent at the knees, and scanned the horizon through our scopes. Then, blending with the night, we made our way to the town and began the search. I took the street level while Moore scanned the rooftops.

"Movement, at our nine," Moore's voice crackled through my earbuds.

"Stay on it." We kept moving. I did a double take when a child stepped out of her house and froze in fear. I held a finger up to my mouth and urged her back inside. I knew the Cartel used children of all ages to do their dirty work, but I wasn't about to take out a kid. For a split second, my eyes moved to the bracelet, and I knew Halim was with me in some way.

We came up the next street, and Mark and Cole signaled us to follow. John, Mike, and Keith stepped in line behind us as we entered a narrow area and came to a stop as unexpected barricades armed by police blocked our route. We knew better than to be spotted by the Mexican police. No one could know we were here. As we watched, one of the officers suddenly jumped off the hood of his cruiser and looked down a side road as though he heard something. He waved at one of his men to go check it out while he pulled out his weapon and picked up a radio.

Cole made the signal for us to split up and follow plan B. We scattered. It was better to be on our own in that situation than all be caught together. Moore and I stayed close enough to keep tabs on each other.

An engine rumbled behind Moore, and both of us dove for cover. Laughter and bottles being thrown against a wall made it clear trouble was nearby. We slowly got up and made our way down a side street, keeping close to the wall.

"I've got company," Cole whispered into the radio. "Three armed men in a Honda. We're staying put."

"Copy that, Raven One," I huffed as I kept my pace. "We have company to the south of us. Moving across the open—" I stopped dead when I saw its shadow even before I heard the sound. Four men in the back of a pickup, AK-47s swung at their sides as they rounded the corner facing directly at us.

"Is that...?" Moore's tone was chilling.

"*Ma Deuce*," I whispered at the large-caliber machine gun capable of destroying a military aircraft pointed in our direction. When I saw the shooter's hand move to load the gun, I knew we had only four seconds to haul ass. I reached back and shoved Moore hard to one side as I ran directly toward the barrel of the gun then dodged at the last second into a side street before they could get a fix on me.

"We've got company!" I could hear Moore inform the others over the radio while I pumped my arms and ran as fast as I could to draw the fire away from him.

Zip, zip, zip, zip! Plaster above my head blew up and rained down over me. I used my shoulder and burst through someone's front door, jumped over a child on the floor, ran through their living room, and then out a kitchen door. I hopped over a fence and landed in a sandbox. After a fleeting thought of *thanks for the soft landing*, I bounced to my feet and shimmied up a pipe to higher ground. More shots could be heard, and I only hoped it wasn't at the family's expense.

"Check in, Beckett!" Moore broke through my wild heartbeat.

"I'm alive."

"Where are you?"

"Just follow the fucking trail of casings!" I jumped to the next building where bullets suddenly sprayed straight up. "Shit!" I took in my surroundings and calculated my options. I knew I needed to head east toward the building where Lexi was supposedly last spotted.

Zip, zip, zip!

I ducked low and studied the skyline then picked up the pace once I spotted the Christ of the City statue. The statue was our landmark if we got split up or lost on this mission. I suddenly found myself teetering on a ledge, and the tips of my boots tilted forward as my brain fought to catch up. I started to lose my balance, so I pushed hard with my feet to propel myself off the ledge toward the next building. I dropped fast, but my fingers snagged the edge of the roof as my body slammed into the side, nearly knocking the wind out of me.

"Shit, Beckett," Keith's voice fought the fog from my head, "I just saw that jump!"

I managed to haul myself up, roll onto my side, then leapt to my feet. I zigzagged a few meters as I got my sense of balance again and kept going.

It always amazed me what the human body could do when adrenaline pumped through the veins.

"Ahh!" someone yelled from behind me, and I whirled around to see a man running at me with a machete. I didn't have a moment to think. He jumped me, tumbling us both to the rooftop. His weapon went flying as we rolled over and over, until I felt the safety of the rooftop disappear under me. The man's wild eyes held mine as we dropped like rocks through the air. I knew I was going to be the one to break his fall, as I was on the bottom.

Suddenly, one of his legs snagged a pole, and his body jerked up away from me. I had a tight grip on his shirt, and the momentum yanked me upward and slowed my fall. With arms spinning, I loosened my knees as I dropped the last several feet to the ground. A cry for help found my ears, but as quickly as it registered, it was gone. On impact, I tucked and rolled until I came to a stop.

Holy shit. My head spun with the possibility that I could have just been spattered on the pavement.

"Could you be any more of a showoff?" Moore stuck his hand out to help me up.

"Fuck you," I grunted through a smile, glad to accept his help to stand.

"I feel like I just witnessed an audition for the next Bourne movie." Mark's low voice behind me had me turning to find Blackstone had seen my dramatic fall.

"You good?" Cole came closer.

"Trust me, that's nothing for him," Moore answered for me, but I gave a nod and did a quick check to make sure I was.

"That's fucking sick." John admired the dead guy dangling by his leg from the pole.

"Lucky bastard. Could've been you up there." Mike shook his head.

"All right, let's move out," Cole whispered. "They know we're here. Let's get going. We need that building cleared."

"Copy that." Mark followed Cole, but I stopped and glanced behind me. My sixth sense was niggling.

"What?" Moore hit Keith on the back to stop. "What are ya feeling, Beckett?"

"Something's bothering me." I scanned the area.

"Like?" Keith came closer and joined me in searching the shadows.

"I don't know."

"Okay," Keith cleared his throat, "let's stay hyperalert."

"Copy that." It took everything in my power to turn my back and follow the team. Something pulled at me to go the other way.

I hated that I ignored my gut.

One more street, and we made it to the building. With little hope, we cleared the shitty, rat-infested building and came up with nothing more than an old box of crackers and some wire. There were no signs of Lexi ever being there. No signs of blood, nothing. The sad reality was we were back at the start, with no leads.

"All this means is we go home and try again." Cole moved over to Keith, who had leaned against the wall as he took a moment for himself. "This is what we do, what we know happens. This isn't over, buddy."

"I know," he nodded, and I glanced over at Moore, who looked just as defeated as we did. You didn't have to know the one you were looking for to feel how fucking heavy the situation was. We all knew that not finding Lexi tonight meant she'd spend another night with those monsters.

John whistled from the side door. "We have to go."

One by one, we slipped outside and made our way

toward the outskirts of town. When the chopper lifted off the ground, a heaviness rooted in our chests as we returned home empty handed.

EIGHT

Twenty minutes earlier

ERIC

"Where?" I cut off one of Castillo's men who frustrated me with his wordy rundown of exactly what happened. "Just give me the street name!" He said the name, and I pointed for Alejandro to take a hard right. "I see them." I tucked my phone in my pocket and jumped out of the car before it had even stopped. I raced over to the wreck; the Jeep had slammed into a flower shop. I knew the owner lived in the back of the shop, and he backed away once he saw who he was dealing with.

"Bitch must've broken the tape off," I recognized the voice of the idiot I'd been on the phone with. "She must've grabbed the wheel or something, and they slammed right into the wall. She took Manny's knife, poor shit. She stabbed Carlo, too," he whined as another of Castillo's men bobbed his head in agreement.

I bent down and eyed her handiwork. The driver wasn't wearing his belt, so his head was smashed on impact. He got off lucky. His passenger must have bled out, as his legs were trapped by the crushed dash. A nasty looking jagged knife was in his hand. He must have pulled it out of his jugular himself. Ugly way to go.

I took a quick glance in the back and saw some blood on the seat. I wondered how badly she might be hurt and how much it would slow her down.

"Where're their guns?"

"I have his." He pointed to the passenger. "Shit, who knows where Manny's is. Bet the bitch took it."

I glanced at the shop owner, who looked like he might shit himself. I reached into my coat pocket and pulled out some cash and handed it to him.

"Which way'd she go?"

"There." He pointed toward the beach.

"Good." I smiled. "He'll," I pointed to the ass I'd just talked to, "clean this up. Use that cash for the repairs."

"Thank you," he repeated a few times as his head bobbed, then he backed inside.

"Deal with this." The ass looked at me in disgust. Clearly, he thought he was above cleaning up such a mess.

"What about the owner?" He had the balls to question me. I knew he was itching to kill the shop owner just because he'd seen the crash and his face.

"You touch him," I stuck my finger in the face, "and I'll use that knife to gut you, and I won't be as kind as she was."

"Fuck!" he cursed.

I approached Alejandro, who had stayed behind the wheel. He knew better than to exit the car unless I said otherwise.

"She headed toward the beach. I'm going on foot, and you circle that way. Filippo, you go that way, and we'll see if we can flush her out."

"Got it." Filippo jumped out of the front seat, and Ale tore off in the opposite direction.

I headed down the street and into the area where there were a multitude of alleyways. I would hide there if I was her. I was a big guy, and I'd learned over the years to be light on my feet. I took pride in my ability to track people. You just needed to be able to think like your prey, get into their head. I factored in their panic, fear, and any injuries they might have had and considered where they'd run. I wondered about this one, how she'd play it out. I was willing to bet she wouldn't make it easy. I stopped and studied the area around me. For most, the beach would mean open water and freedom. It was too easy. I figured she wouldn't go for the obvious.

I stopped when I heard something, I closed my eyes and listened. Footsteps. I swung my gaze to the side and heard them again, but they were louder and sturdier. No way they'd be hers. She weighed maybe a buck twenty, soaking wet. My phone vibrated in my pocket, and I squinted at the screen.

"Noah," I answered.

"Mr. Noah, I need you please to come here." The old guy I paid to be my ears at his shop near the beach spoke quietly.

"Is there a girl with you?"

"*Sí.*"

"Don't let her leave. I'm on my way." I took off in his direction, not caring who might be working the streets tonight. I didn't call my guys. I wanted to get to her first. The last thing I wanted to do was alert Castillo's guys. I didn't need them involved any more than they already were. They'd fucked this whole situation up enough already.

I pumped my arms at my sides as I tore through the streets I knew so well. I took a shortcut and raced through an open beach bar where a sea of bodies pulsed to some crazy new-age music. I knocked over a waitress and pushed aside a drunk guy who had his hands on some young American chick. They were in my way. Fuck me, why did these girls not see that they're just looking for all kinds of trouble? How many of them needed to go missing before they realized they weren't safe? It was such easy money for people like me.

I shook off the anger I felt at all these stupid people as I reached the back door of the shop. I took a moment to catch my breath, then slipped around the side. I could see the vendor through the window. He stood with Lexi, who looked to be pacing in front of him. I slipped away quietly and eased in the back door. I was a few feet from her when she spotted me and tensed.

"What? No!" she cried to the vendor and looked at me as I quickly stepped toward her.

"Come on," I waved my hand, "you can't be here."

"No!" She suddenly pulled a gun from the pocket of her sweatpants. "Stop!"

"Enough," I warned, not wanting to draw attention to us. "Put it down before you shoot yourself." I really wished the vendor wasn't witnessing this whole thing.

"Fuck you!" She squeezed the trigger and shot right next to my foot. She took off running, and to my surprise, she was pretty fast. I raced after her. She crossed the road and disappeared into one of the side streets. As I reached the street, she shot at me again.

"Shit!" I whirled back around and saw she had spotted a few local cops who had a barricade up ahead. "Come on!" I hissed. I knew she'd be safer with Castillo than the fucking local police. As I took the side street, I had a strange feeling and looked up to see someone holding a machete on the rooftop. I didn't even want to think why he was there, but thankfully, he seemed too preoccupied to pay any attention to me. Nothing could surprise me anymore in this crazy, lawless country.

I squeezed through a small area and popped out right behind Lexi. I snagged her around the waist and slapped a hand over her mouth then whirled her behind the wall and out of view of the officers not far ahead of us. I used my knee to knock the gun out of her hand and kicked it out of sight.

"You wanna live another day?" I hissed into her ear. "Because if those officers get their hands on you, they'll sell you to Siberia so fast you'll never have a chance at freedom."

She kicked and bucked, but I outweighed her by a lot.

"Go check it out," one of the officers called. Shit, he must have heard us. I hauled her back into an alleyway out of sight.

"Let me help you, Lexi." I internally cursed as Filippo came up behind us. I shook my head, and he backed off a bit and raised his phone to his ear. I heard him tell Alejandro where we were, then he disappeared around the corner as he talked. "Don't fight me and listen." I loosened my grip and slowly eased her out of my hold. It was a risk, but I needed her to see I didn't want to hurt her. "See, that's—"

Whack! She smoked me in the jaw with her elbow then kneed me hard in the balls and took off at a full run past the alley where Filippo had gone.

"Fuck!" I once again raced after her. It took me a moment, but I figured out where she was headed, where most thought they'd find safety. The church. Little did she know that the *Christ of the City* was an empty shell of a church that had burned down quite a while back. It offered no help to the fallen. Once again, I took a different way around, cut her off, and pointed my gun in her face. I needed to get her out of here before—

"Help!" she screamed, and in desperation, I lunged forward and knocked her out cold. I caught her mid-fall, hiked her over my shoulder, and slipped into the shadows with her. Alejandro raced toward us. I tossed her in back and jumped in the front seat.

"Drive, Ale," I yelled. I'd had enough and wanted to get the hell back home before we had any more company. We eased through the side streets, not drawing attention to ourselves. I glanced at the Christ of the City Church and saw movement inside. Friggin' night junkies probably looking for a spot to squat.

"I hope you enjoyed your evening," I muttered and thought how badly this night could have ended for all of us.

"I did, thanks. Too bad you can't say the same for your balls." Her voice was strong, but I heard defeat in her tone.

"She's back." I smirked and turned to look at her. I made a show of shifting my weight to the side as if to give my balls some relief, and she gave a snort.

We made it back home without any further incidents, and I hopped out and opened the door to help Lexi out myself. Tears brimmed in her eyes, and I looked away. I wasn't going to allow myself to be affected by her.

"Wait outside," I ordered my men as I drew her inside the house. "Are you hurt at all?"

"Fuck you," she spat.

I rolled my eyes and inspected her body. The way she held her arm told me she was hurt. Respectfully, I lifted her shirt slightly and saw some bruising along her side.

"Anywhere else?"

"No." She lowered her defenses with a sniff. "My lower back." Again, I was careful how high I lifted her shirt and saw the bruises that had begun to surface there too.

"Is it from the car accident or from Castillo's men?"

"Car accident." She looked away.

"Did his men do anything to you?" Her eyes went to the floor.

"Other than get some good gropes in, no." I ran my tongue along my teeth at the thought of that and pulled her shirt back down.

"Who touched you?"

"The one with the scar on his neck." Her eyes finally met mine, and I knew exactly who she referred to.

"I'll deal with him."

"Good." She raised her chin at that then winced.

"Let's get you something for that." I looked over her head out the window as I heard engines approach. "Fuck, it's Castillo's men." I watched as they drove up the driveway, then Alejandro opened the door.

"Boss?"

"I know. Take her down and lock her back up."

As the guys came inside, Alejandro took Lexi by the

arm and headed for the stairs. I pulled out my phone and called Castillo.

"Did you find her?" he barked into the phone as I marched up to the cameras.

"I did," I bit out knowing full well he'd been watching me.

"Good, now—"

I cut him off. "No." I didn't even care that I might be about to seal my own death. "You got me involved in this, so let me do it."

"Fine," he snarled.

"And no more fucking cameras." I tossed my phone aside as, one by one, I tore his cameras from the wall to destroy their live feed. For years, I'd been his puppet and cleaned up his reckless mistakes, but not this time. I was finished.

NINE

IVY

Shadows was pretty much the size of a small resort, and when the children were there it was filled with life and laughter and gave you a warm and cozy feeling. But now it felt cold and quiet since they'd moved the children out to keep them safe. The fact that the Blackstone Team was away as well made for an almost eerie silence. Understandably, the wives were worried, and although they all tried their best to act normal, it was a challenge and one they'd never faced before.

I did my best to offer comfort and someone to talk to, but I understood. This was a much bigger situation than they'd ever had to deal with since Shadows was formed. Just the idea that someone could expose the location of the safehouse was a threat to everyone here. I wished I could help more.

At least I had cranky old Scoot to talk to. I had to laugh. He never seemed to alter his shameless way of sitting. Sometimes he'd sit in the crack of the couch cushion, flop his legs wide open, and stare at me as if to say, "Look at how fabulous my manhood is." If anything, at least he gave me a good chuckle.

"Ivy?" Sloane knocked softy on my office door and gave me a nervous look. "May we come in?"

We?

"Sure." I expected to see Savannah behind her, so the fact that it was Frank had me on my feet. "I'm going to guess this isn't a girls' night invite?" I desperately wished it was.

"No," she shook her head, "and I'm sorry, but this does require us to shut the door."

"Okay." I stepped around my desk and held on to the side of it for support.

"I'm just going to cut right to the—"

"Frank," Sloane shot him a glare and shook her head, "perhaps a little softer might be wiser?" He blinked at her and then seemed to think about how he had come across.

"Right, sorry." He turned to me again. "Ivy, last night, Ben Oliver was in your mother's house when she got back from the market."

"She's okay, though," Sloane jumped in and put her hand on my arm as I felt my knees begin to shake. "She's just rattled."

A sudden ringing in my ears made it hard to make out their words.

"He had already broken into her house and had gone through her things," Frank went on, knowing I'd want all the details. "We know he saw the fake letters from you because they'd been thrown back in the drawer. That's a positive because there's no reason to believe he won't believe what he read." A cold wash came over me at the thought of my mom's fear. "Apparently, he waited for her and grabbed her as she came inside. He held a knife to her throat and forced her to tell him where you were." He held up both hands to reassure me again. "You can rest assured she's perfectly fine."

"Did-did—" Mom didn't know where I was, so I hoped she gave the cover story, so he didn't hurt her.

"She did exactly what we'd coached her to do." He read my mind. "She gave him the address in New York City, when he didn't believe she was in California like we lied about before. We have the New York place under surveillance. Hopefully, he's heading that way now. She was very brave and said to tell you she knew you'd worry but that she's fine."

"Thank God." I nodded and felt some of the feeling in my body come back. "I'd like to see her, Frank. You know how close—"

"We leave at zero-four-hundred." Frank stood. I was pleased he'd said that, as nothing was going to stop me from going to be with her after I was the one who put her in danger. "Your mother finally agreed to let us send her somewhere safe. I do think she needs you, though."

"Yes," I whispered. "I'll go pack. It won't take long."

I showered, packed, and was ready to go by three-thirty the next morning. Daniel helped me carry my suitcase downstairs, and Sue asked me to step into the living room for a brief chat.

"How are you doing?" Her warm, motherly smile made me feel as though I could talk to her openly.

"I'm okay," I answered honestly. "A bit rattled, though." I ran a hand through my hair and adjusted my skirt. "I'm just so angry at it all. I mean, this is my problem, and now my mom is caught in the crosshairs of it."

"Frank says she handled it very well," she confirmed with a smile. "Must run in the family."

"She's known to be scrappy." I half chuckled. "I'm surprised she didn't try to pepper spray him."

"From the little I know, it sounds like you have a little of that fire in you, too." I felt the anger rise inside as I remembered the night he'd appeared in my office.

"I knew working with soldiers who suffered from PTSD could be dangerous, but I never expected anything like that. It's making me second guess if I should work alone in my office again."

"Sadly, the world is full of unexpected events, especially when you work with people like that. They have such terrible issues. How you handle it when these things happen is what really counts." She rested her hand on mine. "And I personally think you're handling it very well."

"Thanks." I smiled and squeezed her hand. I was thankful for her kind words.

She seemed to hear something and looked toward the door. "Savi?" she called, and a worn-out looking Savannah came into the room in pajamas, coat, and boots. Her hair was tossed up in a messy bun, and she had her hands wrapped around a mug of coffee. "Everything all right, dear?"

"Yes, it is now." She gave me a little wave as she tucked herself in the chair across from us. "Olivia's all settled at Dusk."

"Dusk? I thought they were going to Washington."

"That was the plan," Daniel pulled his glasses off and cleaned the lenses with the bottom of his sweater, "but the kids weren't having it, so Frank had some of Eagle Eye head down there for added measures."

"It's not ideal, but Mike's family said they'd house them if something came up."

"Always so many things going on, it's hard to keep up."

"I just wished it had been Davie or Quinn who drove her to Dusk." Savi used her thumb and pressed it between her eyes. "I don't know the new guy very well."

"Thank goodness she's back and settled." Sue put a hand on her chest in relief. "So, she enjoyed the camp?"

"She had a great time, but I could tell she was ready for home, and the idea of being sent to Dusk wasn't exactly what she had in mind."

"Once she sees the others, she'll be all right."

"Yes. Brandon met her at the door, and I could tell by

what she said she missed him, too. I'm just glad they have each other and aren't going to be separated."

Sue nodded. "Especially not those two."

"Ready?" Frank stepped in as he pulled out his phone.

I jumped up and tugged the handle on my suitcase. "Yeah."

I hugged Sue and Savannah and followed him out to the car. He took my suitcase and put it in the trunk while I waved at the girls, then he held the car door open for me. I slipped inside and settled in for the long drive to the North Dakota airport. A few times, I second guessed my decision to go without Ty, but Frank was on a call nearly the entire drive, so I couldn't share my concern with him. He spoke quietly, and a few times switched over to a different language, so I assumed the conversation wasn't meant for my ears.

The line for security seemed to take forever, and I found myself looking over my shoulder like Ben Oliver might magically appear. Finally, Frank flashed some form of ID when we got near the front. He must have finally clued in, and we got to bypass the security checkpoint while he maintained his life-long phone call.

I checked my boarding pass to see what gate number we needed to go to. Thankfully, it was right near a coffee shop, and I pointed it out to Frank. I let him know I wanted to get one, and he nodded and mouthed a black coffee for him.

"Two coffees, one with cream and one black, please." I smiled at the young kid behind the counter.

"Make that three coffees," Ty said over my head, and butterflies found my stomach as his hand slid around my waist. "One cream and two black."

"Ty!" I stepped back to check him over. "How—when did you get in?"

"I got the call from Frank that you needed to go, so when we made our first stop," he looked around and skipped over the details, "I flew here to meet up with you."

"You're coming with us?"

"I told you I didn't want you to go without me." He pretended to look mad.

I couldn't help but smile, then stole a glance at Frank, who still had his back to us, so I quickly leaned in and kissed him. His arm hooked around me and locked me in place to extend the kiss a little longer.

"You have no idea how much I needed that," he murmured across my lips with a heavy sigh. "I saw your handiwork on the chopper." I grinned. "It made me feel like you were with me."

"Good." I gave him another quick kiss and wished I had all of him. "How was it?" I whispered, unsure if he was ready to talk about it.

"Eventful." He closed his eyes. "Not at all what we were hoping for. Fingers crossed the informants will come up with something else fast."

"I'm sorry."

"Me too." He slowly let me go when our coffees were ready. "How's your mom?"

"She's okay." I shrugged. "I just need to see her."

"Fair enough." He took Frank's coffee and handed it to him. Frank held it up in a silent thanks but didn't hang up.

"He's been on that phone for ages. Any idea who he could be talking to for so long?" I asked out of sheer curiosity when Frank once again turned his back to us.

"My guess would be to any or all of his contacts with a connection to Mexico."

———

"Mom," I shouted and ran into her arms like I was six again, "are you okay?" I studied her carefully. I knew she was physically fine, but it was the mental and emotional cancer that people often missed. It was why I took my job so seriously.

"I'm much better now." She patted my back, and I breathed in the perfume that always made me feel loved.

"I'm sorry my problems found you." Tears filled my eyes, and I blinked them away.

"Sweetheart," she pushed my shoulders back and looked at me straight in the eye, "what do I always tell you about that word?" I smiled as she swiped a Kleenex across my cheeks. "Never be sorry for something that's out of your control."

"I know." I took her hands and relished being close to

her again. My mother grounded me and reminded me she was all I needed in a parent.

"Sweetheart, I need to tell you something."

"Okay."

"Bronson came by."

"Why?"

"He wants you back." She shrugged, as she knew that would never happen. "Said he loves you."

"Bronson loves what's in front of him in a given moment. We spoke on the phone a few times, and now he wants to get back together." I rolled my eyes. "He'll get over it once Corinne from his office is finished with her fling of the month."

"Maybe you should see him and remind him why the two of—" She looked over my shoulder and then back to me. "And who might this be?"

"Mom," I stepped back as Ty approached, "this is Major Beckett." I sniffed. "Ty, this is my mother, Clara."

"Lovely to meet you, ma'am." He glanced at me. "Are you good?" I nodded.

"Are you the soldier looking out for my daughter?"

"One of them, yes." Mom eyed him and fought a smile.

"Isn't she lucky."

"Mom." I chuckled, and she moved in.

"Thank you," she hugged him, and I caught Ty's surprised reaction, "she's all I've got, so please keep her safe."

"You have my word I will."

"That includes her ex. He never has gotten over her."

"I don't blame him." Ty didn't miss a beat, and my mother swung her gaze to me and my cheeks heated. "I'll make sure no one touches her."

"Thank you." She smiled happily at him.

I coughed with emphasis, and Ty backed away a little to give us space. I wanted to tell him we were fine, but the truth was I felt safe when he was around, and it was nice that he'd come. I changed my mind and waved him over, and he sat down beside us.

Mom relived her horror for me so I could pick her brain. I hoped there might be some small clue that could lead me to know where Ben Oliver had gone. She showed me a photo of a pack of matches that had fallen from his pocket when he'd grabbed her.

"Frank has it, but I took a photo of it before they left," she whispered.

"Moon Slinger." I scrunched my face up in thought. "Sounds like some mythical rodeo bar." I wondered why Frank hadn't shared this with me. "Have you ever heard of it?"

"No, I've no clue," she closed her eyes for a moment, "and I really don't care to know."

"I understand, Mom. I'm sure Frank's all over it." I covered her hand with mine as Ty excused himself and pulled out his phone, no doubt googling the name of the place. "I hate that I have to go." I checked the time. "I'm glad you've decided to stay here for a bit. Once this entire thing gets cleared up, things will go back to normal." Ty's head snapped up from his phone, and he stared directly at me. I knew we'd have to discuss what it would mean when my life did go back to normal. My position at Shadows was never supposed to be long-term. But I couldn't go there yet.

"Here's my direct number." Ty handed her a card. "If you need anything at all, just call."

"Thank you." She hugged him then turned and hugged me.

"I love you, sweetheart. Call me when you get back to wherever you're staying." I knew she didn't like not knowing where I was, but it was for the best.

Ty walked in front of me as we headed to the car. The patrolmen were stationed across the street, and it made me feel a little better about leaving her.

"I'm sure you worry about her being here without family." Ty stared at the house for a moment then backed out of the driveway.

"I do, but it helps knowing she has Reid checking in on her all the time. Oh, and apparently Abby." I rolled my eyes, amazed I'd never picked up on my uncle's secret. "How I never knew about him and Abby still baffled me."

"Reid?"

"My uncle." I pulled out my phone and saw Frank had texted me.

"Do I know Reid?"

"Umm," I opened the text and started to read as I answered him, "Doc Roberts." The car went silent, and I pulled my eyes away from my phone to look over at him.

"What?" I was so wrapped up in Frank's words I couldn't replay my own.

"Your uncle is Dr. Roberts? As in the house doctor?" His eyes widened along with mine.

"Mm," I tried to stall for time, "maybe?" I showed my teeth in a fake smile.

"Fuck," he muttered and looked out the windshield, and then it hit me.

"Did he ever talk to you about me?"

"Yeah, he did."

"He's good like that," I tried not to chuckle, but I failed miserably.

"You find that funny, do you?" He gave me a side eye.

"Maybe a little," I shrugged, "but he is a professional, and always has been. He'll take everything he's ever heard to the grave. It was the number one thing he instilled in me when I told him I wanted to follow in his footsteps."

"Shit," he muttered more to himself, "to think about the stuff I said about you."

"Bad things?" I probed.

"No," he smirked, "just what you do to me."

"Which is?"

"I'll have to show you later." I wiggled my eyebrows and hoped he would. "Does anyone else know who Doc is to you?"

"Just the ones who need to know. The rest of the team doesn't, nor do the wives. That's the way we want it to stay for as long as we can."

"Fair enough." He seemed to let it go, but a few times I caught him glancing my way.

Another text popped up.

Frank: I'll be back at HQ by one. Find me when you arrive.

I read the text to Ty as I wrote him back.

Ivy: Will do.

"Should we stop for lunch?"

"Sure."

During lunch, I couldn't help but feel a sense of normalcy as we ate together. Ty and I talked for a while about regular things, just like normal people.

"So, you met my sister." He leaned back when the waiter removed his dish.

"Yes." I twisted my napkin and dropped it on the table. I was interested in how he felt about that. I knew how private he was. "Shelly seemed very nice." I studied his face. "You don't talk about your family much."

"No."

"Why is that?"

"Is this you asking? Or the doctor asking?"

"It's a normal question to ask." I felt my back go up, but I forced it back down, realizing he had family issues.

"That right there." He pointed to my shoulders. "Most people would get defensive if I gave them a comment like that. You did at first, until the doctor part of you kicked in. Do you think I suffer from some sort of guilt for going to war, leaving them?" I leaned back in my seat and studied him. It was interesting to hear him try to psychoanalyze me. He raised an eyebrow and continued. "Like, for example, I don't want to be here. I like being in Afghanistan. I like living in the mountains, waking up each day knowing I survived yesterday." I couldn't help but feel a little stung by the way he kept using present tense. "I know it's hard on my family, though. I see it on my mom's face whenever I leave. I don't care enough, I guess, because I know it's where I belong."

"What draws you there?" I kept my voice void of emotion.

"So, the doctor *is* at home." He gave a little laugh as his tongue licked his teeth. He suddenly looked annoyed, and I wished I hadn't dug further.

"Says the guy who chose to answer my general question as if he was across the *couch* from me," I tossed back then felt bad about it. "Ty, you brought up your sister, and asking about your family is a girlfriend thing to do. You wanted us to take our relationship to the next level, so that's all I wanted to do. Sorry if I slipped into work mode."

"Yeah, sorry I tripped out. We'll have to have a proper session later." He chuckled his apology, and I tried to shrug off my frustration.

My phone pinged, and I flipped it over to see Frank's name.

Frank: Where are you?

Ivy: Heading back now.

"Guess we better get going." I stood and hooked my purse over my arm.

Ty stood tall next to me and scanned the faces around us. I linked hands with him and gave a squeeze. I wanted to continue to try to keep the rest of our time together light. I promised myself that next time he brought up his family I'd tread lightly. There was obviously a lot there. Lesson learned.

We walked together across the busy street toward the car when two women approached us. One of them looked familiar, and just as it clicked who she was, she held her phone up in my face.

"This is Dr. Ivy Knight." Ben Oliver's ex-wife stood in front of us. She turned to her friend as she spoke like a newscaster. I realized she was videotaping us. Ty immediately put himself in between us. She stepped back and raised her hands to show she wasn't going to get physical. I didn't trust her and frowned as she began to speak again. "Here we are, across the street from The Groove restaurant where she and her," she paused to study us, "boyfriend just had lunch."

"Stop this," I said around Ty's arm.

"Doctor Knight has yet to come forward with any information regarding her relationship with my ex-husband."

"Mrs. Oliver," I tried to move around Ty, but he wasn't having it, "I legally can't say anything."

"Time to leave." Ty's cutthroat tone left no room for argument. "Move or get yourself charged for harassment, lady. Take your pick."

Her face slipped, and I saw the raw emotion on her face. I felt her pain and could relate. She'd suffered a terrible loss, and because Ben had been on the run since it all happened, she couldn't find peace.

"You know what happened to them, Dr. Knight," her chest rose and fell as she tried to keep it together, "so why haven't you gotten them justice?"

"I will," I promised, "just as soon as I can. I'm so sorry. I feel the same way, I can't wait for it to be over. We just have to trust the police will find him soon."

"The police are useless," she cried in frustration as her friend pulled her aside. Ty wrapped an arm around me and used his body to shield me from her as we hurried toward the car. I heard her say a few more words, but we didn't stop.

"Are you okay?" He studied me.

"Yes." I covered my face and sucked in a deep breath. "Physically, I'm fine. Mentally, I haven't been fine since the night he attacked me in my office." I looked quickly at him as I realized what I'd just said. "I've never been so careless with my secrets." I wanted to cry.

"Luckily for you, they're not going anywhere." He pulled me close and kissed my forehead. "I'm not letting anything hurt you," he promised, and I believed him. I looked back at the two women who still stood on the side of the street as we drove away. I agreed with her that more needed to be done to find her ex-husband, and soon, for all our sakes.

Once security checked both sets of our identification, we were allowed entrance into Army Headquarters. I felt myself relax as we stepped into the elevator. This was the one place I knew for sure Ben Oliver would never set foot. Since 9/11, security had been tightened up considerably at all military bases.

When the metallic doors opened, we were met with a set of angry, stressed-out eyes.

"You two need to follow me." Frank didn't waste any time as he whirled around and headed straight back down the hall. He entered an office, and we followed.

Ugh, now what?

He closed the door and motioned for us to take a seat. He had a laptop on the desk and spun it around to face us as he hit play. I felt my blood run cold. There was Mrs. Oliver and her friend on the street talking into the camera about how they'd spotted me having lunch. She called it round two for confronting me. The caption on the bottom said *Justice for My Parents.*

"Apparently, your entire encounter today was recorded live by that woman. This is bad, Ivy. The other woman even said they had more people uploading it, so it'll go viral. She mentioned the previous time when Mrs. Oliver slapped you outside your home and directed them to that video as well." Frank shook his head. "My aide says this damn TikTok page thing is open, which means—"

"There's a very good chance Ben is watching." I finished his thought, and I felt Ty stiffen.

"Exactly." Frank nodded. "I went over both videos a few times to try to understand what she thinks she's doing. Other than the slap, I don't think she's looking to hurt you. I think she just can't understand why you haven't come forward yet with what you know about her parents. She obviously doesn't get how this works. He hasn't even been caught, let alone charged." He glanced at Ty.

"I know nothing, just what Cole shared," Ty confirmed to Frank, and I appreciated that he didn't share my slip-ups in the few weak moments we'd had together. Though Frank would understand, I prided myself on my ability to keep confidences, especially when it came to my clients.

"The first video apparently has over two million hits." Frank rubbed his forehead. "She's getting a lot of atten- tion. I hate to do this to her. I can't imagine all she's been through, but we should involve the police and maybe get a cease-and-desist letter."

I stood and paced the floor as Ty asked a few ques- tions about the video. Frank let the video run out, and just as it ended, Mrs. Oliver's words hit me hard.

"Wave hello to the world, Doctor." You could see it trained on Ty and me as we hurried away.

TEN

I sipped my cool beer as I leaned back against the wall on the balcony outside my room. I watched Filippo below me in the driveway. He spoke to someone on his phone with an excited grin on his face. I hadn't approached him on the topic since I heard he'd tried to get a seller to come in behind Chili that day the girl was handed over to me. Instead, I watched to see what he was up to. Everyone slipped up at some point if they had something to hide. I'd decided to give him some rope and now hoped I wouldn't live to regret it. In this life, everyone was out for number one. I usually appreciated the *wild-west*-style laws here in the way the Cartels did business, but if you wanted to survive, you had to watch everyone very closely. I'd always said to be comfortable meant to be dead.

I smirked when I saw Pedro limping from the security hut a few yards away from the house. He thought it was okay to touch my girls, so I made sure he wouldn't manhandle anyone for a long-ass time. A sprained knee, a cracked jaw, and some mangled fingers should teach him a lesson.

For the hundredth time, I eyed my phone and wondered if I should break my own rules. Just as I hovered my finger over the name, I heard a noise and clicked the screen to black.

"Hey, boss," Alejandro called as he entered my room and placed my dinner on the table. I stepped back inside as he came to join me, as I didn't want to draw attention to Filippo. "The new camera looks good." He handed me my tablet to show me that he'd installed it exactly the way I wanted it. I was pleased to see how well I could zoom in on the woman. "Better than the other ones, that's for sure."

"Indeed." It had felt good to get rid of Castillo's cameras. I'd dumped them, wires and all, in a box and sent them back to him. I wasn't opposed to using cameras—shit, I had a few in the other rooms with cages—but they were for me, not someone else. I never did my job under a microscope, and I wasn't about to now. "Good." I set the tablet down as I picked up a taco from the plate.

"Want to hear something crazy?" He leaned back with a shit-eating smile.

"Okay."

"Guess who was in town the exact same time we were chasing the girl through the streets?"

"Who?" I squeezed a lime over my carne asada.

"Blackstone." I dropped the food back on my plate and stared at him. "Yeah, boss, my buddy is friends with Hugo, and he said his brother almost shot one of them with their *Ma Deuce*."

Holy shit.

"Yeah, he got away," he shook his head, "but not before he killed Mario's little brother."

I couldn't believe the coincidence that they were there at the same time we were.

"His brother. Is he the one who's always on the rooftops?" I tried to piece it all together with what I'd seen that night.

"Yeah, they called him the Flying Machete. He was something else." He shook his head at the loss. "The army guy was lucky, though. They fell off the roof, and Machete got snagged by a pole right through his leg. Crazy, hey? If it wasn't for that, the army guy would be dead, too."

"Did someone actually see it?"

"A couple kids saw from their window, and I think the rest they pieced together. What a way to go. I wonder how they'll get him down. He's still hangin' up there." He gave a low in-drawn whistle. That would explain why I felt I wasn't alone that night. "Someone saw them run into the Christ of the City Church." He leaned back and pulled his shirt from under his plump belly. "Isn't that where you said the girl was heading?" I blinked at him, shocked beyond words she'd been racing toward them. Did Blackstone know she was on the loose? Was she somehow communicating with them and knew they were there?

"That's crazy," I mumbled when I realized I hadn't spoken for a couple of moments.

"Well," he sat and kicked his feet up, "at least they didn't get the girl."

"No," I flicked my hand at his boots, and he lowered them, "but I want to know how the hell they knew to be there in town, that night, after she just escaped."

He shrugged but nodded and pulled out his phone.

Later that evening, when the sun went down, and the temperature had finally cooled enough, I headed back out to the balcony and settled in for a quiet evening. I pulled up the basement camera to see what the girl was up to. My mind had been in a constant loop since Alejandro shared what he'd discovered. She seemed to be asleep. I was about to close it when I caught movement. Leo moved toward the cage and seemed to inspect Lexi asleep on the bed. I felt my temperature rise. Only Alejandro and I knew about the new camera, and everyone knew I had removed Castillo's. I leaned forward in my seat to watch him. He used the generic code to open her cage door then went inside and set a fresh cup of water on the small table next to her. *Okay.* Then he slowly pulled back the blanket and exposed her naked thigh. *Hell, no!*

I jumped to my feet, raced out of the office, and pounded down the stairs. I heard a loud yelp as I pushed the door open. Pain exploded in my gut as Lexi elbowed me hard in the belly then again in the mouth. Instantly, I tasted tin. I took a swipe at my mouth and saw blood. She came at me again, but I blocked her hit, grabbed her wrist, and slammed her against my chest as she bucked and kicked. Her heel drove down into the top of my foot, and I lost my balance for a split second, just long enough for her to wiggle free and run to the far wall.

Leo groaned, and I saw the broken dinner tray she must have used on him. He lay on his side with a hand clutched to his gash.

This chick is gnarly.

She frantically raced around to find something to defend herself with. She took a hard swipe at the TV. It wobbled then fell and smashed as it hit the floor. She tore her sweatshirt off and wrapped it around a big piece of glass to protect her hand. She stood there in her bra and sweatpants, balanced with her legs wide and waited. I could hear her harsh breathing as she stared at me. Her hair hung partially over her face and her eyes blazed with hatred.

"Impressive." I purred as I reached back and pushed the door closed. "I see the pain meds have kicked in." I eyed the bruises that hugged her side and lower back. The click of the door as it locked behind me made her face slip, but only for a split second.

"All I need is your fingerprint," she hissed at me as I tapped the button behind the tile on the wall. So, she thought this thing used a fingerprint to open. Little did she know, the tile didn't lock or unlock the door. I don't know why I found that amusing.

In one smooth motion, I pulled my t-shirt off. Her eyes widened and she backed against the wall, no doubt worried I was about to do something she wouldn't like. I was built and was bigger now than I'd ever been in my life. Working out was the only thing that kept my mind in check. Well, that and Talya, and now that she was gone, I'd doubled my workouts. She let her eyes slip down my chest, and I raised my brows as I caught her gaze.

I stood there for a moment and let her think about what I could do. I hoped she'd back down, plead with me, and put the glass down but she just stood there. I groaned in frustration then began to wrap my shirt around both my hands, ready to come at her.

"Believe it or not," I tried to distract her by talking, "I'm the least of your worries in this whole thing."

"Are you tryin' to gain my trust, Eric?" She used my name to distract me back.

"Here's the thing, Lexi. I don't need your trust." I played along, but the truth was her trust would make this a hell of a lot easier. "What I need is your ass back in that cage."

"And all I need is to cut your thumb off so I can get the hell out of this place."

"I'm not sure how to tell you this, sweetheart, but you're outnumbered once you step outside the door." I jumped out of the way as she took a swing at me. "One," she jumped at me again, "two," she went for my gut, "three," she tried to kick my chest. I grabbed her ankle flipped her around and pinned her down on her stomach. I held her hands against the floor on either side of her head. I tried to be careful and leaned down and whispered in her ear, "I don't want to hurt you."

"Then get the fuck off me," she cried as she struggled.

Enough already, this is getting tiresome.

"Come on." I kept a tight hold on her hand and tugged her up off the floor. I quickly opened the cage where Leo still lay. I couldn't tell how badly he was hurt, but figured he'd hope for a sympathy vote. I grabbed Lexi around the waist and held her tight with one arm. I shook my head as she never let up and kicked and thrashed as I carried her inside. I yanked Leo to his feet with my free hand and tossed him outside the cage door then dropped her on the bed and backed out, quickly locking the cage behind me.

"You bitch." Leo screamed at her as he began to stand. I pulled my gun and shot him in the head.

"Holy shit!" Lexi cried and curled into a ball on the bed.

Leo was a loose cannon, and clearly, he couldn't be trusted. His death was justified.

"I just finished what you started." I shrugged. "What did you think would happen?"

"I don't know. Jesus." She looked at Leo's body with wide eyes but said nothing further.

I called Filippo to come down as I grabbed my shirt from the floor and slipped it on. "Now," I pulled up a chair and sat down near the cage, "I get it, and I can appreciate what happened here." I waved toward Leo. "I'm impressed by your will to fight for your life. I really am. But I know how Blackstone thinks. This isn't my first time up against them, and given your fighting skills, they've trained you well to protect yourself. But you should know I'll win, so don't come at me again. That being said, everybody else here is fair game." I smiled, amused at my comment.

"Good to know." Her chin rose, and I was pleased to see that Leo's death no longer affected her. She'd already moved on. *Impressive.*

"Boss?" Filippo came in, and Lexi quickly tugged the blanket over her bra. He then did a double take at the sight of Leo's lifeless body on the floor.

"Clean this up," I ordered and took the suit jacket he handed me.

I studied Lexi as Filippo cleaned the gory mess from the floor, and as she watched, I could see a tiny part of her began to struggle. Her shoulders sagged, and her hold around her knees slackened. When I saw some of the color drain from her face, I felt something tug at me briefly. Normally, I'd retreat to my office where my drink waited, but something told me to stay.

"Anything else, boss?" Filippo's voice was strained, and his hands were sticky with blood. The smell of bleach hung thick in the air. When his gaze swung to Lexi, I clucked my tongue to pull his focus on me.

"No." I nodded for him to leave, and he scurried

away. I sat there a moment then pulled out a clean sweat-shirt from the bin. The one she had on had some of Leo's blood on it. I carefully opened the door and set it on the bed next to her. Then I quickly closed it again. I wasn't about to chance any further action on her part.

"Do you need anything?" She shook her head, and I saw she fought to control herself as her chin quivered. I tapped my fingers on my leg and felt a bit off. I'd never given a second thought about the women we'd run through here. I just did what I had to and moved on, but this whole situation was different. I didn't like the way I felt, but I turned and left her there without another word.

I thought Castillo was crazy to kill her once we got information from her on Blackstone, I wanted to sell her to Chili and be done with it. This whole thing bothered me. I also hadn't felt I was completely in the loop with the girls who were being brought through my tunnel lately. Chili was my buyer, but I had control of the tunnel. Lately, I'd heard rumors that some girls had been moved through the tunnel on days I wasn't there. If that was really true, I trusted Chili and knew it wasn't him who bought them, so that meant someone was cutting me out of the equation. I had very little to go on and no proof of anything. I knew I needed to be in control here or shit would go sideways fast. I made a decision.

I sent a text off to Alejandro, and a moment later he brought me two glasses and a bottle of whiskey. I still needed to maintain my use of text messages so Castillo didn't suspect I was on to him for bugging my line.

"Do I want to know?" He gave me a confused look as he handed me the bottle and glasses.

"No." I turned and went back downstairs.

I let the door lock behind me, tapped the tile again, and she sat up quickly. I could see her eyes as they flitted around the room as if to find some new escape route. I removed my jacket and took a seat on the floor close to the bars then leaned back against the wall. I decided to skip the chair this time to bring myself down to her level. I wanted to appear less of a threat, and without my jacket, I hoped I appeared more relaxed and casual. I showed her the bottle was sealed to prove it hadn't been tampered with it. Her eyes went to slits, but she didn't say a word.

"I'm not even going to guess what's going through your head right now." I pushed a glass through the bars then the long neck of the bottle and poured her a double. Then I did the same for me. "I do know I need one of these right now." She watched as I took a sip of the amber liquor, then she must have decided it was worth the risk because she began to move. She quickly snatched the glass and moved to the opposite side of the cage and sat on the floor against the bars.

"Here's to a fucked up, cruel world," I toasted her, and she shot me a glare as we both raised our glasses. She threw back the entire drink, and I smiled. I found myself impressed with her for the second time tonight. She slid forward and nudged the glass toward me, careful not to get too close. I poured her another, and this time she nursed it.

I had to admire this woman. She still managed to look good in spite of her time spent here in the cage, the time she spent hiding in the streets, and even after she'd killed a man.

"Is this where you ask me for information about Blackstone?" She tried to keep her voice strong, but her eyes gave her away.

"No," I chuckled, "I wouldn't believe anything you told me, anyway."

"Smart man," she muttered, and we both went back to staring into our respective glasses. I hated how bright I'd made the room. It figured it had served its purpose, so I used my phone to dim the lights then changed the color to a warm orange. "Thank you." She whispered, and I actually felt bad that I hadn't thought about adjusting them earlier. I never usually gave someone down here a second thought. *I couldn't.*

"You didn't eat. Are you hungry?"

"No."

"You should eat."

"Why?" She sighed. "I only ate to be able to fight."

"Your escape was pretty impressive." I nodded and held up my glass.

"I know," she gave a dark chuckle, "but not good enough, because here I am."

"You took down two Cartel with your arms tied, ran through the streets, and got to where you thought you'd get help. Sorry he was one of my guys." I shrugged. I chose my next words carefully, as I wanted to see how she reacted. "Honestly, you did really well. You almost made it, too, what with Blackstone there the exact same time as you were—"

She sat up and looked right at me, and I saw shock then defeat wash over her.

"They were there, when I was there?"

"Yes." She hadn't known. Her reaction was real, and the way her face twisted in pain made me wish I hadn't even said it. Sometimes it bothered me how much I fucked with people's heads to find out the truth. I looked away for a moment, not liking the hold she had on my conscience.

"He came for me," she said softly in disbelief. "Oh, my God, after all I did." She started to cry, and I forced myself to look at her again. She covered her face and drew her knees to her chest and sobbed.

Shit.

"Lexi," I moved closer to the cage, "I honestly didn't mean to make you cry."

"Eric," she crawled over to me and held on to the cage with white knuckles, "please, let me go. I've done so many things wrong that I need to make right." Tears streamed over her pretty cheeks, and I allowed myself to feel her pain again, just for a moment, because it had taken years to become like stone inside and any softening scared the shit out of me.

"I—" I cleared my throat and wondered maybe, just maybe if…

"Boss?" I hadn't even heard Alejandro open the door. "I need to speak with you."

Suddenly, the spell of that moment broke, and I snapped back to reality.

"No, no, no, no, please!" Lexi begged, still on her knees, and Alejandro looked at me, confused.

I got to my feet as she sobbed harder, then gathered our glasses, my whiskey, and jacket.

What the hell was I doing?

Once we were upstairs, Filippo stood and ended his call when he saw me coming.

"Boss, I just got off the phone with Sal, the guy who runs the girls in and out of Castillo's house."

I waved impatiently at him to speed it up. "I know who the fuck Sal is."

"Okay, well, he overheard Castillo talkin' about the girl. I think he's got another plan in mind for her."

The fuck he does.

I felt my temper rise. The last thing I needed was more attention on Lexi. I wanted Castillo to get his head out of his ass and see that my idea was better than anything he wanted to do. The guy just wanted to show the world he was fuckin' king shit. I needed my deal to go through, the money to be paid, her to be handed off, and my fucking job to go back to normal. I couldn't wait until the day I could rise above that idiot and get him the hell out of my life.

"Did he say anything else?"

"Just that Castillo gave the green light to something that was put on standby."

"What are you, fuckin' Blackstone?" I tossed the glasses into the bar sink and heard them shatter. "Find out what the hell is on standby!" I knew Castillo had to be up to something big. He was like a toddler with a new toy to show off. "Who was he talking to?" Filippo shrugged. "Don't shrug. Find out who the fuck it was."

I vibrated with anger, and my tone must have alerted Alejandro because he came into the room.

"Just give me a minute." I shook my head to warn Alejandro I wanted to be left alone. I needed to think without everyone in my head. With my keys in hand, I shoved one of Castillo's men out of my way as I headed to the SUV.

I turned the engine over and sent some stones flying as I flew down the driveway toward a local pub. It was only a short drive but gave me a few minutes to calm myself down. The place was a small local dive, with shit music, cheap drinks, and low lighting. Just what I needed to get myself back in check.

"*Tres tequilas,*" I mumbled, and the bartender snapped three shot glasses on the bar, ran a lime along the edge of each, then dipped the rims in salt. He knew how I liked my drink. It was far from my first visit. He flipped the bottle and overfilled them each to the top with no room to spare. He took the other half of the lime and sat it at the end of the row of the shot glasses.

"No man should drink alone." I nodded at him then at the bottle, and he poured himself one as well.

"*Amigo.*" He held his glass and took his shot as I downed my three then sucked a quick bite of lime at the end. "*Mese?*"

"*Sí.*" I ordered two more shots and went to the back of the place and took a seat by the exit. Moments later, the shots arrived, and I finished those off quickly as well. It wasn't often I ever allowed myself to drink like that, but I sure as hell needed it. There was so much at stake, and I needed my head on straight. The liquor calmed my head as I relaxed in my chair.

I leaned back and pulled out my phone, but my hand froze as I heard *her* voice. It filled my head and immediately brought back memories of us together I'd finally managed to push out. I looked over at Talya, who sat at a table with some men. No doubt they were some of her father's clients.

Cresta de Burro was one of the best kept secrets in town, a place the tourists didn't know about. A place a guy could drink in peace, and the fact that it was less than a minute from my house was a major perk. That she was here at all pissed me off, but that she was here with people from out of town burned even more. She wouldn't have even known about this place if it wasn't for me, and that made it worse still.

She caught my stare and pressed her lips together as she processed that I sat across from her. Then she tossed her hair over her shoulder and went back to the clients. She laughed and threw compliments at them as they sat around the table.

What were the fucking odds she'd be here tonight?

The lone waitress came by and handed me another shot.

"I didn't order this."

"I know." She moved her gaze across the room to Talya and then placed a napkin in front of me and tapped on it. I saw the familiar handwriting.

Should I leave? Or will you throw me out again? - T

I scoffed at her note, downed the shot, and headed out back. I hoped the balcony would be less busy. It was just as busy and filled with locals, so I slipped into the back room in hopes I could find a quiet place to sort things out. I kicked the door shut hard, and it rebounded back. I reached to close it again when Talya stepped in. She had on a short black dress, her breasts proudly displayed as usual. She had her hair long and wavy like she had been caught in the rain.

I shook my head. I'd always loved that look on her. I knew I couldn't be that close to her right now. She was quicksand for me. Talya and tequila had never been a good mix.

"Are you following me?" she asked quietly.

"No."

"Are you trying to hurt me?" Her eyes were beautiful as they studied me.

"No," I rubbed my face, not needing this right now, "I never meant to hurt you."

"You should have thought of that before you slammed the door in my face." She moved closer, and I closed the door as she did. "I deserve an explanation, Eric." She did, but I couldn't give it to her. "You made me fall in love with you, then you shattered that love into a billion pieces. Is it that hard to let me in?"

"Yes," I lied. I never wanted Talya to love me like I loved her.

"Wow," she looked away and brushed away a tear with her fingers then let out a long breath, "you could have at least given me a chance to say goodbye."

My head shot off in different directions, Castillo, Lexi, the fact that my house was crawling with men who would love a reason to put a bullet in my head, to—

I didn't even notice that she had moved so close. Her hands slid up my chest and around my neck, and all the while my head spun off its axis and set off every nerve in my body.

One smell of her perfume and I crumbled. I bent down and hooked her lips with mine. One hand went under her thighs as I lifted her and sat her on the table. She pulled her dress up and pushed her panties to the side, then her fingers clawed at my belt until I was free.

This is a bad idea.

I didn't wait for her to get ready. I knew if I paused, I'd stop, so instead I gave in to my weakness that was Talya and sank myself deep inside of her.

Home.

She knew me so well and kissed my neck the way I loved. Her little noises drove me on as I moved against her with no mercy. Because she knew I loved to watch her body when we had sex, she untied the front of her dress and lay back on the table so I could have a good show. I studied her stomach as her muscles flexed when I dragged my erection over her sensitive, greedy nub. Her breasts bounced wildly, and her neck strained as she built toward her orgasm.

I hated how much I wanted her. How much I needed her.

"Eric!" she moaned, and I bit my tongue, on the edge of wanting to share my truths. I fixed one hand on her small hips and moved one to cover her heart. It was as if my unspoken words flowed through my arm, down to my hand, and passed them straight through to her heart. She would never know how much she meant to me or how much I loved her.

As the sadness kicked in, I thrust harder, taking my pain out on her, wanting her to see how much this broke me, too.

Her nails clawed at my arms as she attempted to hold on.

"Eric! Yes, more!" She had no idea of the war I kept from her. All she saw was lust, but behind my eyes was a man saying goodbye to the only woman he ever truly cared for.

"I'm going to explode!" Her legs wrapped around my

waist as I hauled her upward and devoured her mouth as she came. I squeezed her harder as I came right behind her with everything I had.

When we both came back down, all that could be heard was our heavy breathing. I slowly pulled out, tucked myself away, and reached down for her shoe. I slipped it back on her small foot, and when I looked up, I found her watching me.

"I think we can make thi—"

"Goodbye, Talya." I kissed her once more and walked quickly out of the room. I nearly ran into the waitress, who looked over my shoulder at Talya with her wild hair and flushed, brokenhearted face.

"You good, boss?" Alejandro appeared. I tossed him the keys as I walked past him, and he followed. He knew I'd be looking for a drive home.

"Yeah." I rubbed my head and fought the urge to have one more round with Talya.

Quicksand.

"What did Filippo find out?"

"He got hold of Sal, and he's still tryin' to find out. He sent a girl to his room, paid her extra to go through his phone."

"I need to know who the hell that was."

"I know." He held up the keys. "Ready to go home?"

"Yeah, come on."

I tossed some bills at the waitress to assure her silence, not that she'd probably care about what she'd witnessed. I threw a wave to the bartender, and we stepped out into the hot, stuffy air.

The back of my neck prickled, and I looked back to find Talya's eyes on me. I let the door slip from my hand, and it closed with a slap.

At least we had our goodbye.

ELEVEN

"Ty, relax." Ivy poked the tiny black straw between her deep red lips and drew the colorful drink into her mouth. "We're in a building with at least fifty soldiers. If Ben was going to show himself, this wouldn't be the place."

"It's not just Ben I'm worried about," I glared at the guy who came up to gawk at Ivy's outfit, "and though I appreciate you wearing jeans, this scrap of fabric you call a top doesn't make my life any easier." I allowed my gaze to roam over her sheer black halter top. It barely covered her breasts, and only a little fabric found its way down her back into her tight-as-sin black jeans. "And with those high heels, you look like you're heading to a *Maxim* magazine shoot."

"Why do men always get protective when we ladies

dress sexy? I can handle myself, but I'm just going to take that as a compliment." She rolled her eyes. "I mean, jeeze, if you had it your way, I'd be in an oversized hoodie and sweats."

"And your point is?" I scanned the room, waiting for my opportunity to speak to the bartender. I made eye contact with Ned and Alex, who'd been sent to watch over us via Frank. He wasn't overly pleased Ivy insisted on joining me tonight, but she wasn't having it. So, he quietly told me we'd have extra eyes tonight.

"My point, Ty, is that I'm twenty-eight and single."

Her words repeated in my head until they broke through my consciousness.

"Single?" I eyed her, and she gave me a playful look.

"I just wanted your attention."

"That's the problem." I leaned down and brushed my lips against her ear. "When you're in the room, you're the only thing I can focus on." She used her free hand to caress my side and pressed her nearly bare breasts into my chest. They were so soft, and my hands begged to cup them. "You're dangerous for me to be around." I chuckled.

She pulled back, and her gorgeous eyes sparkled with dirty thoughts. "I think I want to solve that problem." She sipped her drink then touched her bottom lip to catch a drop of wine.

"Don't do that," I begged, as it took all my control not to devour her. "You're flirting with my control, Ivy."

"Am I?" The corner of her mouth went up, and I

snagged my arm around her waist and pulled her front to mine.

"This is getting painful," my erection pulsed against her tight little body, "so between this and the fact that your breasts are on display not only for me but the whole rest of the bar, I'm about ready to throw you over my shoulder, take you back to our hotel, and remind you, Dr. Knight, that you are *not* single."

"Is that a promise?"

"Yes, it is." Her gaze slid down to my phone that had just lit up on the bar top. I saw her eyebrows twitch at what she saw. I scooped it up and opened three text messages from my sister. She wondered when we could meet up and would I bring Ivy to meet our folks.

Ty: Out of town. I'll be in touch.

Shelly: I won't hold my breath - xo

I cringed at her response because I knew she was right. Chances were I'd never respond. I hated that I was so distant with my family. I loved them, I knew that much, but I really didn't know why I felt the way I did about them. I tucked that thought away once again and knew one of these times I was going to have to figure out that disconnect. I glanced at Ivy, who wasn't even trying to hide the fact that she'd seen the texts. I didn't comment, and she looked at me for a moment then said nothing. I appreciated that.

I looked away from her and surveyed the bar. The

Rusty Nail was frequented by the military, but there were a lot of younger couples and a group of girls dressed to kill who noisily flirted with some guys at another table. It was a happening place.

Finally, the bar slowed a little and the bartender seemed to have a free moment. "Excuse me," I called, and she moved down the bar to where we sat at the end. I leaned forward and spoke as quietly as I could. "Do you have a moment if I wanted to ask you something about your husband?" Her face fell, and she blinked a few times, but then motioned for me to step to the side with her.

"Don't leave this chair," I warned Ivy, who made a face at me then nodded.

"Look, I'm sorry for your loss, and I promise it's not anything to disrespect you or him," I started the conversation. "My name's Ty, and I just could really use your help." Her gaze swept the room, and she looked nervous, but at least she didn't immediately say no.

"I have someone coming in to help me out in about fifteen minutes. You can meet me over there." She pointed to a door that looked like it led out back.

"Thank you. I won't keep you long, okay?" I tried for a kind smile.

"Do me a favor." She leaned in. "Be careful who you talk to about Philip in here."

"I'm only interested in talking to you," I assured her. That seemed to relax her a little, and I left her and made my way back to Ivy.

Ivy's hand reached for my arm as I climbed back on

the stool next to her, and I instantly went to high alert. She spoke quietly into my ear. "Promise me you'll behave?"

"Why?" The hair on the back of my neck rose as my sixth sense screamed at me to turn around.

"Please, keep your back turned." She played it cool, but her voice told me otherwise. "Remember your promise that you wouldn't cause any trouble when I was with you tonight, so don't get into a fight. Promise me." Panic laced her voice, and it took everything in me not to turn and find out why. Then I caught his face in the mirror over the bar. He sat by himself only a table away, but so far, he hadn't spotted us.

"Ty, will you let me handle this? This could be your only opportunity to talk to that guy's wife. He won't do anything here, anyway. There're too many witnesses."

I hesitated but knew she was right. He was too much of a coward to do anything with people around.

"All right," I nodded, "but if he even so much as says anything, you look my way and I'll be there in a flash." I could feel the hatred burn through me at the thought of her being anywhere near him. She squeezed my shoulder as she got up and quietly walked across the room as if looking for the restroom. She turned and walked back toward his table so she approached him at an angle that would take his view plane away from where I sat. I could still see his face. *Smart girl.*

She caught his eye as she walked toward him, and he looked up at her in surprise, half rising in his seat. I concentrated so I could read his lips in the mirror. The place was packed, so I figured he wouldn't notice me at the bar, but I sat hunched over my drink a bit just in case.

"Dr. Knight, what in the world are you doing here?" I could just hear his nasally voice above the noise.

"Carson," she snickered, "oh, wait, it's Hill, isn't it? I guess it really doesn't matter who you are. You mean nothing to me." I smiled to myself at how cool and collected she was.

"Now, Ivy," he mocked her like a parent, "it was a simple misunderstanding."

The bartender suddenly flashed me a quick glance then looked over at Ivy as she talked with Hill. I nodded slowly as though I understood her concern with Hill and placed my finger to my lips. She gave me a thoughtful look then moved farther up the bar.

"Save it, Hill," I heard Ivy say as she waved him off.

"Or we can try it again." He spoke a little louder, as if to hold her there. I curled my fingers into a fist. "Look, I'm really sorry you got caught in the crossfire between me and Beckett."

"The crazy part is, Hill," she emphasized his name, "we weren't even dating, so you used an innocent person for your reindeer games."

"And for that, I'm sorry." I could see him work his jaw. I assumed Hill wasn't used to a woman standing up to him. "You were important to him, though, so that's why you were my target."

"No one is important to Ty," she said in a crisp tone,

and though I knew it was an act, it still hit my gut hard. "He's not interested in anyone. He has his eyes set on one thing, and that's getting back to Afghanistan."

That was the hook she needed. I saw his shoulders straighten as he pulled in his chin to stare right at her.

"Is he going back?"

"Yeah, the last I heard, he was." She was good. "Why do you care?" She put her hands on her hips. "I'd think you'd want him as far away from you as possible."

He eyed her for a moment, most likely trying to figure out what she knew.

"Why'd you say that?"

"Ty said you two weren't meant to be in the same country. I just figured you were both type A assholes, and the struggle for power was just too much."

"Hill." Dustin appeared out of nowhere. "A word?"

"Did I say you could approach me?" Hill snapped, then backed off as he must have realized his true colors showed. His face rearranged into a friendly one as he backpedaled. "What's up, buddy?"

Ivy stuck her hand out and introduced herself to him. "Ah, hi. I'm a friend of Hill's."

He wiped a hand over his chin. Just then, a big group came in singing football chants, and I lost my view of them. When the crowd cleared, Hill was gone, and Dustin walked away from Ivy. She approached the far end of the bar and ordered a drink without looking my way.

"I'll give you ten minutes, that's all." The bartender leaned in then motioned for me to follow her out back. I tapped Ivy on the back to follow as we headed for the door.

"Not her." The woman glared at Ivy as we stood in a low-lit kitchen area.

"Why?" I asked before Ivy could. "Because she was talking to Hill?"

"Exactly."

"You misunderstand. I'm with Ty." Ivy stepped forward. "We're trying to find out information on Hill." The bartender closed her eyes and chewed her bottom lip while she thought. "I'm a psychologist with the US military. You can look me up. I'm not someone you need to be concerned about, honest." Ivy opened her purse and pulled out a business card and pressed it into her hand. "Please, we just have a few questions."

"Fine." She tucked the card in her back pocket then folded her arms. "What do you wanna know?"

"What happened to your husband?" I took over. "How was he killed?"

"Do you want the story they fed the public or the real one?"

"Real."

"Hill shot my husband straight through the heart." Her eyes watered. "All because one night they were having drinks here when Captain Flex came in with some girls. Hill was all over one of them, and I swear she wasn't a day over sixteen. Phil tried to intervene at the end of the night. The girl wasn't even into him. I saw the entire thing. She was tipsy, and it was obvious she couldn't handle him. Anyway, one thing led to another, and Hill tried to take her home. Phil outright asked in front of everyone if she wanted him to drive her home. She said she did, and all the guys gave Hill shit for losing the girl to Phil after that. Didn't matter we were friggin' married at the time. My husband was a good guy. He had three sisters, and his mom raised him to look out for them. Look where that got him." She sniffed.

"But how do you know Hill shot your husband?" I cut in. "Do you have any proof, witnesses, camera footage?"

"Do you want a reenactment? Shit." The woman was on the verge of losing it. I looked at Ivy for help. I wasn't good at being gentle with stuff like this.

Ivy came to my aid. "We're sorry. The truth is Ty and Hill were in Afghanistan together, and Ty lost one of his men to Hill, and he's trying to find a way to prove he killed him."

"Really?" She looked up at me, and I saw her defenses lower. "Let me guess. He did it without any witnesses around?"

"No American witnesses, anyway." I swallowed sharply. "There was an Afghan mother and her two daughters, so as far as the military goes, it's my word against his, and now some of his friends have spoken up and backed up Hill's story."

"Same." She nodded, but that just confused me. How was it the same? Ivy slowly shook her head and went on to dig more.

"If there were no witnesses to your husband's death, how do you know it was Hill?" Ivy asked gently.

"I didn't know for sure at first, but people talk when they drink and, much like you, Doctor, I knew the right questions to ask after they'd had a few. Soldiers like to brag." She looked at me. "No offense, but they do. Over the past couple years, I pieced the story together. Then one night Hill sat right here and bragged about how he was untouchable because of who his brother was. Someone muttered Phil's name, and he laughed." She paused to hold back a sob. "He actually laughed and then made the action of raising a gun and made a pop sound like he'd shot him."

"Holy…" Ivy's sympathetic expression brought out the woman's sob, and she pressed her hands to her mouth to stop herself. "I'm so sorry." Ivy placed a hand on her shoulder. "I promise you we'll do everything in our power to take him down, not just for Ty's friend, but also for your Phil."

"It's like an unstoppable loop inside." She dropped her arms heavily at her sides. "I need to accept that Phil is gone, but without justice, it's like I can't. I feel like I'm fighting my own war and there's no end in sight. No one will listen to me about Hill, and what can I do? I have no evidence." She put a hand on my arm. "But if you could really do something. Well, maybe I could take a step forward, put this behind me. I know that's what Phil would want."

"It's exactly what Phil would want you to do." Ivy smiled warmly.

"Which guys hang out with Hill?" I asked as softly as I could. "Which ones do you think might talk to us? If any."

"Ahh," she thought for a moment, "yeah, actually." She pulled out her notepad and scribbled some names. "I'm Pam, by the way." She smiled as she realized we hadn't had a proper introduction. "That's my number at the bottom." She looked down at Ivy's card. "I have your number Dr. Knight, so if I hear anything, I'll let you know."

"Ivy," Ivy corrected her and gave her a pat.

"And I'm Major Ty Beckett. We'll do the same and let you know if we come up with anything," I promised. As I turned toward the door, I looked back and realized Ivy had stayed behind, so I stepped outside to give them a moment. Truth was, everyone could use a little Ivy in their lives. She genuinely cared about people. I loved that about her.

"Ty?" a female called, and it took me a few seconds to place the voice.

"Melony?" I turned to find Moore's cousin and her group of friends. They pushed through the crowd toward me. "What are you doing here?" I wasn't ready for her hug, and it lasted a little longer than I was comfortable with.

"Are you kidding me? We're here all the time." She grinned at her friends. "Everyone, this is Captain Ty

Beckett." She paused when she caught herself. "No, wait, it's Major now, isn't it?"

"Yeah, I guess it is." I shrugged then leaned against the bar top. "How've you been?" Melony practically lived at Moore's house. I knew his mom's brother, Mel's dad, was always in and out of rehab, so Moore's family had helped raise her.

"Just living my best life at twenty-three." She giggled with her friends.

"At a bar?" I questioned and arched an eyebrow at her.

"Men in uniforms, Ty. This place is loaded with 'em." She laughed.

"Mm." I shook my head.

"I blame you," she tossed playfully at me, "you in your camo." She fanned herself, and I was taken aback by her flirting. I'd never really looked at Melony that way. She was my buddy's cousin, after all. I just never went there in my head.

"I see." I cleared my throat while the other girls blinked up at me with their doe eyes. "So, you're on the prowl, so to speak?"

"Sort of, yeah."

"Tell him," her friend urged her. "Tell him about the guy. She met him last time we were here, and he's here again today."

"Who?" I immediately wished I hadn't asked. I didn't really want to know, but maybe I should.

"No way, because if you know him, I know you'll get all big brother on me."

"No, but if you don't tell me, I'll tell Moore you're here and let him question you."

"That's dirty," she huffed and rolled her eyes. "His name is Matthew Rivera." My blood went cold, and I know she saw it on my face. "Don't start, Ty."

"If you knew what was good for you, you wouldn't talk to him again."

"I love that you're protective, Ty, but you can't stop me from talking to him." Her hand moved to cover mine, but I pulled it away.

"Look." I moved her away from her friends. I leaned close and lowered my voice. "He's connected to Brown's death." I watched her face drop. "Yeah, he's up to his neck in it, Melony. Please do your cousin and me a favor and stay away."

"Damn, I didn't know." She sighed. "It would explain why he was asking questions and seemed so interested in where my cousin had disappeared to." She squinted. "Where is he, anyway?"

"He's on another mission," I lied, suddenly furious they were targeting our family members now. "You need to leave, Melony."

"Why don't we hang out with you tonight instead?"

"I'm leaving."

"Maybe I could come with you?" She ran a hand down my arm, and I shook my head, taking her hand. "Come on, Ty. I've always had a thing for you."

"Good lord, Melony, I never knew that. Besides, I'm seeing someone, and my life is way too complicated for you." I tried to be nice. "You deserve better than someone like me. My life is and always will be about the military."

"Ty, you don't date, and seriously, that's a rejection if I've ever heard one." She chuckled. "But okay." She went to leave, but something bothered me, so I hooked her arm.

"How did you and Rivera meet?"

"We were here having drinks, and he approached me. Well, he and his buddies. One of them was a real cocky ass, but Don was nice. He asked a lot of questions, but he made it seem like he and my cousin were close."

"They're not, believe me," I hissed. "Did he ever say anything about Brown?"

"Not really, but his cocky-ass friend kept trying to show off. He was doing anything to get my attention. He bragged like he was God's gift to the Army." She thought for a second. "He was really nasty to one of the other guys, too, named Duncan?"

"Dustin?"

"Yeah, that was it. Every chance he got, he made fun of him. I kinda felt sorry for him."

"What was Rivera's reaction to it all?"

"He ignored the whole thing. He was focused more on me. He honestly seemed nice." She sighed.

"Trust me, he's not, and they were playing you. Promise me you'll stay away."

"I will." She leaned in for a hug. "Thanks for caring about me."

I patted her back in a friendly way, but when she glued herself to my body, I pulled back.

"Okay, I have to go, and you and your friends need to hit up a different bar." I eyed her in what I hoped was a parental way. "So, at least for now, stay away from here, right?"

"I will." She reached up and touched my face tenderly. She really was sweet. But I gave her a little push toward her friends, and she laughed at me over her shoulder as she left.

She reminded me a bit of Demi. She knew exactly what she was doing, but she was kindhearted.

I heard Ivy's voice and turned to find her talking to a guy at the bar. I made my way toward her, but when she saw me, she slipped off the bar stool, said goodbye, and met me. She handed me a piece of paper.

"Friend of yours?" I glanced at the guy, who watched us as we walked away.

"No, I was just waiting for you to finish up talking to your friends." She pointed to the paper. "These are a few more soldiers we should talk to, and I think I have an idea of how we can do this without being obvious."

"Great." I glanced at the paper again. "I know a few of 'em, so we'll have to play it carefully." I tucked it away and took her hand. "Let's get out of here."

"Yeah, I'm ready to leave."

Once outside in the cool night air, I shifted gears from watching for Hill to watching for Ben Oliver. I hailed a cab, and we settled in the back while the driver took us back to the hotel. Ivy suddenly put her phone to her ear and mouthed *Doc Roberts*, then she turned away to look out the window as she spoke quietly, leaving me to my thoughts.

The lobby of the hotel was quiet, and she pointed to the cart at the edge of the bar and poured herself a glass of water as she ended her call.

"Sorry about that." She sipped the lemon water. "He wanted to hear how Mom is."

"Is your mom his sister?"

"Yeah, but he's really more like a father to me than an uncle." I nodded and looked over at the few people who hung out near the bar.

"Did Pam say anything else after I left?" I followed as she made her way toward the elevator.

"Yes, actually. She said Hill suspects she knows something, and he makes it a point to come to the bar to scare her into staying quiet. He sounds psychotic." She hit the button then rubbed her arms like she was chilly. "Maybe we can tip him over the edge and get him to unravel."

"Spoken like a true psychologist." I tapped my forehead with a chuckle. "That's my plan, though." I lifted my hat and ran a hand through my hair. I felt uneasy about what happened at the bar. "The girl I was talking to is Moore's cousin," I told her as we waited.

"Really? Does she go there often?"

"I think so. But what bothers me is that Hill's buddy Rivera has been hitting on her, asking her questions and the like. That means Hill is doing what he can to get to me." I turned and looked at her.

"That's scary."

"Yeah, it is." I stepped in front of her. "Just so you know, nothing ever happened between her and me."

"I never questioned if it had."

"I know, but I don't want you to think that was something back there. I mean, she got all close and huggy." I made a face. "I didn't know she had a crush on me until tonight."

"Ty, you're sexy and smart. I'd never blame a girl for being attracted to you. I mean, look at us. Insane sex in the woods to—" A few people came and stood next to us. The woman pressed the button a couple times in spite of the fact that it was already lit up. Human nature, I guessed. It finally arrived, and we got in first and stood at the back of the car. I took the opportunity to run my hand over the curve of Ivy's bottom, and she smiled up at me.

Finally, the steel doors opened, and the people got out. When the doors closed again, I pulled Ivy to me and kissed her deeply. I could feel her smile again through the kiss. The elevator stopped on our floor, and I pulled away, snagging her arm in the process.

"I need my brain to stop. I need you behind closed doors," I nearly growled as we made our way down the long hallway. She stopped by my door and leaned against the wall as I searched for the room key.

"So, Hill took the bait and thinks you're going back to

Afghanistan." She spoke softly then put a hand on my arm as she arched her neck and leaned up toward my face. I dragged my gaze from her moist lips, down her slender neck, to her plump breasts that seemed to beg for release from her top, and kissed her again. "And Dustin gave me a warning to be careful with Hill." She breathed hard against my mouth as she fought to get the words out. She pressed her hands against my chest to push herself away slightly. When she licked her lips, I reached over and wrapped my hand around the back of her neck and thumbed her jaw as I deepened the kiss. I needed air.

"I've had to behave all night," I panted. "I'm not sure how much longer I can take it with you in this." I tugged on her top, then slid my hand over her breast and rolled her nipple through the fabric.

"Then we should get me out of this." She pushed my shoulder, took the key card out of my hand, opened the door, and headed inside with me hot on her heels.

The moment the door shut, I tossed my hat and pulled off my shirt. She clicked on some music, and *I Put A Spell On You,* by some guy I didn't recognize, filled the silence. I came up behind her but stopped at the sight of her sexy silhouette on the back wall. She saw me look and made her silhouette do a sexy little dance. She drew my eyes back to her and took off her shirt and tiny scrap of a bra to let her breasts bounce free, then she turned to show off how her silhouette looked. I didn't know which way to look. Her hands gracefully undid her jeans, and the sight of her bottom when she bent over to pull them off at the ankle had my eyes zoom to the real deal. I was done with the silhouette. I squeezed my fists and desperately tried not to lose control. My hands itched for her, and they landed on her bare hips where I twisted my fingers into her lacy thong.

She reached back and drew my head to her neck while she swung her hips to the sexy beat of the song. I dropped kisses behind her ear, down her neck, to her shoulder. A moan vibrated her chest, and I pressed my painful erection hard against her lower back. My skin heated as I walked my fingers over her smooth stomach, past her pelvic bone, and dipped between her legs. She was wet and ready for me.

"You're so damn gorgeous." I nipped at her ear, and she wiggled her hips. "So perfect for me," I confessed. "I never knew I needed someone until I met you." She tilted her head back and tenderly kissed me to let me know she'd heard me. She reached for my hand and cupped her breast with it. I caressed it while we deepened our kiss. My body hummed with need, and I fought to focus on what I was doing. She must have sensed my need because she broke free, spun around, and walked backward to the bed. She lowered herself onto the mattress and seductively inched her way backward up toward the wall. I dropped my pants along with my boxer briefs and crawled over the top of her sinful body, dropping kisses as I went.

Her feathery touch ran along the groove of my back muscles, and I had to grit my teeth to maintain what little control I had left.

"I have no control when I'm around you," I mumbled. "It's terrifying but addictive all at the same time."

"So, be an addict." She smirked. "Feed on me." She raised her arms over her head as if to give herself over to me. I paused for a moment then reached over and whipped my belt off my pants and made quick work of her wrists. I straddled her waist and found her opening.

With one hand holding her hands down, and one on her hips, I gave in and slowly fed myself into the one woman I couldn't get enough of. Her chin lifted toward the ceiling and her lips formed an O. Everything inside me tightened, and I felt my erection throb. I drew back slowly until I was almost out, then reached down and caressed her bud. Her delicious breasts rose and fell with her short breaths.

I leaned forward, brushed her hair back, and started a slow, deep kiss. When she tried to pick up the pace, I pulled away and started again. She tried to behave, but my little strokes in and out of her drove her crazy. I chuckled into her mouth, and she whimpered with need.

"Tell me what you want," I whispered.

"You, Ty, I want you."

I took pity, lifted my hips, then rolled them like a wave. Little moans escaped her lips, her skin turned pink, and then her head thrashed around, and I knew she was close. I picked up the pace a little, and when she least expected it, I pulled her straight up to sit on my legs.

"Oh!" Her hair was wild as she wrapped her bound

wrists around my neck to hold on as I thrust up into her from below. "Yes!"

I couldn't get enough. I felt crazed with my desire to be tender but wild with the need to take her at every angle. I spread my hands on her bottom and squeezed. She lifted and let gravity push her back down.

Nothing in life mattered when I had her like this. The sound of her desire, the smell of the leather, her slender neck exposed for me to suck on were my heaven.

"I'm so close!" she screamed. "Ty, please, I can't hang on!"

I wrapped my arms around her body and pressed her to me as I thrust into her with all my strength. She screamed and shook, and I came with her with such force it lifted us both off the bed. We both came again a few moments later, and somehow, she was on top with her head on my chest and we both breathed like marathon runners. I released her hands and tossed the belt aside.

"We can't ever break up," she panted with a chuckle, "but if we do, we need a sexual agreement because I've never almost blacked out during an orgasm before. I think I might've just met Jesus." That made me laugh, and she rolled to look up at me. "I've also never let anyone tie me up before."

"It was sexy." I hugged her. "Thank you for trusting me." She nodded, and we lay in silence listening to the music while we enjoyed the buzz of our sexual high. I thought she'd fallen asleep, but she stirred and started to draw circles on my chest.

"You should know that Dustin also told me Hill's been back to Montana twice since you punched him."

"Is that so?" I puffed out my cheeks and slowly let out a breath.

"Yes." She turned to look at me. "You might want to find a way to talk to Dustin. He obviously isn't totally on Hill's side in all this."

"Seems that way."

"I wasn't trying to ruin the mood here tonight. I just wanted to make sure you knew everything that was said tonight."

"I appreciate that," I rubbed her back, "and trust me, nothing could ruin this night."

"Good," she got up on her knees, "because now it's my turn to play."

TWELVE

While Ty was busy filling in Frank on what we'd learned the day before, I set up shop in an empty office to prepare for my video conference with Mark. Cole had texted and asked me to check in on the team and see if anyone needed a session. To my surprise, both Mark and Keith asked to have a thirty-minute session with me.

Mark needed to talk; that was clear by the way he started the session off. He hardly took a breath until he finished what he had to say. He smiled once he got it all out, and I could see as he took a deep breath he already felt better. The gist of it all was his worry about how badly misinformed they were with the intel they'd been given by one of Frank's informants. It apparently had led them directly into a potential ambush and almost got Ty killed.

That got my attention.

I knew the guys would have already talked this out with Cole in their debrief, and he'd probably be in touch with Frank himself, but I promised him that since I was here in Washington with Frank, I'd mention it. He hesitated but agreed he'd like me to.

I took some quick notes and filled out my usual patient spreadsheet like I did after every session while I waited for the alert that Keith had logged in. When it came, I immediately switched to the chat and took a deep breath to reset my head as the video call came up.

"Hi," I waved and immediately noted the heavy dark circles under his bloodshot eyes, "I'd ask how you're doing but I think your face says it all." He nodded with a small smile and pinched the bridge of his nose as if to seek some relief.

"Headache?"

"Migraine."

"You take your Maxalt?"

He shook his head. "Don't like taking shit like that."

"I get that, Keith, but what helps you get rid of all that sludgy crap inside when you're hurting?"

"Training."

"Can you train when your head is splitting in two?"

"No." He seemed to hear me because he reached over and popped a Maxalt out of its tinfoil pouch and stuck it under his tongue to dissolve.

"Suffering in pain isn't going to help you or anyone else right now."

"I know." His voice showed how weary he felt with it all.

"While that's working its way into your system, why don't you tell me about how you felt about the mission? Truth be told, I know a little from Mark."

"I know. I was in the room with him when he had his session." That was news to me. I knew the guys were close, but the fact they were that comfortable with one another was huge to hear. It meant they talked openly with each about their sessions, and that was extremely uncommon in men. Once again, I was in awe of the enigma that was Shadows. "You got the story from Mark and our frustration with the informants."

"I got that, yes. Let me ask, though, do you trust Frank?"

"I trust Frank with my life." He didn't miss a beat. "It's just that I'm not sure I trust the information he got. The location was clearly not where she was being held. I want to know why we were sent there. I want to know if it was a fluke we got ambushed by the Cartel. And why were the police standing around just a street over from where we were heading? Things aren't adding up." He paused like he needed a moment, so I gave him one. These guys dealt with life and death situations, and they needed to share their feelings about their missions with me, but I had to tread lightly. It was a gray area I had to move in between helping them emotionally while never giving them anything that might undermine their faith in their superiors.

"Maybe the information was right, but they just moved her before you got there."

"I don't know. Call me crazy," he fought his emotions, "I just thought maybe for once things would align and she'd be there."

"That's not crazy, Keith, that's staying optimistic."

"Optimistic," he repeated with a head shake, and I could feel the darkness inside him fight to take over. I knew what he needed, but sadly, I wasn't there to get him to punch the wall again, so I played dirty and prayed it would work.

"Or maybe she's gone forever, dead or sold off." I hit him low in the hope I'd smack him back in line again.

His face snapped up, and he looked like he wanted to hurt me. I lifted my chin and looked at him. *That's right. Get angry.*

"What did you just say?"

"You heard me. It's the truth, isn't it?" I shrugged and kept going. "I can see it in you. The words I just said are playing with your head. You think she's dead. You think it's too late to do anything."

"No," he whispered, but he wasn't fooling anyone. I picked up my iPad and started to take notes.

"You know what'll happen if you let yourself get pulled down into that dark place in your head." I eyed him through the screen of the laptop. "Cole will be forced to sit you out on the next mission."

"Are you threatening to report me to Logan?" He started to move about like the reality of what I'd just said hit him hard. Because he knew it was the truth.

"No," I tossed my iPad aside and leaned toward the camera, "I'm trying to prove a point here. Don't let yourself go dark. You'll hate yourself for it later. I can promise you that. You're a Blackstone soldier in an awful situation, so man up. Even if you believe, deep down, she's gone. Your kids need to know you did your very best to get their mother home again."

He stood straight up and sent his chair flying backward as he covered his mouth and took a few deep breaths. Slowly, his hands moved to the back of his head, and he squeezed his eyes shut.

"Jesus," he said to himself, and I could see it took all his willpower not to scream out his pain. "This wasn't how it was supposed to be."

I felt my own emotions rise to the surface, and I blinked back the tears that prickled my eyes. My heart ached for this man who had done so much to save the woman he loved, only to have her fall out of love with him and then be taken from him this way. She was snatched out of thin air. No person deserved that, especially not a man like Keith.

He paced back and forth then he pressed his palms down on the desk as he leaned forward, and his face filled the camera.

"Okay," his jaw flexed, "I've got myself back in check."

Good.

"At the risk of sounding condescending," I switched it up, "I'm incredibly proud of you for having a meeting with me today." I softened my tone. "I'm starting to see how your head works, and you're strong Keith. Remember that when you find yourself slipping."

"Okay." He nodded, and I knew he was himself again.

"Good. Now, let's talk some more."

We ended up talking for well over an hour, and I didn't care. He needed it, and that was what I was there for.

When we were finished, I packed my things and left the office the way I found it. I headed down the hall and saw Frank's office door open and decided to check in with him. I wondered where Ty was.

"Frank," I knocked on his door, "may I have a quick word?"

"Sure." He tossed his glasses on his desk, and I closed the door behind me. "What's up?"

"I had a session with Mark and Keith today."

"Good."

"Yes, Mark's was interesting."

"I bet." He chuckled slightly.

"He has concerns."

"Let me guess. It's about the info my informant gave me and what happened in Rosarito?" I nodded and leaned against the table by the side wall.

"I'm sure you know a lot of things, and I'm sure you can't share everything with them."

"That's right, I don't."

"But you trust your informants?"

"I do." He hesitated, and I knew he was trying to decide whether to continue the conversation. I knew he certainly didn't have to explain anything to me.

"You know I'm only trying to understand so I can do my job, but I totally understand if I'm overstepping."

"I have informants all over the world, Ivy. Six informants in Rosarito alone," he said as he leaned back in his chair. "Three Blackstone know about, and three they don't and can't know about."

"Why?" I pressed.

"It's my job to protect the men whenever they step foot on Mexican soil. I don't share everything with them because it's on a need-to-know basis, and they don't need to know."

"I understand."

"Ivy, there are things I simply can't share with the men. It would change how they view their mission. They probably wouldn't like the idea of who some of my contacts are." He gave a dark chuckle then held up a finger as I opened my mouth to speak. "Look, it's just like how I can't press you for all the things the men might share with you. It's for their own protection. For you, too, for all of them."

I knew I couldn't argue with that.

"I know, I totally get it." I flexed my back. "I just want you to know it's playing on their minds. They feel they were fed the wrong information, and they don't trust where it came from. They don't need any more distractions right now."

"Understood, Doc." He gave a firm nod, and I knew our conversation was finished.

"Do you know where Ty went?"

"He saw someone he knew and headed that way." He pointed to his left. "How's Keith really doing?"

"Exactly how you'd think a Blackstone member would be in his situation."

"Do I have any reason to pull him from the mission?"

"You don't," I gave my honest answer, "and if you did, I think the damage would be catastrophic. He needs to be involved."

"Is that your professional answer?"

"Would it be anything different?" I raised a skeptical eyebrow.

"Very well." He backed off. He needed to know I would never let personal feelings for a patient affect my judgement.

"I appreciate the talk." I smiled as I tugged the strap of my heavy bag over my shoulder and headed out the door. I sent a quick text and hoped I made the right call.

When I turned the corner, I stopped short.

"Hello." A man blocked my path and gave me a smile that rather reminded me of a vulture eyeing its prey. "Dr. Ivy Knight. I hoped we'd get to meet in person." His brown hair was cut in the classic military style, but his brown eyes warmed his demeanor as he studied me.

"And you are?" I matched his repertoire. I thrust out my hand and waited for him to take it.

"Rivera. Donald Rivera." I swallowed back my nerves and gave a polite nod. He wasn't stupid; he knew I knew exactly who he was.

"Ah, yes, I've heard a bit about you, too."

"I'm flattered." He grinned wider and made me chuckle. He had a Mark feel to him. "I'm not shocked you have, with you being Beckett's girlfriend and all."

"I'm hardly that." I was interested to know who fed him that detail.

"Well, then, it's my lucky day."

"Perhaps." I played along, curious to see where our conversation would go.

"So, where are you headed?" He shifted topics.

"Ah," I checked the time on my phone, "I'm about to grab a very late lunch."

"Great. I'm starved." He moved next to me and offered his arm like a gentleman. "May I escort you?"

I hesitated then figured this might be a good chance to gain some information.

"I suppose that couldn't hurt." I switched my bag to the other side and cautiously put my arm through his.

He acted like a tour guide and had me in stitches as he made up fake names and jobs for the people I knew and greeted as they passed. He certainly had charm, and if the situation were different, I think I'd have hung out with him. He was light and funny, and, especially in my profession, that held its own appeal.

I grabbed a turkey sandwich, water, and an orange while Rivera decided on an apple.

"That's your lunch, huh?" I made my point as we sat in the middle of the room. I chose a seat that faced the door like Ty always did. I didn't want anyone to be able to sneak up on us.

"I had a late breakfast." He chuckled as he sat across from me. "Maybe I just wanted to get you alone."

"You've achieved that." I eyed the room and took note of who was around us. My luck, Hill would approach, and things could go south quickly.

"Do I make you uneasy? Am I losing my charm?" He winked playfully.

"I was the one who agreed to this lunch." I unwrapped my sandwich and took a bite and made sure I didn't send any signals that I was the least bit interested in him. I knew I'd need to fuel my body for this conversation to stay sharp. Charming or not, he was still on Hill's side. "And no, you don't make me uneasy." I figured I should add that last part.

"Thank God." He made a show of acting relieved.

"Though I'm curious why you sought me out."

"How long have you and Beckett been together?"

"Like I said before, we're not dating." I dabbed the corners of my mouth. "Why would you care anyway?"

"Besides the obvious?" He shrugged like his open flirting was natural for him. "I've known Beckett a long time, but I've yet to meet anyone he'd actually date."

"Ty's relationship status seems to be the topic of

conversation a lot lately, and I'm really not sure what you're going to gain by asking me that question." I cocked an eyebrow at him as I chewed.

He leaned back in his chair and tapped his fingernail on the table. "I'm just trying to figure out if you *were* dating, how close you two are."

I chuckled lightly. "That would be a pretty personal thing to ask someone you don't know."

"For fun, let's say you *are* dating, because let's be real, you're gorgeous, and if I was lucky enough to work with you, I know it would be near impossible for me not to make a move on you. Also, I'd think, given your profession, you could get people to open up and share things. Share things they think are true but aren't."

"Is there a question here?"

"Has Beckett ever told you what happened on his last assignment?"

"I'm not his doctor."

"Okay, but as a girlfriend or *friend,* did he ever share anything?"

"Yes. As a friend, Beckett and I talk, but just so we're clear, I don't dig inside my friends' heads unless they ask me to, and he's never asked."

"I see. You're a smart woman, Ivy. I'd think you wouldn't play games."

"You're right, I don't." I eyed his nail as it drilled repeatedly into the ceramic surface. An uncomfortable heat crept around my neck.

"Can you tell me what he's shared with you?"

"About?" I spun the cap off my water and waited for him to come out with it.

"Are you always this obtuse?" He tapped harder. Flashes of Ben Oliver tried to force their way forward, and I blinked them back. He misread my silence and kept going. "Are you going to sit there and tell me he didn't share his story with you?"

"He's shared some things, some good, some not." The sound of his incessant tapping overtook the sounds around me as he went on.

"Ivy," both his hands covered mine, and I felt the tension in my shoulders the moment the tapping stopped, "I'm just looking out for Beckett. Hill's not someone to mess around with."

"That, I believe." I looked down at our joined hands and slid mine back away from his.

"So, you understand he needs to back off. Let what happened with Brown go."

"That's not up to me. I can't sway Ty. Maybe you should speak with him directly."

I pulled out my phone and saw it was time for me to find Ty. I didn't want him steamrolling this little encounter.

"I'm sorry, but I have to go."

"Did you know Brown was sleeping with Demi, and on our last mission, Beckett found out about it?"

"I haven't heard that version." I shook my head, annoyed he'd tried to plant the idea in my head. "But given the way Ty's been affected by Brown's death, I'm going to say that's fake news." I stood, tugged my bag over my shoulder, and plucked the tray off the table. "Thanks for your company, but I think we should part ways now."

"Ivy."

"I can smell your bullshit a mile away, Rivera, and so will any judge."

I went to the corner and tossed my trash in the can then set the tray on top of the others. As I brushed my hands free of some crumbs, I turned to find Rivera too close to me. He grabbed my arm and pushed me into the wall, out of sight of the rest of the room.

"You've no idea what kind of trouble could happen if you can't get Beckett to back off Hill." All signs of his previous charm and humor evaporated in that moment.

"I think it's you who needs to back off." I held up a hand, but he pushed it down and held it to the wall.

"I tried to do this nicely, but since you're a prissy bitch, we'll do it this way." He smirked when I lifted my chin to show I wasn't scared. I wasn't; I was petrified.

"I said let me go." I tried to yank my arm away, but it only intensified his hold.

"I saw that TikTok video, and I know your story with Ben Oliver." I licked my lips, hating how I'd become some sort of internet true crime celebrity lately. "What are the chances he saw it, too?" The food I used to fuel my fight threatened to come back up.

"Are you threatening me in some way, Rivera?"

"No, Dr. Knight, that wasn't a threat, just an observation." His gaze made my blood run cold. "Here's what's going to happen. You're going to tell Beckett to stop looking into Hill."

"Why would I do that?"

"If you don't, Dustin and I will come forward and say we saw the entire thing. Say we saw our captain raise his gun at his best friend and shoot him between the eyes because of a shared lover. And when Hill, Dustin, and I came in, he tried to pin it on Hill. It's no secret they hate each other, so it seems natural he'd blame him."

I wanted to lash out, slap him across his face, and knee him in the balls so he would think twice before putting his hands on another person the way he did with me. But then I saw something flicker over his face, and I stopped struggling.

"I'm confused then, Rivera. Why haven't you come forward with that already?"

His face shot back, and he blinked a few times. "What?"

"Why haven't you just done it? Say Ty killed him. I mean, if you guys are all prepared to say you witnessed it, what are you waiting for?"

"Stop talking." I was clearly throwing his head for a loop.

"Why's Hill trying to stop Ty from proving he's guilty? Why not come forward now and end it all?"

"Because—" He stopped himself.

"Because what? There's a missing piece to this story, Rivera. And if I can see that, so will a judge." I raised an eyebrow at him and felt his hold on me loosen. So, I went in for one last try. "Does Hill have something on you?" I tried to read his face. "Because that's the only logical reason you'd want to help Hill send an innocent man to prison."

"Stop." He pushed me into the wall a little harder. "Just," he came closer, "get Ty to back the hell off!"

"Rivera?" Dustin was suddenly behind him, and Rivera stepped back with a snarl.

"Jesus." He shook his head like he was losing it then turned on his heel and left me wondering what would have happened if Dustin hadn't shown up.

"Fuck, are you okay?" He came toward me, but I held up a hand to stop him. I didn't have a whole lot of trust for any of them at this point.

"I don't get it." I sniffed as another thought came to me. "If Hill's so scared of Ty, why doesn't he just get his JAG lawyer brother to toss the case out?"

"His brother's made some bad moves in the past. He wants to lay low. I don't think he's got the pull he used to," Dustin muttered.

"That's not what I hear."

"Yeah, well, things aren't always what they appear." The way he held my gaze made me once again question why these two men were so loyal to Hill.

"There are no witnesses, no weapon, just *he said, she said*, so why is Hill that worried about Ty digging?" He picked up my bag from the floor and handed it to me. I took it without making contact. I was too wound.

"People get comfortable when they get away with stuff enough times," he whispered.

"Dustin," I shifted my bag, "does Hill have something on you and Rivera? Because—"

"You may want to leave, Doctor." He cut me off and stepped back. He used his head to point. "Company's comin'."

Shit.

I gave a quick nod and rushed out of the room as I spotted both Rivera and Hill heading my way.

My steps quickened as I burst through the doors with my stomach in my throat and ran right into someone.

"Ivy?" Ty grabbed my arms and stopped me from falling. "Where've you been?"

"Ty." My voice gave me away.

"What happened?"

"Not here." I grabbed his arm and tried to get him to follow me, but he read me like an open book. "Please, Ty, don't do anything."

He looked through the window, and I saw his shoulders stiffen. I knew he'd spotted the others.

"Ty, seriously," I begged, "don't go in there."

"Tell me what happened."

"I will, but we need to get out of here first, please." He struggled and looked one more time through the window and swore. Then he took my hand and walked me away from the mess hall. I whooshed out a breath, relieved he was with me.

He found an empty office, closed the door, and

listened to what I'd just gone through. The entire time, his jaw twitched, but he didn't interrupt.

"You're always talking about you listening to your sixth sense—your gut, right?" He nodded. "I'm telling you I feel that if we dig more into other tours Hill's been on, we might find more evidence that he's killed before. We might be able to get enough to at least have someone higher up look into it."

"It's worth a shot." He rubbed his face and reached for my waist and pulled me to his chest. "I can't have anything happen to you, Ivy. Promise me you won't go off again, even if it's here in this building."

"I promise." I wrapped his arms around my waist and relaxed, knowing I was safe.

My phone pinged, and I leaned back to pull it from my purse. I took a deep breath and turned it to show him the screen. He took it from my hand and read the text. "What did you do?"

"What I needed to."

"Are you sure, Ivy?"

"Yes," I stood straighter, "I can do this."

"All right, but do you understand what this means?"

"I do."

Within an hour, we stood in the elevator. We barely said two words as we crossed the busy street, then just as we stepped on the curb, a phone was thrust into my face for the second time that day.

"And here I am again with Dr. Ivy Knight," Mrs. Oliver yelled above the sounds of the city. "Dr. Knight, why won't you share what you know?" Her voice was full of anger. "I want justice, and I deserve it!" she screamed. "Justice, justice," she shouted, and her followers closed in until Ty stuck a hand up and shielded me from her posse of people. "What if you were me? Hey!" Her cry had me stop mid-stride. "What if it was you who lost everything?"

"I did." I whirled around and matched her glossy eyes. "My entire life has been uprooted because of your ex-husband." I pressed my hand against her arm, and she lowered her phone, so it pointed down away from us.

"Then help me. Just show me where." Tears leaked over her eyelids and streamed down her cheeks, and I felt my heart break for her. I knew I needed to break my silence to finish this for her. When I didn't answer right away, she tried again. "I don't care about Ben. I hope he's in the ground or at the bottom of a well somewhere, but please," she took my hand, "please show me where they are."

"All right, all right." I finally nodded and stepped closer. "Meet me at the mill off Connolly Road."

THIRTEEN

ERIC

I waited for her eyes to close then peeled myself off the floor and onto the comfort of the leather chair. I'd spent the last couple of nights downstairs with Lexi. I learned a lot about her and listened to her talk about what life was like above the border. Of course, it was all general, nothing too specific. She was very careful and didn't give me anything I could pass on to Castillo. Nothing about the location of the safehouse, how the men operated, the other wives, nothing at all.

Years ago, I'd made the decision to stay here and work for the Cartel. It was easy money when you gave in and stopped caring. Plus, the way the Cartel ran their business wasn't at all like the United States. It was more of an *anything goes to get to the top* kind of life. How ruthless could you be? I was still finding that one out.

Since Lexi's arrival, I'd allowed myself to reflect a bit, and I wondered what I'd do with my life if I wasn't here transporting women from point A to point B. When I arrived here, I was determined to do whatever it took to get myself into a position where I could make money and gain some power. I had the option to work with Talya's father, but he had just begun a working relationship with Grim, and I didn't trust Grim any more than I did Talya's father. Grim was new to the game and was pushing hard to make his own connections via his father's request. Now, years later, I knew my gut was right. The guy was a snake.

Though some might look down at what I do, I knew that when the women were with me, they were well looked after. Well, the best they could be while in a cage. I had a solid, reliable buyer in Chili. He lived by the same code of ethics I did, and I'd never heard a single complaint about how he treated the women.

I remembered when I first met Chili in the middle of the desert. It was nearly a hundred and ten degrees that day, and I had a load of girls who needed to be moved in a hurry. At the time, Castillo played the bigshot even more than he did now, and I wanted them moved before he decided to play with them. I was tipped off that an American was looking to buy from a solid source, and I made the call and set up the meet.

He told me he'd spent most of his childhood in TJ, Mexico, in spite of being born in the USA. His dark aviator glasses and Green Bay Packers ball hat hid his face, but I had a good feeling about the guy and trusted my instincts. He didn't say much when I handed the girls over, and the payment was made with no fuss. We both just stood there while our guys moved the girls from my truck to his. I remembered how the sweat dripped down our faces as we made the exchange, each of us worried the other might make a wrong move, but since then our relationship had grown with each shipment through the tunnel. Over years, our trust in each other proved lucrative, and we'd become close almost to the point of friendship.

I shifted in the chair and glanced over at the dark shadow on the bed and hoped Lexi slept as more memories flooded in.

"Stop," I whispered out loud to shut down my head. I needed a distraction to stop the pull of old memories. Those memories were way too dangerous for me to pick at, and I stood up.

"Will you stay?" Her soft voice found me, and the memories shot back behind closed doors. I could barely see her in the low light of the basement. "I don't want to be down here alone." Her words had me settling back down into the chair.

"I thought you were asleep."

"I wish." Her sigh was genuine and proof this place had taken its toll on her. "Every time I close my eyes, I see my kids' faces the last time I saw them. Hurt and confused why their mother didn't love them the way a mother should."

"I'm sure they don't think that." I knew I wasn't

convincing because, truth be told, kids felt more than we gave them credit for.

"Trust me, they did." She sniffed, and I brightened the room just a tiny bit so I could see her better. "Why can't I feel the way my parents did? They loved me unconditionally. When they were murdered, something just snapped inside me. Like I'm—"

"Like what?" Even though she was careful not to give me anything I could really use, it gave me insight into who she was. I rather enjoyed talking to her. She was smart and tough and had been through a lot in her life.

"Like I'm scared to let myself feel that side of me." I heard the bed squeak as she cried into her pillow for a moment. "Look at Keith," she started up again. "I treated him like shit when all he ever did was love me, give me two kids, and a safe place to live." She paused like she thought about what she just said, but I didn't push. She'd already proved she wasn't going to give up the location.

"Sounds like Keith is a good guy." I leaned my chair back and crossed my ankles to get more relaxed.

"I was so in love with him when we were teenagers," she let out a shaky breath, "but I made him work for it. God, I was hard to love."

"If you could do it all over again, would you marry Keith?" I yawned.

"No." She paused, and I leaned my head to study her. Her confession wasn't what I expected. "He deserves so much better than me." She went on, "I only hope he can see that and move on." She lowered her head sadly. I found myself intrigued. I wanted to dig deeper into her head. She interested me. She was so raw, and I could almost feel her pain.

"If he was here right now, what would you tell him?"

"Besides to stick a gun in your face and get me the hell out of here?"

"Yeah," I chuckled at her dark humor, "besides that."

"I don't know." She sat up and leaned her back against the wall. She pulled her knees up to her chest and pulled the blanket over herself. "Is this something you're going to use against me later?"

"I may be cruel but only when it's necessary," I assured her. We sat in silence for a few moments, and I wondered if she was deciding what words to say. She was careful.

"I should say thank you." She finally spoke, and I arched a brow at her. "Thank you for showing me a side of me I didn't know I had. I only wish I could keep those feelings at the surface instead of buried deep. Maybe I'd have been happier."

I thought about what she said, and a part of me could relate. I'd suppressed a lot over the years, made a lot of sacrifices to be with the Cartel. Though I wouldn't change it now, there was a time I'd battled with it and wondered if I could live this life. I tuned in to the faint smell of bleach and thought about fucking Leo and knew this was where I belonged.

"I'll see what I can do about passing that along."

"Thanks," she dripped with sarcasm, "yeah, you do

that." I smirked, and she huffed out a breath. "Can I ask you a question?"

"I can't guarantee an answer, but you can ask," I shot back. I didn't really care what she asked. I just enjoyed her company over the men upstairs.

"Have you ever been in love?"

"Yes." I reached for my drink. It was cold, but I took a sip anyway, needing to do something.

"Didn't end well, huh?"

"What makes you say that?"

"You gave me the truth, but you quickly moved on. That proves you're uncomfortable with the question."

"No," I cleared my throat, "it didn't end well."

"Was it your fault?"

"Yes."

"Why did you end it?"

"Because—" I started to lie but stopped myself and figured maybe admitting the truth would help the ache in my heart hurt less. "Because I have a past and a life that could hurt her."

"That's very noble of you." She genuinely held my gaze with her puffy eyes. "I know, I'm the last person who should give out relationship advice, but have you ever thought about admitting it to her? Give her a chance to decide if she can handle it?"

"She won't be able to."

"Sounds like you're giving up to me."

"Trust me," I shook my head and forced myself to clear all thoughts of my past from my head, "I'm not."

"For what it's worth, I'm sorry." She averted her gaze. "Being the one to hurt the person you love, or should love, is more painful than being on the receiving end."

"Yeah, well, she's moved on, so—"

"Has she really? Or is it an attempt to get your attention?"

I wasn't sure. Alejandro had reported to me that he'd seen Talya the very day after we had sex at the bar hanging off the arm of Grim Gates. It hurt like a bitch to hear it, but it was my own doing, regardless.

Suddenly, the door burst open and the lights flipped on, almost blinding me. My gun was in my hand, ready to fire, before my eyes had even adjusted. Then I lowered it with a hiss.

"What the fuck is this? A slumber party?" Castillo glared at me, and I settled back in my chair, unfazed by his frustration. He should know what I was doing, so I didn't grace him with a reply.

"Do you ever check your damn phone?"

"It's two a.m. I didn't think anyone would need me." I sat forward slightly and glanced casually at Lexi, who was wide-eyed at our intruder.

"You fuck her?" he snarled, and I shook my head in disgust.

"You know me better than that. I've never touched any of the girls who have come through here." I was insulted he would even accuse me of such a thing. I was a professional and had my standards. "You wanna talk, let's go upstairs." I jerked my thumb toward the door. He ignored me and stepped toward the cage, and Lexi scurried to the far back wall where he couldn't reach her.

"She's a pretty little thing, isn't she?"

"She's scrappy too," I warned him. I wouldn't put it past Lexi to take a swipe at him. I could see her contemplating the idea, so I stepped forward, unsure what Castillo would do if she did.

"You know I like it rough." He let out a nasty laugh, and I cringed at the sound. Castillo was a good-looking man and could have used it to his advantage, but he smoked heavily and sounded like a sixty-year-old with a hacking cough and a wheeze. Shit, he hadn't even hit midlife yet. I thought I saw him briefly eye the lock on her cage.

"You see the chick Filippo brought?" I hoped to lure him upstairs. "She's got tits bigger than a basketball." She was all plastic, just what he loved.

"No." His eyes sparkled with interest as he turned toward me. "Let's see his treat."

I waved toward the door, and as he walked ahead of me, I glanced back at Lexi, who mouthed the word "thanks" to me. I flipped off the light without a response and followed him back upstairs. Alejandro nursed a bump on his head and shot me a look that told me he'd tried to stop Castillo.

"Drag Filippo's girl in here," he ordered Alejandro. "I wanna see her tits."

Alejandro looked at me, and I nodded but gave him a signal to give me ten. I needed time to get Castillo to focus and tell me why he was here. He left, and I headed for the bar and poured Castillo his favorite drink. My phone buzzed, and I quickly glanced at it.

> Alejandro: Filippo said the girl he hired to go through Castillo's phone didn't return for her next shift. We have no answers, but we're still digging. No clue why Castillo's here.

Fuck!

"What brings you all the way here at this time of night?" He took the drink and sat in a chair as I settled into the couch across from him.

"I've changed my mind."

"Oh?"

"I don't want her dead yet." He loudly slurped his drink. "I wasn't pleased about your tag on the proof of life." He eyed me hard, and I leaned back and crossed my ankle over my knee. "I'm gonna show her off a bit, share my story on how I found her." That caught my interest. I didn't know that story either.

"Fair enough." I shrugged. "Then what?"

"Then you wait for my command, Eric." I could tell he didn't like how comfortable I seemed to be with this situation. Castillo's original idea to kill her was stupid, so maybe he'd made a hasty decision and now thought the better of it. "Say it," he spat out.

"What?"

"Like you said, I've known you a long time, Eric.

Enough to know you must have a feeling on what's going on here."

"My view hasn't changed. We've got someone big here. We could sell her off to the highest bidder and make millions of dollars, but instead you wanted to stick a bullet in her head just so you can go down in history for killing a Blackstone woman."

"You said yourself, she's not gonna give up their location."

"And I still stand behind that. She's been trained, brainwashed never to tell the truth. You'll get nothing from her. I've been inside her head, opened as many doors as I could, but it is what it is. She'll die before she tells us anything useful. We could use her and lure Blackstone to us, but truth be told, they're smarter than us. So, show her off, make your mark in history, but be smart and get rich while you do it."

"So, how do you figure to play it?"

I knew I had to be careful. If Castillo thought I wasn't up to the job, I'd be replaced and any of the money I'd banked on for the woman would be gone. I leaned back and played it cool while I pretended to think. I licked my lips and tapped my fingers on the armrest. Then I shot forward like I had a new idea.

"Death might not scare her, but a price on her head and the idea of disappearing deep into Siberia with God knows who just might." He ran a finger along his lips as he considered my words. I quickly kept going before I lost him. "I say kill two birds with one stone. I'll sell her off to

Chili, you'll make your money, and as I take her to him, I'll give her one last chance to talk. The fear of the unknown can be worse than death. Maybe she'll give us something after all. Either way, we'll have the cash."

"Have you spoken to Chili about this?" Just the way he said it confirmed what I'd thought. My phone really had been bugged.

"No, I just told him that this chick was yours and left it at that." I held his piercing gaze, and I tossed my phone on the table so he could *see* for himself. "We got this, Castillo. This'll work."

A wicked smile traveled across his lips as his gaze latched onto mine.

"I like it."

Good.

"But first I get to tell my story."

Yes, get your glory, and then we get paid.

"My place, seven p.m. this Tuesday."

I nodded, leaned forward, and tapped my glass to his.

"It's a date."

FOURTEEN

IVY

I stood back and watched Frank, Ty, and Sergeant Chamness mutter among themselves. Sergeant Chamness seemed like a nice guy. He had come to town from the Dusk safehouse specifically for this meeting, along with Corporal Davie, at Frank's request. Davie was sweet and was more than pleased to help out.

I tightened the tie around the waist of my coat and scanned nervously around the grounds. The mist was thick, and the fog sat low. It made anything more than a few feet away difficult to see, but the chill I felt in my bones came from more than the temperature. My whole body was on high alert, and I shivered despite myself.

I checked my phone for the time, and when I looked back up, I saw Ty watching me. His eyes were shaded by his ball hat, and his ticking jawbone told me he felt just as nervous as I was.

A light flickered and caught my attention, and a moment later a text message came through.

Unknown: I'm here. Look for the light.

I tapped on the passenger window, and when it went down, I rested my hands on the open sill.

"Hey, Davie?"

"Mm?" He was studying a map.

"I'm going to join Ty for a moment, okay?"

"Okay." He nodded with his eyes on his screen, and I watched him send off a message. I stepped back as his window went back up then used the SUV for cover and slipped down into the ravine. I made my way toward the light that could just be seen across from a wooded area.

As I drew closer, I saw Jennifer Oliver's panicked face. She latched on to my arm and looked down at me.

"What are those?" I eyed the bizarre looking rings on all of her fingers.

"Defense rings, one swipe of either hand, and pain will reign." She gave a dark chuckle. "I got them when I heard Ben was coming home this last tour."

"Smart." I, on the other hand, had a phone and a stun gun ready to go. "All set?"

"Show me." I knew this was about to be the hardest moment of her life, and I only hoped I could offer her some kind of peace. "By the way, I'm really sorry, Dr. Knight." She kept her voice low as we awkwardly made our way toward the old mill. "Social media was the only way I could think of to get your attention." She caught my arm to steady me as I slipped on some moss. "No one would listen, and until Ben's finally caught, I felt like they only cared about him and not what happened to me." She started to cry.

"I don't blame you." I patted her hand that still clung tightly to my arm. "I'm sorry, too. It's awful that I've been told I have to stay quiet and basically allow myself to be hunted just because I tried to help. I never wanted any part of all this."

"I see that now." She sniffed. "I blamed you for not reporting Ben and his behavior, but I realize now you did. The truth is he was showing signs of PTSD two tours ago. I begged him to get help, but he said he was. He'd gone to see you."

"Yes, I only started seeing Ben as a patient on those last two tours." I moved her hold on me from my arm to my hand, but her rings still hurt. "I could see he had problems, but we only get to see each patient for an hour every week, if we're lucky. It's hardly a window into their lives."

"I understand." She let out a shaky breath. "Can I ask you something?"

"If it's for another favor, let's see how this one'll go first." I wiggled my fingers a little, and she took pity on me and let go of my hand and let out a little laugh. Her laugh was cut short when a twig snapped underfoot and the realization of where we were headed sank back in. The damp air that seeped through our clothes had us both shivering.

"I know why you're doing this tonight, and I'm happy you're doing it, but isn't it going against your oath as a doctor?"

"Yeah," I felt my heart trip, "but I realize more each day that there are gray areas, and this is one of them."

"Did he hurt you that night, you know, after…" She trailed off, and I cleared my throat of emotion.

"Yeah, he did."

We both stopped as we came to a small rock wall. The old mill stood tall, dark, and abandoned as it had for nearly a lifetime now. I scanned the edge of the woods, and I was terrified to my very core. But I knew I could do this.

"Is this where?" I heard her swallow with a gulp.

"Yes."

"My God," her voice cracked as she took another tight grip on my arm, "do you think he's—"

"I do."

"Are you sure we should be doing this?"

"No," I whispered, but just the same, I patted my cell phone in my pocket to remind myself I wasn't alone. My location was on. "But I can't do this anymore, and neither can you."

"Okay, let's see if we can find them." We both stepped out of the protection of the woods and climbed over the small rock wall. I fought back the memories I'd been fed about this place by Ben.

My teeth chattered as I pushed open the old door and reached back to take the flashlight she pressed into my hand. The hinges squealed loudly enough to wake the entire forest from its misty sleep. The sound seemed to vibrate through my bones.

"I've heard about this place." She seemed to want to talk to hold back her jitters. "Watch your step." She pointed to some rotten wood at the entrance then followed in behind me.

I scanned the pitch-black building, unsure of what we'd find. The temperature seemed about twenty degrees colder inside. I knew this part of the mill had caught fire back when it was still in operation in the forties, and part of the roof was missing, along with some of the upper wall.

"Do you think this place is haunted?" She blew into her hands as her flashlight bounced around.

"No."

"They say when the place caught fire, everyone got out but three young men. They got trapped in here." She pointed around. "Can you imagine? Apparently, they called for help, but no one could go back in because the flames were too high. It was shut down after that. Eventually, the land was sold, but whenever crews moved in to clean it up, unexplained things started to happen."

"Like?" I lifted a wooden cover and looked inside the barrel as I held my breath.

"Like whenever they'd come back to clean it up or tear it down, someone would get hurt. It didn't take long for the mill to get the reputation for being haunted."

"Any idea why Ben would pick this place?"

"No, other than maybe because most people would stay clear of it." Her voice shook. "Can you tell me again what he said to you, please? I just need to understand what happened that day."

"Are you sure?" I asked, and her flashlight went still then she pointed the light at her face. I saw her nod and took a deep breath.

"He said he knocked on your door and your mom answered." I hesitated and felt my stomach tighten. I had already crossed a line I promised myself I never would. "She said he couldn't come in, but he forced his way in anyway. Then he gagged her and held his hand over her mouth and nose until she passed—" My flashlight suddenly flickered and went out. Jennifer tripped and sent her flashlight across the room. "I can't see anything." I tried to get my eyes to adjust as my nerves took over.

"Dr. Knight?" Her panic sent a chill through me. Something above us creaked, and we craned our necks to search the floor above us. Something fell, and we both ducked and covered our heads.

"Take my hand." I reached in the direction of where she was, and she took my hand. "I think maybe we should get back outside." I shuffled my feet so I didn't trip as we inched toward the door. I wobbled a bit as I tuned into her hold on me and flexed my fingers as I realized she wasn't wearing her rings.

People talked about different levels of fear. There was seeing fear, hearing fear, and feeling fear. As my brain spun to catch up, I felt that entire cocktail flush through my veins.

"Say something," I choked out.

"You've been saying enough." Ben's voice trapped the air in my lungs. I felt terror rip through my body. "You've been a bad doctor, Ivy."

"Jennifer!" I somehow managed to scream. "Stay where you are!" He grabbed my arm, and my instincts kicked in as I desperately reached back with my free hand, my fingers felt wood. I swung it hard in his direction and hit him on the side of the head. I heard him crash into something as I raced around a half wall I'd spotted in a sliver of moonlight. I felt around for anything I could toss to make a loud enough noise to alert the guys of my exact location.

My cold hands desperately felt around shapes and surfaces for something to throw, but nothing would move. Everything was either nailed down or welded together. The fog of what was happening tried to shut me down, and it was a great challenge to not let it.

"I can smell your fear, Dr. Knight." He chuckled, and I held my breath and flattened myself between two steel beams. Maybe if he walked by me, he wouldn't notice I was there. My heart pounded so loudly I was sure he could hear it. Everything told me to run, but my body was locked in place. I held very still, but the steam from my warm breath could be seen in the moonlight just inches from my nose.

"Imagine my surprise when I saw you were in town," he sounded closer, "and that my wife kindly advertised your location with her little 'justice for her parents' thing. The power of the internet is amazing, isn't it?"

He was so close now that I could feel the heat from his body. I carefully sucked in a deep breath and held it. I clenched my jaw so he couldn't hear the chatter. *Pound, pound, pound*, my heartbeat tried to out my location, and my throat begged for moisture. *Stop*. I needed to control myself and not let panic take over.

I stared straight ahead and willed myself to be one with the building. Then I saw a single white puff of air. It brushed by my cheek, and I felt my heartbeat slow as the blood drained to my toes.

"Don't move," Ty whispered in my ear, and I almost cried out in relief that he found me in this house of horrors.

"You shoulda stayed hidden!" someone called, and Ben's footsteps suddenly stopped. I allowed myself to turn and look in his direction and saw why. Several red dots peppered his chest, then in a sudden flurry of movement and confusion, several shots were fired. In the seconds that followed, I felt the warmth from Ty's body as it cloaked mine. He'd pulled me down and shielded me from it all. He held me tightly to his chest for several minutes, our hearts both pounding together. I shrieked as more shots fired, terrified they might miss and hit us.

"It's okay." I felt Ty brush back my hair in the dark, then he ran a hand over my body to make sure I was in one piece. "You're okay," he said. "We were here the entire time." I wrapped my arms around his neck and took a deep, relieved breath. We had gone over this plan many times; it was staged from the moment we'd arrived at the mill. We only hoped Ben saw me as I slipped away from Davie, who had let the others know I was on the move. I saw Agent Chamness give us the signal from the tree line that all was in place and to move inside the building. I knew they needed Jennifer and me to separate to see who Ben would follow. What I didn't expect was for Ben to take my hand. In that instant, I forgot what I was supposed to do.

"I'm sorry I missed my mark," I apologized as I nearly shook out of my skin. I was supposed to draw him to the far wall so Davie could take me out of the building.

Lights from several flashlights flickered around the inside of the room, and I could see Ty's relieved face as he helped me up.

"We anticipate changes in scenarios." He rubbed my back. "You did great." I saw Davie take Jennifer outside and was relieved she was unharmed. Though we both would have a journey to recovery, I knew hers would be far worse than mine. I couldn't imagine what it would be like to lose both my parents to that man, especially with the knowledge that she had brought him into their lives.

"I want…" I pulled back and closed my eyes, completely rattled. "I want to go back to Shadows," I confessed as I was hit with a sudden epiphany. Even before Ben Oliver came into my life, I'd never felt so safe and content, and the warmth and love on that mountain suddenly became all I wanted.

"And that's exactly where we're going, just as soon as we can." He used the backs of his fingers to dry my tears. I grabbed his hand and held on to it like an anchor as he moved us outside the mill and back toward the others.

Frank didn't miss a beat and whisked us back to Washington Headquarters that night. I decided to skip dinner and crawled into bed after a hot shower, but even that didn't do much to help my shakes. Frank made sure to set up a meeting with Jennifer's lawyer the next morning so I could give my statement. In spite of my rush to get back to Montana, I was glad I didn't have to deal with it right away.

The only thing I was disappointed about was that Eagle Eye hadn't killed Ben Oliver. Apparently, he'd only been wounded. Frank explained they'd mostly fired over his head in an effort to subdue him rather than kill him. He said Ben didn't deserve death; he deserved to sit in a six-by-six cell and live with his punishment. I saw his point, but I still hated the fact that he still breathed. I knew as a doctor I should have had some sympathy for him. He was obviously mentally ill, but as a victim, I couldn't find it in myself to be that kind. Especially after all he'd done.

Ty's shadow flickered on the wall as he quietly entered the room. He quickly undressed and slipped under the covers and pulled me into his arms. When he felt the fabric of what I had on, he peeled back the blanket.

"Is that my shirt?" I nodded. "You brought it with you?"

"I wanted you with me," I whispered. He made a sound that let me know he was pleased with my answer.

"I really love that you did," he dragged it off my body, "but I want to be skin to skin." I didn't protest as he removed the shirt and tossed it on a chair and then snuggled back in.

Both of us were silent as we listened to the weather outside. A snow-rain mix had started on our way back to the hotel, and it was nice to be cuddled together as the freezing pellets hit against the window. Ty's warmth finally began to thaw my tightly wound body. Every few moments, he'd lean down and kiss my hair as if he needed reassurance that I was still there. I imagined he and I both replayed the night's events over and over in our heads.

"Thank you," I whispered against his chest as the constant memory of what had happened finally stopped doing replays. "You risked a lot to make sure this ended for me."

He rolled onto his elbow and looked down at me with such a tender expression it melted the rest of the ice from my bones.

"I would risk everything for you." He tenderly traced my eyebrow, down my cheek, and to my lips.

"You know what scared me the most tonight?" I caught his hand and pressed it against my lips. "The realization that you're in that kind of danger every time you go on a mission." I swallowed as my voice caught. "I never want to experience that again, ever, yet you run toward it." I sniffed and squeezed his hand.

"Hey," he must have felt my body tremble because he covered my chest with his warm hand and pressed gently, "everyone's wired different, but we're a lot the same, you and me. I might save them physically, but you save them mentally. Both jobs are important, and," his eyebrows went up and he tapped my forehead, "apparently both are dangerous." I gave a smile, but I didn't fool him. He could see how raw I still was. "I can tell you one thing. I'd be terrified to deal with the stuff you do. All that gettin' in someone's head and all that personal stuff. No way."

"Does anything else scare you?" I barely recognized my voice.

"You," he chuckled, "gettin' inside my head." He nodded emphatically. "Yup, I'll admit I'm a bit scared you won't like what you might find in there."

"How so?"

"Let's unpack that another night." He yawned, and I didn't push. I could feel my own exhaustion hit me. He rolled back and pulled me close and tucked the blanket around us. My leg hooked over his waist as his hand stroked my thigh.

"I'm okay," I whispered after a few moments to reassure myself. The panic still simmered just below the surface. "I'm safe," I said a little louder. "I guess I needed to hear that so I could really believe it."

"When you're with me, you'll always be safe." He held me tight, as if he, too, needed confirmation that we were okay. The last thing I remembered was his soft breath on my cheek.

———

The next morning, we were out the door by eight, but I still felt like a zombie. We met Frank and began our prep for the afternoon session. Somehow, I got through everything and felt mildly better about what was about to happen. I just needed all this behind me.

By four-thirty, I was standing outside the courtroom full of people waiting to hear my statement on all that had happened with Ben Oliver. The only positive thing that came from the previous night besides Ben being caught was that Frank was able to pull some strings to put me on the stand today instead of having to return in a week or so. We all hoped Ben would be declared unfit for trial, but it remained to be seen what he'd end up being charged with.

"I have to ask this," Frank glanced at Ty quickly, "but they'll ask questions you might not want Beckett hearing the answers to. This is your last chance to decide if you want him in there. How much you want your boyfriend to know?" I nearly blushed that Frank knew Ty and I were dating. "Give me a little credit, Ivy, I've known him for a few years now, and you're the first woman I've seen him with." I sneaked a glance at Ty, who watched me intently. "Just know this. These guys will try to twist what you say to work in Ben's favor."

"I can handle it." I set my face, and Frank nodded at Ty to come over.

"You can be there, but no matter how nasty they come at her, you say and do nothing. Don't give them a reason to come at you, too, Beckett."

"Copy that." Ty was all business as he turned to me. "No matter what happens in there, he can't touch you because he'd have to get through me first."

"Okay." I swallowed the lump in my throat and reached over to squeeze his hand one last time to ground me.

"All right, let's go." Frank opened the door, and we walked in. Whispers hummed as my heels clicked on the wood floor. Ty, who was in front of me, took a seat while I continued to the witness stand. I held up my right hand and placed my left on the Bible. I took the oath to promise to tell the truth, then on wobbly legs lowered to the chair. I'd been in court before but never like this. This affected me in such a personal way. I inched toward the mic and rolled my chair closer, so I didn't have to strain my neck. I glanced at Ty, who sat next to Frank near the wall with a few others. Introductions were made, and within ten minutes it was my time to share what really happened that night.

"Please start from the beginning, Dr. Knight," I was urged to begin. "Tell us how you met Mr. Oliver and what happened after."

I nodded and licked my lips, suddenly glad for all the prep Frank had put me through.

"Ben Oliver was assigned to me two tours ago. We had six sessions in total. After his first tour, I determined that although he had a few problems with what he'd experienced, it wasn't anything beyond the usual stress soldiers feel after a tour in Afghanistan. I had no reason to think he was unfit for duty. I told him I wanted to see him as soon as he got back." I took a sip of water. "However, after the last tour, I wasn't prepared to sign off on Mr. Oliver. Something had definitely changed. He showed signs of extreme PTSD and displayed some aggression toward his family."

"Such as?" my advocate asked, and I closed my eyes and unlocked the memory.

"Welcome back, Private Oliver." I wasn't expecting him. I stood from behind my desk and approached him with my hand out, but I dropped it when he didn't take it. He'd been escorted in by one of the soldiers who patrolled the floor. As I closed the door, I noticed my secretary was packing up her desk. It was late in the day, and she often left early on Thursdays to pick her son up from her ex-husband.
I instantly picked up on his frazzled state when he arrived. His boots and pantlegs were muddy, and his

hands were stained. He perched on the edge of the seat on the far-left side of the couch. On previous visits he'd sat on the right, closer to me. He sat upright and rested his hands on his knees then cleared his throat a few times but made no attempt to speak. Suddenly, his eyes flicked around the room. I was instantly on high alert.

"I can only give you a few minutes, Ben." I eyed his obvious distress. "How are you?" I asked as I sat in my chair and used my thumb to open my tablet to take notes. He shrugged, and I held his intense gaze.

"Okay, just give me three words on where you're at."

"Irritated, frustrated, and pissed."

I used my pen to draw the line to number nine on the mood scale. I gave his appearance another quick glance and decided to wait to ask about it.

"Want to tell me why?"

"It's Jennifer's parents. They're getting all up in my face. Meddling where they don't belong again."

"Why this time?"

"And who is she to tell me to pick between the Army and my marriage?" he shouted, and I slid the line from the nine to the ten.

"She, meaning?"

"Jennifer," he grunted at me like I was stupid, "my dumb bitch of a wife. She saw what it was like over there, she saw the bullshit that happened to my team."

I quickly scribbled, expressing signs of psychosis.

"But how could she see that, Ben? She wasn't on your tour. She was back here in Washington waiting for you to come home." I tried to steer him back.

"What?" He shook his head. "No, she was there. Until I found her in bed with Private Jimson."

"You caught your wife cheating on you?"

"Are you listening?" He leaned forward quickly, and I tried to hide my flinch. "Yes, the night I got home to the States, I caught Jennifer in Jimson's bed."

"I'm sorry to hear that."

"Not as sorry as her parents were," he mumbled and started to tap his nail on the wooden side table like he'd often done in our previous sessions when he had something to share. Only this time I wasn't sure I wanted to hear it.

"What does that mean?"

He blinked at me a few times then sat calmly, minus the tapping, "I got into a fight with my in-laws over the phone because Jennifer was supposed to meet me at the restaurant. She didn't show. So, I drove to their house. Her bitch of a mother answered the door and wouldn't let me in." He chuckled darkly. "She was always nervous of me." He shrugged like he didn't care. "When the old bat tried to close the door on me, I pushed her inside. I was ready for her. I knew how to put her down. We're trained in all that stuff."

"Ben," I huffed in disbelief.

"I did the same to her father. They both pissed me off, wouldn't give up her location." He smiled, and a cold shiver shot down my back. "I stuffed them in the trunk, drove 'em out to the old mill. When they came around, I gave them another chance. Asked them where she was." I eyed my emergency button, but he shook his head at me, like he knew what I was up to. "Come on, Doc, let me finish my story first."

His nail tapped harder.

"Then what?" I tried to sound normal, but I knew I was in trouble here.

"Then I shot them both and buried them in that bog at the back. Low enough they won't be seen but high enough that the animals will sniff 'em out over time." He seemed to think a moment then looked right at me. "Then I came right here to chat with you about it."

I took a deep, steady breath and tried to calm my nerves. My tongue stuck to the roof of my mouth, and I worked it around a bit before I attempted to speak. "Why tell me?" My heart pounded.

"Because you're my doctor. You're the only one who listens to me and won't judge."

"Except I have to report you, and I think you know that."

He leaned back and started to tap louder and watched me, then something changed in his face and he suddenly seemed to take in where he was and what he was saying. "Oh, my God!" He jumped to his feet. "Dr. Ivy, what am I doing here?"

I couldn't tell if he was truly having a bipolar moment or not.

"You're here because it's your scheduled time for your session, Private," I lied and spoke as calmly as I could.

"Why am I all muddy?"

"It's raining outside, and your car broke down. You had to walk here."

"Oh." He sat down but went right back to his tapping. The sound seemed to drill every word about the murders into my brain. I knew he was trying to play me. It was written all over his smug, murderous face.

"Time's up." I flipped the cover on my tablet over.

"I'll see you again next week."

"Great. You have a good night."

"You too." I didn't move until he shut the door, then I scrambled for the phone. I needed to call Frank. It took two tries to unlock my phone with my face ID, but my hands shook so hard I couldn't think straight. Then the door flew open, and Ben Oliver came at me in a full-out charge. He grabbed hold of my shoulders and sent me flying into the wall. Just before everything went black, all I could think of was if this was it. Would I live to see tomorrow?

When I came to, my head hurt. I didn't know how long I was out. I was relieved to see I was still in my office and not stuffed in his trunk on the way to the old mill.

Was he gone?

I strained to listen, too scared to move. Silence. My teeth started to chatter as pain made its way through my consciousness. I felt it build as I lay there.

"Oww," I started to cry but instantly went quiet when I heard a noise. I was simply too terrified to move as I stayed where I had been left, by him.

"You know what I'm capable of, Dr. Knight." His threat came back to me in one horrific flash. Even trying to breathe nearly overwhelmed me. He'd held up my ID and pointed to my home address. "You open your mouth, and I'll kill you."

I blinked as I came back to the room. I realized it was silent, and I looked for Ty's face. It was set in stone, but when he saw me looking, he nodded, and his lips stretched into something of a reassuring smile.

"My office was trashed," I continued. "I made it to the door, and I locked it then called Dr. Roberts."

"Why not General Brandon," he pointed to Frank, "like you were originally going to do?" my advocate asked.

"Dr. Roberts is my uncle. At that moment, I needed my uncle more than the general."

"Okay. Then what happened?"

"My head hurt, and I felt a goose egg where I'd hit the wall. I saw blood on my fingers. My uncle picked up after a few rings." My memory went back to that moment as I continued to tell my story.

"Ivy?"

"Uncle," I tried to make sense, "I, I don't know what happened, but he was here, and—"

"Who was there?" His voice turned serious. "Where are you?"

"I'm at my office. Reid, please…" Suddenly, my office door opened, and his murderous eyes found me.

"Noo!" I screamed.

Someone's hands were on my arms, and I struggled and screamed, then realized it wasn't him. It was one of the patrol soldiers who'd come by to do a swipe of my area. He'd found one of his men unconscious outside my office door.

I shook my head free of the memory and quickly wiped my eyes with a tissue. My focus came back to the courtroom. Frank's eyes were on Ty who leaned forward in his seat.

"No further questions at this time." My advocate nodded at some paperwork in his hands.

Ben Oliver's advocate stood, and now it was his turn to fire away. He asked a few questions about Jennifer and her TikTok videos, and I answered them the best I could.

"Let's back up here for a moment," he said as he looked at his notes. "What happened after you spoke to your uncle about what happened?"

"The next day, Dr. Roberts found me another position out of state."

"Which is?"

"I can't say."

"Please, Dr. Knight," he basically rolled his eyes at the witness stand, "we need that information to move forward."

"If you'd like the location of where I'm staying, you'll have to speak to General Brandon Frank." She pointed across the room at Frank. "Like this case, I'm bound by the law to keep some information private."

"But you didn't keep your word, Dr. Knight, did you?" Ben's JAG lawyer lifted some papers and read something. "You—"

"I did, actually," I cut him off. I knew where he was headed. "I made a deal to use myself and Jennifer Oliver to lure Private Oliver out into the open so we could do what your people, sir, could not." Ty and Frank tried to hide their amusement. "I tried to help your client, but he was too far gone before I could help him. I didn't see the signs before his last tour, and that's something that will weigh on me for the rest of my career. But don't sit here and question my professionalism. Not until you, sir, have sat in my chair."

"Dr. Knight, if you—"

"I've answered all your questions willingly and did my part for you in this case," I interrupted. "I know my rights and what was expected of me here today. If you have any more questions regarding me, the whereabouts of where I'm staying, or anything else, you can contact my JAG lawyer, Sloane Black." He pressed his lips together and looked irritated. He knew he couldn't press on because I'd done my part and then some. "I'm now finished. The rest is up to you."

"I have no further questions for you, Dr. Knight, and we thank you for being here today." He inclined his head with a grim face.

I hooked my bag over my arm and stood with relief. I looked at Ty, and he got up along with Frank, and we all walked quickly out the door. I was happy in the belief that I could leave that chapter of my life forever.

FIFTEEN

TY

Chamness and Davie, who decided to return home as well, were in the SUV ahead of us. I wanted as much alone time as possible, so it worked out well that Daniel had left his SUV at the airport the day before and we got to drive it back.

"Feel better?" I threaded my fingers through Ivy's as she tucked her phone back into her bag.

"Yes, I really do. I filled Sloane in on everything, and she'll be ready if Ben's lawyer should come back at me for the location of the house. I've also made an appointment with my uncle to make sure I keep on track up here." She tapped her head.

"You impress me, Dr. Knight." I squeezed her hand, amazed by how assertive she was. "So many people refuse to consider their mental health, but you face it head on."

"Because I know it works, and I know how important it is when you ignore it." She looked out the window as if she slipped into a memory.

"And you're okay with the fact that your uncle is the one you go to?" I wondered how that worked between them.

"My entire life, my uncle has been the one I talked to about anything like that. When he feels I need more in-depth help, or he feels he's too close to the situation to see clearly, he refers me to a good friend of his."

"Have you ever had to do that?"

"Just once." She sighed and kept her eyes on the window. I followed her gaze, and we took a moment to watch the first snow of the season spread a light blanket over the gently rolling landscape of Montana. She seemed lost in it, and I stayed silent and waited for her to elaborate. "When my father left," she continued in a soft voice, "my uncle was, in a word, livid. I felt he wouldn't be the best person to talk to about it."

"Smart move," I chuckled lightly.

"He's a good man. He's always been there for me, but he's as professional as they come. He'd never allow himself to put his own anger ahead of my well-being."

I like this guy more than ever.

"There's a good reason the Logans keep Uncle Reid on. He's the best of the best, and I only hope someday I'll be as good as him."

"You are."

"Says the boyfriend." She glanced over at me with a raised eyebrow.

"Yes, says the boyfriend, and it also comes from the guy who sees you keeping a brother sane through one of the worst situations a guy could ever go through. He'll make it through this, and it'll be because of you."

"Keith wants help. It's easier when they're open to it."

"Still," I shrugged, "I think it's pretty amazing."

"Thanks." She smiled then turned back to the window and pressed her forehead against the cool glass. Ivy usually showed pride and accepted compliments when it came to her job, so the fact she seemed less receptive told me she was worn out. I hated to see her like this, but I understood it. I reached over and ran my hand over her leg to let her know I knew where her head was.

"I love the snow," she breathed and let out a small sigh. "I guess you love the heat and sand?"

"It's what I'm used to," I shrugged, "but I like both."

"Was there ever a time..." She stopped mid-thought, but I shook her leg to keep her going.

"Was there ever a time, what?"

"Was there ever a time where you thought you wouldn't make it out of a situation alive?"

"Many." I hit the wipers to clear the snowflakes.

"You say it so casually."

"Because it became the norm for me."

"How did you deal with that day in and day out?" I felt her eyes on me as she tried to understand.

"At first, it was a struggle, but I soon turned it into a challenge. If I lived to see the sun fall and the moon rise, I got a point. I just kept a tally. I'd scratch a line into the back of a notebook I carried on me. At the end of each mission, I'd start a new page. The sight of all those scratches kept me positive."

"Did you do the same thing when you got back to the US?"

I met her gaze, confused by her question. "Why would I do that?"

"Because you act like it's a war for you here, like you're just trying to survive until you get back to Afghanistan."

I felt my brows pinch together as I thought about her words and just how spot-on she was. I'd never looked at it that way.

"I never thought about it like that," I admitted. She went back to the snow outside the window.

I left her with her thoughts while I sorted through my own.

A few minutes later, we rolled up to the safehouse and I saw her shoulders relax.

Davie and Chamness parked ahead of us and waved as they hurried inside.

"What's up?" She looked at me as I pressed her shoulder against the seat to hold her there a second. I slid close, cupped her head, and pressed my lips to hers. Our tongues danced, and I savored her taste and inhaled her fresh scent. I slid my hand up her bare thigh and she shivered at my touch. She moaned and opened her mouth to take more of me. She put her hand in my hair and her fingers drove me into a frenzy. It took everything in me to pull away.

The more I had her, the more I craved her, and I wasn't sure how to get my head on straight without another fix.

"You good?" I muttered against her lips.

"Of course." She tucked our conversation away and reached for the door handle before I could stop her.

"Where ya going?" My erection strained against my zipper.

"I can't have you getting sick of me, Beckett." She reached for her bag, and when she leaned over, I got a good show of her plump breasts. I groaned and reluctantly opened my door with a curse and joined her.

"For the record, I'd never grow sick of you," I murmured into her ear.

"Mmhmm," she laughed. "Listen, you, we need to get inside and get ourselves back into the mindset of the house." She chuckled again when I quickly leaned in from behind and pecked her neck. "You're not helping." She giggled as I cupped her ass. "Waiting will make it that much better." She winked and opened the door. We both stepped inside the warm house.

"I wonder where everyone is." Ivy shrugged. "I'm going up to change." She jogged up the stairs. "I'll see you in a few." I wanted to talk more about her comment on the notebook, but now wasn't the time. She was right; we were back in work mode.

The place smelled like fresh cookies, and it captured

my stomach's attention as I closed the door behind me. I could hear Moore's voice and headed toward it to find him with John and Mike in the living room. When he spotted me, he quickly crossed the living room to meet me at the door. Mike and John both hit their phones.

"Hi. So, it's great you're back, congratulations on taking down a psycho killer, but we're dealing with our own problem here."

"Which is?" I dropped my bag at my feet. I was all ears, as I could feel his concern.

"Keith's son, Brandon, is missing over at Dusk."

"What?" My gaze flew to Keith, who sat at the dining room table on the phone with a map in front of him.

"Keith says he's got to be still on the grounds. The kids are under orders not to leave the property. All the guys there are out looking."

"Maybe it wasn't the best thing to send the kids there." I chewed my lip. "At least Brandon. Maybe he needed to be here with his dad. I mean, his mom being taken and all, he's probably all messed up in his head." I couldn't imagine what might be going on in the kid's mind.

"Yeah, but it was necessary." Moore shook his head. He might be new here, but I could tell he'd already become part of us.

"Yeah, you're right." I rubbed my eyes. "Poor Keith, he can't catch a break right now."

"And no," he read my mind, "nothing new has come in on Lexi. Mike had a meeting with Cole this morning.

Something's going on, but we haven't been told anything yet."

"Okay." I caught sight of Ivy as she came toward the room. She had changed into a red dress with tights, and it made my mind slip for half a second. I might live and breathe the military, but just one glimpse of that woman filled me with need. "Ahh…" I fought to get my head in the game, and Moore smirked.

"My shoes were in your closet," she said quickly. "I hope it was okay I went in your room."

"Of course." I was surprised she even mentioned it. I forgot I'd tucked her shoes in there after we'd showered together. "Are you okay?" I saw something in her face and reached for her hand. She was about to speak, but she had picked up on the vibe in the room and hesitated. I prompted her.

"Um, I couldn't help but notice…" Her words trailed off and she looked down.

"Notice what?" I was curious as to what was on her mind.

"What's going on?" she asked quietly, and I could see she had slipped into work mode, so I dropped it and quickly filled her in on what was happening with Brandon.

"Oh, my, that poor boy. Okay." She headed toward Keith, who had just put down his phone to study the map again. We followed her. As soon as he saw her, his eyes softened and I noticed a look of vulnerability that I'd never seen up to now. "Tell me everything." She sat down beside him.

"Quinn said he didn't show up for target practice after lunch, and he's been missing for," he looked at his watch, "over three hours now. Three hours and twenty-six minutes, to be exact."

"Cameras?" I caught his eye.

"Yes, there are, but a strong wind came through this morning and knocked three out, so all we know is he was walking in this direction." He drew a line with his finger on the map. "Olivia said he's been checked out even more than usual lately. He's distanced himself from the other kids."

"Makes sense." Ivy nodded. "So, remind me again, you and Mike spent time there for a bit, correct?"

"Yes, and my Nan is there, and they're really close, but I never should have left him. God," he smacked his forehead, "will I ever get things right?" He was nearly at his breaking point, and Ivy put a hand on his arm.

"Does Brandon—"

Keith shot out of his seat when his phone rang, and we all waited to see who it was.

"Okay, thanks." Keith closed his eyes, and his shoulders sagged with relief. "Put him on the phone, will you? Please." He waited for a moment, then without having said a word he handed the phone to Ivy. "He, ah, wants to talk to you."

She took the phone and muted it. "This is good,

Keith. It means he's looking for help. Let me talk to him, but I won't hang up until you hear his voice."

"All right." Keith watched her as she tugged open the sliding glass doors. I followed her out, and as she turned with a question on her face, I shrugged off my jacket and wrapped it around her shoulders. She gave me a small smile before she did what she did best. I stepped back inside and closed the door behind me.

"I just heard." Cole came racing into the room. "Where was he?"

"In a tree." Keith shook his head slowly. "He only went a few miles from the house, then I guess he climbed a tree and hunkered down. Quinn said he just needed to think."

"How'd he sound?" It was evident that every child in this house was loved by every adult as if they were their own. It was incredible, and for a moment it made me think of my own parents and how much I insisted on keeping my space from them. I had a moment of clarity as I accepted my part in that relationship.

"No clue," Keith muttered, hurt evident in his voice. "He wanted to talk to Ivy."

"Oh," Cole gave me an impressed look, "well, that's good."

"It is." Keith snatched up the map of Dusk's grounds.

"It's a vagina thing." Mark shrugged from the doorway where he stood with a fist full of cookies, and to my surprise, Keith burst out in a full-blown belly laugh.

"The shit you say, Lopez." He laughed harder, and it

immediately evaporated the tension in the room. Keith could have gone two ways right then—burst into tears from emotional exhaustion, which no one would blame him for, or laugh to the point of tears. I, for one, was glad he chose the latter.

"It's true. It's a scientific fact." Mark went on like Keith's laughter didn't faze him at all. "Women have a strong maternal instinct, and when kids are struggling inside, they know a woman's the one who knows how to pull out what's wrong with them and make it better." He happily chomped on another cookie, oblivious of the crumbs that fell around him. "Mia does that shit to the twins all the time. It's like friggin' witchcraft or something."

"Mm, and don't you forget it." Mia pushed by him with a platter of steaming carrots, potatoes, and ham and placed it on the table. She pushed up on her toes and gave Keith a kiss on the cheek as Mark snagged a slice of ham. "Glad that B is back at the house. Let Ivy work her magic." She glanced at Mark and gave him an *I dare you* look, as his fingers reached for the plate again. "And he'll be looking for his dad in no time. Now, clear away that stuff," she eyed the maps and pencils in front of Keith, "and let's get some good solid food into all of you."

I grinned at Moore and could tell he saw what I did about this place. It was warm and comforting at the hardest of times. Everyone had each other's back, and we were all part of a big family, not just a military unit. Rank meant something here, but it was never used as a power trip, and no one disrespected orders. I could see myself here long term, and I knew it was time I used what little downtime I had here to search harder for the perfect team. I knew more than ever it was what I wanted.

"You're wrong." Mark shrugged from the doorway of the kitchen. "Cookies all go to the same place, my belly. So, putting them neatly in a tin or a box or lining them up on top of each other in a Ziploc bag like you did is just a waste of your time."

"Marcus," June sighed as she came into the dining room and rolled her eyes.

"This is me helping, June. I'm here to make your life easier."

"Are you, though?" She dripped with sarcasm.

"Yes." He snagged another cookie off the dessert table near where he always sat. *That's convenient and makes sense.* "Cookies don't need to be stacked neatly. That's a myth. Toss them in a bag and call it a day. But," he got in her way again, "they should really be hidden away for me, and only me. None of this 'save some for the grandkids' crap. If I knew my kids were going to get in the way of my cookies, I would have—"

"Would have what?" Mia piped in.

"I would have had more, sweetheart." He smiled widely, and when she looked away, he looked at June and mouthed, "Thought twice about having the little monsters."

"I heard that."

"My apologies." June placed both hands on his shoulders and smiled. "I won't waste my time stacking them neatly."

"That's all I'm asking for."

"Done. Now, is there anything else I can do to make you feel better?" June asked him in a serious voice. Savannah chuckled from where she sat, and Cole shook his head at the rest of us.

"Yes, as a matter of fact." He put his hands on his hips. "Three times now you've left the house at nine p.m. and returned twice at two a.m., and another time in the morning. I want to know where you're going." June looked at her sister Abigail and then over at Doc Roberts, and Mark looked around at all three of them.

"What? I know that look. You're keeping things from me."

"This is better than TV," Moore whispered under his breath.

"Cole?" Mark swung his gaze over to him.

"I know nothing." Cole raised his hands, wanting no part in one of Mark's moments.

He tried again. "Mom?"

"Marcus," June took control of the conversation, "I'm a woman in my sixties, and I have needs that can't be fulfilled with some simple triple A batteries."

Mark's face fell, and his cookie dropped dramatically from his hand. "A lifetime of therapy just flashed before my eyes." He spoke like he was stuck in a trance.

"I have found someone who has the same needs as

me, and I'm not willing to share who that is, as long as you, my love, will stay out of it."

"Needs?" He swallowed hard.

"Yes, sex."

"I need to go lay down." He eased into his seat, and June looked at Abigail with a smirk. She'd had fun with that.

"Shall we eat?" June beamed at all of us, and the laughter broke out as we all sat down at the table, and as conversation hummed, I glanced out the door where Ivy leaned against the rail and talked on the phone. I turned and began to chat with Moore about some ideas I had for the team.

"Keith," Ivy had come into the room and handed him the phone, "Brandon would like to tell you what's going on."

"Thank you." He pulled her in for a hug then slipped away with the phone pressed to his ear.

"Told ya." Mark, who made a miraculous recovery from a few moments ago, made a V with his fingers then a T at me, and I chuckled. Ivy shivered and headed toward the kitchen.

"Excuse me for a sec." I hastily got up and followed her. I came up behind her as she blew into her hands to warm them. "Here." I took her icy fingers and pressed them to my stomach as I pulled her in for a hug.

"You're so warm," she sighed and snuggled against my chest. I rubbed her back to create some friction and hoped it helped. "Thank you." I felt her body vibrate with a giggle. "You'll do anything to get your hands on me."

"While that's true," I laughed, "Just tryin' to help. I hate seeing you uncomfortable."

"That's a nice thing to say." She pulled away when a burst of laughter came from Mark's table. "Sounds like Mark's at it again. Come on. We should eat."

With Brandon back at Dusk safe and sound and Ivy's stalker behind bars, the house enjoyed a quiet evening. The conversation stayed light and fun, and it kept our minds from slipping to the dark shadows that constantly haunted us.

"Okay, hang on. I have something to say." Savannah leaned back as June removed her dessert plate. "Thank you, June." She smiled warmly at her and focused back on us. "Moore, I think it's only fair that you know we've heard all about the Tinder account." I went to speak, but she shot me a look.

"I thought we were even!" Moore hissed at me, appalled I'd give up such a story. "Did you know he gave out my mother's number, and she got some sex texts!"

"I mean, what you did was pretty bad…" Savannah shrugged and played her lie well.

"One guy told her that he wanted to eighty-four me, and my father thought it was wise to look up what that term meant."

"What does it mean?" Sloane glanced at Savi who shrugged.

"Let's just say it involves one of us to sit like a crab."

Everyone covered their ears and groaned. "Yeah, well, try having to explain that while at Thanksgiving dinner with all my cousins sitting around researching what it actually meant."

"Don't you think it was fair? I mean, for what you did. How did it happen, again?" Savannah's face was pure evil.

"How was I supposed to know he'd be stark na—"

"It's a trap. Abort, abort," I hissed behind my napkin, and the entire table broke up. Moore looked at me then at Savannah, and it clicked.

"Oh, you're bad!" He pushed to his feet and tossed his napkin at her. "And I thought you broke our code!" He pointed at me. "Fuck me." He held his chest like he might have a stroke. "My life could have gotten so much worse if I finished that sentence."

"No, I think you should share it, Moore." Ivy joined the girls' team. "You see, as a doctor—"

"Nice try!" I shook my head. "Don't even try." I laughed. "Remember, I know where you sleep."

"I suppose that's true." She raised a sexy eyebrow.

"All right," Mike stood next to Moore, "I'm beat, and bed is calling." He turned to leave but then faced Moore. "Oh, and ah," he placed a hand on his shoulder, "suck it, sucker. You're it."

Moore looked around as everyone scattered in all directions.

"What the fuck does that mean?"

———

I woke with a jerk to find my body wrapped around Ivy's. Her flowery shampoo filled my senses, and I felt instantly needy. I positioned our naked bodies just right and slipped between her legs, taking her from behind. I was granted a throaty moan.

"This is my favorite place," I ran kisses along her shoulder, "so warm and snug."

"I'm surprised you can still fit after how many times we did it last night. I was filled to the brim." She wiggled her hips, wanting more friction.

"Just leaving my mark." I thrust a few times and felt my skin break out in goosebumps. "You're the most beautiful woman I've ever met. I see how many men turn their heads when you're around."

"I turn for one." She pulled my hand from her hip and kissed it.

"That's right," I grinned and tugged her chin to look up at me, desire flickering around her gorgeous face, "and I'll always keep you satisfied."

Someone shouted from downstairs, and we both stilled to listen.

"Who's that?" She flipped the blanket off, but I pulled them back over her, reluctantly slipping free from her.

"Stay here." I whipped out of bed and snatched my watch off the nightstand. It was only three in the morning. I tugged on my pants and t-shirt and snagged my phone from its charger. I squinted at the bright screen to read a missed message from my buddy Rowe.

> Rowe: I wanted to let you know I'm now officially a law enforcement officer for the City of Redstone. Hill's been talking to people about you and Brown. We should meet.

"Fuck," I muttered as I closed the door behind me. I'd love to have one day where Hill didn't prey on my mind.

Again, someone's voice hissed loudly from downstairs, and I pushed aside my own demons to find out what the hell was going on. I took the stairs two at a time and found Keith in the dark in the dining room staring at his phone. The light from the kitchen just allowed me to make him out, and as I opened my mouth to talk to him, I heard Frank's voice.

"Think about what you're doing, Keith." Frank's tone told me he was treading carefully.

"I told you. I've been here before." Keith's shoulders were rigid as I came into view of the two of them. They didn't move or look at me.

"But never to this extent." Frank stood by the sliding glass doors with a suitcase in his hand. My bet was he never expected to find Keith up at this hour. "You're talking Elio Capri here. Don't forget the Capris are mafia, too, no matter how you look at it. I'm just saying think about it, Keith. If you open that door, there could be repercussions for the team."

Elio Capri. The Italian mafia boss. Savannah had told

me about him. I shook off the bad feeling that came with the mention of anything mafia.

"Any!" Keith shot out of his chair and slammed his fist into the table. "Any of my brothers would call the devil if they thought it would help to get their children's mother back!"

"And I would, too." Frank lifted his hands in a gesture of understanding and for the first time acknowledged my presence. "Just give me twelve more hours, and—"

"No."

"Keith, you need—"

"I had to listen to my son sob on the phone tonight because he thinks he's the reason his mother left." He swallowed hard. "He begged me to bring her home to him, but I can't because some savage took her and more than likely has already thrown her body into a river somewhere!"

"What about Mike?" I stepped into his view, and his murderous expression swung over to me. "I don't mean to overstep, but awhile back Mike told me about his friend, that motorcycle dude. Didn't he help you once before? Can we use that guy? Maybe start there before you call *him*." I pointed to his phone.

"I already called Trigger." Keith's shoulders sagged. "He's dealing with a situation in Vegas. I'm waiting on a call back."

Frank closed his eyes and cursed under his breath. "Look," he huffed, and I could hear the stress in his voice, "I can't hear this. I know nothing. Good God, Keith, who else are you planning to share this with?" Before Keith could answer, Frank threw up his hands to stop any come-back. "You know I'm doing everything I can to find Lexi. At least, please, for God's sake, wait for Trigger before you contact someone you might forever be in debt to."

"I can't promise that, Frank." Keith shook his head. "I'd risk everything to get her back."

"I know, just hear me when I say, I'm risking a lot here, too. I can and have turned my head for a lot, but involving the mafia is a whole different level. Just," he paused, "wait for Trigger. He's bad enough." He turned and hastily headed for the door after giving me a look to help reason with Keith.

As the door closed, Keith sank back into his chair, and I sat across from him. We both stared at his phone as the screen grew dim. I watched him from the corner of my eye and thought about all the times I had bent the rules. I never did it lightly and always justified it as necessary at the time. I couldn't imagine what he was going through with his wife missing, let alone with kids involved.

He finally spoke while keeping his eyes glued to the phone. "Catalina has this favorite movie she watches all the time. It's about a guy and a girl who fall in love but fight like crazy all the time. They just can't seem to make it work for very long. They break up but always find their way back together again. It's messy and confusing, but at the end of it all, they love each other. They die together at the end. That's how I always saw me and Lex. Fighters but lovers 'til death parts us."

"It's not over yet, Keith." I tried to think what Ivy would say, but that was all I could come up with.

"Blackstone's been through unimaginable things," he said quietly. "We built a fortress to protect the ones we loved, but there was always some part of me that knew it would be Lexi who would be the one to test it." He cleared his throat. "She was always one to live on the edge. She loved hard, but she had a side that was cold as ice too."

"No doubt, wherever she is, she's kickin' ass, then." That made him chuckle.

"Yeah, she'd never go down without a fight."

"Look," I leaned forward so only he could hear, "I'm with you if you want to call Elio Capri, or anyone else you want. I'm with you if you want to leave tonight. Guns out, shoot first, repercussions later. Just make sure whatever you do, you can live with it afterward. Because whatever the outcome is, you have two kids who need you, too."

Pain showed on his face, and I knew he'd heard me. He opened and closed his eyes as he thought about it or thought about who else he could call. Keith was a smart guy, and I knew once he settled and had a good night's rest, he'd see what he needed to do. He reached over and squeezed my arm. I could see the battle that waged just below the surface.

He let out a long breath and slowly stood then held out his phone.

"I need sleep, and right now I don't trust myself." He

urged me to take it. "All I ask is answer if Trigger or Dusk call."

"You've got my word." He looked away, then nodded and dropped heavily onto the couch where he sprawled out and covered his face with his arm.

I lowered my head, pursed my lips, and silently thanked the stars he hadn't made a deal with the mafia tonight.

SIXTEEN

ERIC

"So, you're telling me you had a Blackstone member's wife sitting in your basement this entire time?" Chili looked at me from behind his glass. The ice cubes clicked together as they touched his teeth.

"Yeah."

"And why is this the first I've heard about it?"

"Because I've been like a fuckin' bug under a magnifying glass. Damn Castillo's got me paranoid. I got rid of his cameras, but I'm sure my phone, office, bedroom, even my truck is bugged." I patted my pockets and gave him a palms up, to show him I hadn't even brought my phone with me. "I don't dare make a move."

"I got wind she'd been picked up but didn't make the connection you had her. The four girls I got were all from Seattle, so I just assumed."

"Yeah, it was a surprise to me, too."

"Blackstone must be flippin' loosin' their minds."

"I'm sure." I shrugged as I scanned the perimeter of his house. Chili had sensors everywhere, but I still didn't trust that we were alone.

"And how is it you're here now?"

"Well," I turned to look at him, "that's what I needed to talk to you about."

"I'm listening."

"His plan was to kill her." Chili's face twisted in disbelief. "I know, asshole move, right? But I think I've convinced him to put her up for sale."

"He's gonna open it up for a bidding war?"

"That's what he says, yes," I leaned my forearms on the railing and looked out over the crystal blue ocean, "but I'll believe it when I see it."

"Did you stroke his ego?"

I chuckled. "Of course. Is there any other way to get through to Castillo?"

"I'd asked if you seduced him, but you don't have fake boobs, so…"

"Mm," I grunted. "Can we make this happen or what?"

"It would certainly up me in the buying world when I win." Chili pressed his lips together as he thought. "How much are we talkin'?"

"A lot." I dropped my head and thought what Lexi might be worth. "Don't cap me. It's now or never to make this buy. If you don't step up, he'll find someone else, and chances are his top buyers will be there, including Roman Sanchez."

"I fuckin' hate that guy," he snarled.

"Yeah, well, don't cap me, then and we'll both win."

"I guess I'll make some calls."

"Yeah," I tucked my hands in my pockets and thought about how much crazier shit was about to get, "just make sure you and your guys are on stand-by. I've no idea what Castillo's up to. He's drunk on power and wants everyone to see it."

"I understand." He cursed. "Castillo and his fucking parties. I've never seen someone so obsessed with having the spotlight on him." It was true. He hosted parties as often as he could, the bigger the better. It was ridiculous.

"Speaking of which, have you heard anything about Castillo giving the green light on some plan he's got in the works?"

"No, but I'll keep my ear to the ground. Can you give me anything more than that?"

"No, not yet." I thought for a moment. "Just that one of his men overheard something, and I've got a bad feeling Castillo's working this whole Lexi thing from a different angle."

"Like if the bid doesn't go well?"

"Maybe?" I shrugged. "I wouldn't put it past him. He's an egomaniac at best."

"Me either. I'll see what I can find out."

He pulled out his phone, and I left Chili to do his

business. I was relieved Chili knew what was going on and would be ready for the bidding war.

Chili and I went way back. I trusted him with my life, and he'd proven he felt the same toward me. That was why this deal needed to go down right. If not, I wasn't sure what the repercussions would be, but I knew it wouldn't be pretty.

Things were silent as I waited for the phone to ring, it had been nearly twenty-four hours with no calls or visitors. I was concerned that Castillo had changed his mind, but several days later, he gave the order. He wanted the girl cleaned up and ready for that night. I felt a sudden rush of anxiety when I opened the bag he'd sent. The fact that Castillo wanted her dressed in something ridiculous to show off her sex showed me how short-sighted he was. I held up the scrap of fabric that was supposed to be a dress, it looked about the size of a napkin and you could see right through it. I didn't need someone bidding against Chili with their dick. It wasn't enough. Sex brought in money for sure, but this woman needed to be in the spotlight in the right way. That was when the wallets would really open wide.

"Filippo," I waved him over, "go get the woman some jeans, a shirt, and a pair of sneakers, size seven." I handed him some bills. "Nothing slutty, and hurry back."

"Sneakers for this event, boss?" He looked at me like I was crazy. Filippo had been around long enough to know that wasn't how things were done.

"Fine. No heels, but something with straps or some

shit to hold them on. Nothing slutty," I reiterated and gave him a *don't fuck with me* look.

"Nothing slutty, got it." He raced off, and Alejandro hiked himself off the couch and joined me by the basement door.

"Boss?"

"I don't want any of Castillo's men coming inside the house unless I know about it. Understood?"

"Yeah, but what's going on?"

"It's time to get paid," I smacked his shoulder with a grin, "but first she needs to be ready."

"Ah, got it." There wasn't a shower downstairs, so she'd have to do it up here, and I didn't trust any of Castillo's animals not to try to make a move on her. They were a pack of dogs, no respect for anyone.

"Watch the cameras," I ordered as I disappeared downstairs.

I hesitated when I stepped into the room and saw Lexi on the bed staring at the ceiling.

I hope she doesn't run.

I quickly typed in the code, and the door unlocked. I stepped back and waited for her to look at me.

"Let me guess. I'm free?" she joked darkly. "Or is it a 'run and I'll hunt you' kind of thing?"

"It's time for a shower."

"Now you're suddenly concerned about my smell?" She studied her dirty nails, then she looked at me and her mouth drooped, and her arms fell heavily to her sides. She knew it was something bigger than just a shower. "Where am I going?"

"I'll explain everything later."

For some reason, I felt nervous, too, maybe because I didn't have any idea how tonight would go. I was as prepared as I could be to win the bid, but Castillo was unpredictable. I wouldn't put it past him to change his mind again and make a spectacle like shooting her in the head in front of everyone to show off his power or just because he felt like it.

"Come on." I pointed at the door with my head and waited for her to step outside the cage. She swung her feet around and slowly stood. I could tell she was contemplating her options. "Listen, I hadn't planned to tie you, but the house is surrounded with Castillo's men. Men who won't be as kind as me. So, if you plan to run, I'll tie you now and take you to the bathroom like a dog on a leash. Up to you."

She eyed me carefully. "Please tell me I'll be showering in an actual bathroom." She tried to sound like a fancy lady, but I could see the flicker of fear in her eyes. Up until now, she used a small area in the basement that looked like a dressing room with a white plastic sheet for privacy.

"They might be animals," I pointed to the ceiling, "but I'm not."

"Time will tell, won't it?"

"We're going up the stairs," I decided to explain to help smooth things for her, "across the living room, and into my office." Her eyes darted to me. "Where I will lock the door behind us, and then you can go into the bathroom alone and shower."

"Can I say no?"

"No." I kept my voice calm and matter of fact as I tried to anticipate her next move. She studied me for a moment and tried to hide the fact that her hands shook.

"Fine." She stood, squared her shoulders, and walked past me. She stopped in front of the basement door and waited. I opened the door, and she huffed as she realized it wasn't locked. I waved her through, and she looked cautiously at the steps before taking the first one.

"I feel like I should be walking down not walking up," she hissed. It took me a moment to realize what she was saying.

"You're not walking to your death, Lexi."

"Says the man who's had me locked in a cage in his basement for how long?"

I didn't answer.

When she opened the door at the top, she came to a halt, and I saw Alejandro on the chair holding a gun.

"We good, Ale?"

"Yeah, boss, we're good." He kept his eyes on Lexi. She jumped when I wrapped my hand around her arm to keep her moving. The last thing I needed was one of Castillo's men looking through the window and getting any ideas. I pushed her through my office door and closed it behind us.

She went to make a move but thought better of it.

"Can I—can I have a little?" She pointed at a bottle of water on a side table.

"Yes." I watched as she spilled a bit of the sparkling water when she tried to pour it into a glass. She used the bottom of her shirt to dry it, and I hid my amusement at her sorry attempt to clean it up. "If this is really it," she closed her eyes as she drank, "I need something other than booze or water in my stomach." I shook my head and waited for her to finish. It wasn't lost on me she was checking out the room. I really didn't care what she did in here. Nothing was important. My house was meant for guests, so anything important was kept out of view anyway.

"I can get you something to eat."

"You're not like the others." She lowered her glass and placed it on a coaster.

"Others?" I wasn't sure who she was referring to.

"When the other girls speak about the Cartel, they always said how scary they are or how rough they are, but I don't get that feeling from you."

"It's an illusion." I shrugged.

"Is it?"

"Yes."

"Are you gay?"

"No," I shook my head slowly, "though sometimes I wonder if my job would be easier if I was," I admitted. Pain impaled my chest when I thought of Talya.

"That right there," she narrowed her gaze on me,

"that's why you're not like the others. There's a kindness behind your mask."

"I can assure you any kindness I had in me left years ago." I knew I had to prove my point before Alejandro came in or someone else got the wrong idea. I reached over and picked up the one thing I knew would explain it all to her. This would hit hard. "You feel comfortable with me because I look more like the people from back where you came from, but I can promise I was meant to play on this team." I handed her the photo, and she gasped in horror.

"Was he your brother?"

"My cousin," I corrected and watched her head trip out at her new discovery.

"They said he died in prison," she whispered.

"Everything's an illusion, Lexi. We needed Blackstone to focus on something else while we worked a different plan."

"Oh, my God," she held her stomach, and tears filled her eyes, "this will tear Savi in two." She put a hand to her mouth. "You're related to The American, and I thought maybe, just maybe, there was a shred of good in you. Now I see that can't be fucking possible." I held her wild gaze. "How can anyone want to be a part of your world?" She shook her head in disbelief.

Her words stopped me from saying anything. I moved across the room and opened the door to the bathroom where I saw Filippo had dropped off the bag of clothes. I'd already cleared it of anything she could use as a weapon and tossed her a towel. She held it tight to her chest as she forced herself to walk toward me.

I decided to explain. "There're a lot of reasons people do what they do, and I have a very good reason for my actions."

"Which is?"

For once in my life, I felt the urge to share my truth, but as quickly as the weakness came on, it dissolved.

"You've got twenty minutes. I'll have food out here for you when you're finished." I closed the door and listened until I heard the water turn on.

I opened the door and motioned for Ale to order some food. He didn't question it he just dialed and made a call.

I sat at my desk and woke my computer, but any attempt at work just didn't happen. Instead, I watched my phone, watched my cameras, waited for any sign of something out of the ordinary, but nothing came. My head spun like a top as the minutes ticked by, we were so close to making the biggest deal a Cartel member had ever made, but something felt off. I got up and looked out the window then turned and eyed the cross on the wall. Funny how such a simple shape could mean so many different things to so many people. I needed to go back—

"Boss?" Ale held up a fast-food bag.

"Leave it on the table."

"You good?"

"What would make you ask that?"

"You just have that look you get when you're deep in

thought." I looked away, hating that he'd seen something I didn't want others to see in me.

"Thanks for the food, Ale." I started to pull the food out of the bag and place it on the table. Alejandro had just left when the bathroom door opened behind me and pulled me from my thoughts. Lexi looked like the typical American woman. Dark jeans, a soft red blouse, and slip-on shoes with a tiny strap that looped up behind her heel. Nothing fancy but not overly casual either. Her hair was toweled dried, and by the way it hung I could see it would dry nicely, so I skipped the offer of a blow dryer.

"Your taste in makeup sucks." She made a wry face and lifted her chin at me. I gave a huff at the fact that Filippo had even thought to get some. "I'm not wearing it."

"Fair enough." I checked the time and realized we had to get going. "It's time to leave, anyway." Her gaze shot to the door, and I could see the panic pump through her again.

"Will I be coming back?"

"I believe so." I opened the door and waited for her to walk through.

"Eric," she looked up at me with such a raw expression I felt a shot to the stomach about what was about to happen to her, "are you guys going to hurt me tonight?"

Unlocked feelings burst their way from my core, and I felt like I was about to drown in my own hell.

"No." I somehow pushed through the internal battle

and put my hand on her back and gave her a little push to get her to move along.

"Wait," she stopped me, "what if you kept me here?" I could almost smell her brain frantically trying to work out what was better, here with me or wherever the hell she thought she was going. "What if I promised not to run. I could wear a tracker, or chip me if you want. It wouldn't be the first time someone said they'd do that to me."

"I need you to trust me on this, Lexi. What's about to happen is what's best for you."

"Eric, please." Her chin quivered, but I couldn't let my guard down. "Please."

"Come on." I urged her to move.

Alejandro and Filippo held up their weapons and made it clear our men were well-armed as we approached the SUV. They stayed near Lexi, and I kept a close watch as we walked. Castillo's men circled us, but I knew he wasn't with them. Castillo would be back at his place talking up the buyers, and although we were all there for the same reason, to get her safely to the meeting place, I didn't trust anyone but myself. Once we were inside the tinted-out vehicle, we joined Castillo's convoy and we all moved through the streets of Rosarito. The police had been paid well tonight and had done their job of clearing the streets of wanna-be gangsters or other Cartel families who might have gotten word of our plans.

We drove slowly, and I could feel Alejandro's nervous energy as he sat behind the wheel. His head was on a swivel, and he glanced at me several times in the mirror.

"Just keep driving, Ale." I glanced at Lexi, who hadn't said a word since we left. I never bothered to blindfold her. She'd already been through most of these streets the other night.

"They're branching off." The leather seat flexed under Filippo as he twisted around to look out the back window. "They're going off the main road." His voice went high.

"That's the plan." I kept my voice calm.

"I didn't know that." Alejandro echoed Filippo's anxiety.

"I'm aware." I nodded. "Just keep going."

"I love how you guys are the ones who are nervous." Lexi snickered from the back seat. "You're not the one they all want a piece of."

"That's the problem," Filippo grunted. "In this business, you can't trust anyone but yourself. Everyone else is out to get you."

"You mean like bringing in other buyers when your boss already has one he works exclusively with?" She chuckled, and I raised a brow at him.

"That was a mistake." Filippo licked his lips and looked away in what I hoped was shame.

"You only get one strike," I whispered.

"One strike?" Lexi sighed. "Guess you better watch your step, Filippo."

I cringed when she used his name. Ale glanced at me in the mirror, and I shook my head at him. It was the first time we'd ever let one of the women know our names.

The situation had become what it was, and at this point, I really didn't care.

"Did you just use my fucking name?" Filippo twisted in his seat, and I was ready to crack him if he tried to touch her.

She let out a dark chuckle. "Here's a tip. Don't use your names in front of the ones you kidnap. Jesus, you suck at your job." Filippo strained to look at me.

"Can she talk to me like that?"

"She just did." I kept my eyes on the street.

"Fucking amateurs," Lexi muttered, and I hid my smirk with my hand. I had to give it to her, she was feisty at times in spite of the fact I knew she was terrified by the way her hands fisted and unfisted on her lap and by the way her shoe tapped on the car floor. If she wanted to piss off Filippo to get herself through this, then so be it. Besides, Filippo could handle it.

A short time later, we were buzzed through the protective gates of Castillo's driveway, and we drove down the lane to his house. Lexi went very still, and I fought the urge to comfort her. Fuck me, I was slipping.

The place positively blazed with lights and fancy cars. As Alejandro parked, the tension was thick in the SUV. We weren't on our own turf here.

"Take a breath." I touched Lexi on the forearm. "You're just here because Castillo wants to introduce you to some people."

"Well, if that's all," she dripped with sarcasm, "let's

hurry inside to show me off." I waited for the others to exit then leaned toward her.

"I give you my word, you won't be hurt here." She rolled her eyes at me as I helped her out.

"Promises from the man who's kept me in a cage like an animal." She shook her head. "Yeah, that's comforting."

"Meet us at the door," I ordered Ale and Filippo. "Have I hurt you?" I stared down, careful not to touch her. "Have I starved or not protected you when others tried to hurt you?"

"Whatever you need to say to let you sleep at night, Eric."

"You need to curb that mouth when we're inside," I warned her. "I'll take it, but Castillo won't. And right now, he's looking for any reason to drill a bullet in your head, so shut up and behave so we can get through this night."

"Nice to know I have options," she snarled, and I grabbed her arm and whirled her around to look at me.

"This isn't a fucking joke, Lexi," I spat at her. "Don't fuck this up."

"What's in this for you?" She ripped her arm from my hold, but I quickly grabbed her again. "Is it the money?" I blinked at her words, and she shook her head and closed her eyes almost as if to calm her temper. I felt shitty that we were in this situation to begin with. I'd never allowed myself to feel for any of the women; they were faceless to me. I'd allowed this one to get under my skin by letting myself talk to her. I knew it was a mistake. "Please, just tell me I'm worth more than fifty grand?"

That was a punch directly to the gut, and I couldn't find my voice. I opened and closed my mouth, unsure how to respond.

"I'd like to think I'm worth more than that." She widened her eyes at me. "At least tell me if I'm worth it for you."

"You're worth a few million," I managed to choke out as I urged her along. "Now, get moving."

Once inside, we were escorted to the grand ballroom. When the doors opened, we were met with a waft of fine cigar smoke, expensive bourbon, and waitresses in nothing more than thong underwear. *Classy as always…*

"Who didn't he invite?" Alejandro snickered behind me. He was right; all the bigwigs were there. This world brought out the worst of people. Women fawned over their men and took turns pleasuring the scum they lusted over.

There seemed to be about seven to ten potential buyers, plus their wives and mistresses. I knew most of the women here would know each other, or at least know about each other. There was no loyalty here; it was all about money and power. Then, of course, there were all of Castillo's right-hand men and his soldiers lining the wall. The place was like a fortress.

I spotted Grim Gates, and to my utter horror Talya hung off his arm. I swallowed back my anger and focused on what I was here for. I moved my attention and spotted Talya's parents in conversation with Roman Sanchez.

"Of course, Roman's here." Ale spoke close to my ear as if I hadn't spotted the three right away. "She's talking with Elva and Jerry." He referred to Talya's parents, who glared at me as soon as they saw me. They never liked me, and at this point I didn't blame them. I'd been an asshole to their daughter.

Roman was one of the oldest buyers Castillo worked with, and he had a real problem with me. When I started to work with Castillo, I came in with my own buyer, Chili, and I refused to work with Roman in spite of his very deep pockets. I simply didn't trust the guy.

Finger foods were served from silver trays, and drinks were thrust into your hands the moment your glass was nearly empty. There was a Vegas vibe here, no windows so you'd lose your sense of time. Castillo knew alcohol and finger food took the edge off sharp decision making, and he played it up well, especially when he knew he had something particularly appealing on the hook. The people here would understand the tactic. It was the lifestyle of the Cartel.

"Welcome!" Castillo called as he clapped his hands to draw everyone's attention to himself. He wore a huge smile, and it was easy to see he was enjoying all the attention.

"Everyone," he whirled around and made sure all eyes were on him, "our very special guest has arrived!"

"Eric?" Lexi panicked and grabbed for my arm.

"You're okay," I whispered.

Castillo made his way over to us and reached out for Lexi's arm, but she jerked it back. With a lunge, he grabbed it roughly and yanked her from my grasp. He walked with her to the center of the room. She locked eyes with me, and I inclined my head at her to behave. "I have quite the story to share with you in a few moments, so please drink up and enjoy some of this wonderful food." He gestured to the waitresses. "I'll soon be ready to begin." He held up a glass and smiled then tugged Lexi back across the room and shoved her back at me. She stumbled into my chest, and I used my free hand to steady her.

"Keep this bitch on a leash," he hissed as he turned to talk to someone.

"I need to get out of here." Her words came out in a rush. "I've been through enough, Eric. Please, please let me go. I'll disappear and never say a word to anyone."

"Lexi!" I snapped her from her spiral. She couldn't do this now. I couldn't afford this shit to unravel. "Pull it together. Do you want Castillo to beat you in front of all these people? Or shoot you in the head? Because you have my word, he will."

"But, Eric—"

"Stand up straight, keep your chin up, and don't show any weakness. They all thrive on torture and humiliation, and you don't want to give him that pleasure." *I refuse to consider what will happen if this plan fails. We're so close.*

I spotted Chili in the corner, and relief filled me as he gave me the thumbs up.

"Hey," I threw down one last card before I left her with Alejandro, "do you want to see your kids again?" I saw the fire reignite inside her. "Then man up because Castillo just might change his mind and end this for everyone." I pointed to Chili. "Be desirable and do your best to get that guy's attention."

"I'm being sold off?" Her voice was incredulous as she stepped back. "I thought you guys were just after the ransom."

"Sold off or six feet under, you make the call." I shrugged.

"Holy…" She covered her mouth, but when she caught Castillo watching us, she pulled it together. "Fine, sell me, so I can make their life a fucking hell."

"Excellent." I waved for Alejandro to look after her then made my way across the room to Chili.

"Should I be worried?" he breathed as I got close.

"I was going to ask you the same thing." I raised a brow at him.

"After you left yesterday, I had a visitor."

"Oh?" I jerked my head to look at him.

"I did. One of Castillo's men wanted to extend an invite to tonight's event."

"Oh, did he, now?" I glared in Castillo's direction. Chili was my buyer. I'd found and sourced him, and we'd worked together for years. In our world, that meant something. You didn't mess with buyers and sellers. There was an unwritten but well-defined law for it.

"I'm not sure if it was a coincidence that he showed up the same day as you did, or he wanted to let me know that he knew you would be here. Nonetheless, I accepted the invite. I'm just keeping a low profile."

I shook my head at a sudden realization that my control could slip away on this entire thing.

"Let's just get through this." I ran a hand through my hair. I looked over at Lexi, who still had her eyes glued on me. I also noticed that Grim Gates hadn't taken his eyes off Lexi. I didn't like the way I felt protective of her, so I gave myself a shake and kept my distance.

"She's an attractive woman," Chili said, more as a concern than an observation.

"Yeah," I looked away, "I'm afraid she is."

SEVENTEEN

TY

"Live or die. The elements are always against us, whether or not you see it, feel it, or sense it. It doesn't matter. It can creep up on you if you aren't on your toes. Death waits for you where you least expect it. Our playing field shows no mercy, and as your leader, neither will I." Cole fought to keep his voice strong, to talk us through this exercise. Our muscles screamed to shut down and lock in place. "Black, are you with me?" Cole shouted.

"Where else would I be?" Black shouted back, his voice strained with the effort.

"Keith?"

"Yeah."

"Lopez?"

"Unfortunately, yes."

"Irons?"

"I think," Mike yelled through a clenched jaw. He ran a hand over his bald head and blinked hard a few times to clear the water from his eyes. The wind blew ripples across the water and lapped at our exposed skin, and our blood ran cold as we fought the elements.

Cole continued to check in. "Moore?"

"Yes, sir."

"Beckett?"

"I'm just glad I can see what's under me." I threw a choppy chuckle at Moore when I caught his eye. He knew exactly what I referred to. This was immensely better than the dark water we used to hide in.

"It was a hell of a lot warmer, though." Moore's teeth chattered as he spoke.

"I almost feel bad for sipping hot coffee." Ivy grinned at Mia as they both basked in their enjoyment at our discomfort. Mia kept a close eye on us to make sure she could step in if needed. Steam from the barrels filled with hot water taunted us. They were so close by on the bank, but this was a test and not one I was willing to fail.

"Laugh it up, ladies," I shook my head at Mark then shot a tight grin at Ivy, "but I'm coming for you, sweetheart, to get warmed up." Ivy's mouth dropped for a hair of a second, surprised that I so openly showed affection to her in front of the others. I didn't care. She was mine, and they all knew it, anyway. Besides, just having her this close helped heat up my insides.

"I can outrun you." She winked, and I heated a little more at the thought of how fun that would be.

"Hey, Logan," John coughed as he fought for breath, "I was thinking maybe the ladies should train with us, too."

Cole laughed. "That's not a bad idea."

"But who'd be there to warm you when you get out?" Ivy called, and I pulled in my chin, amused by the tight little package not that far in front of me. It was odd to see her in jeans, but the way they hugged every curve, along with that cream-colored sweater, reminded me of what I had woken up to that morning before being summoned for this merciless trial at the lake.

"Jesus, Logan," Mark shook as a tremor ran up his body, "my swimmers have officially taken residence in my stomach. Could we move this along?"

"Yeah, okay." He grunted, and I knew he felt our pain. "On my command, you know what to do," Cole called and waited another painful beat. "Up."

We raced out of the icy lake, dove into the powdered snow, and rolled like an ice cube in what felt like warm snow. It was bizarre and hurt like hell, but I knew it wouldn't last for long. With stick-like fingers, I shimmied into my clothes and fumbled to hold my weapon correctly.

I felt Ivy's eyes on me, and it kept me moving. She had the ability to make me do and think crazy things.

Focus.

Four men with paintball guns were ready to fire if we

exposed our locations before hitting the assigned targets. I hurried to the first point and dropped to my knees while the others did the same at their marks. I breathed out long and slow as I lined up the scope with the bullseye and squeezed the trigger. Blue paint shockingly hit the center of the target. I heard the others fire off their colors but didn't see who hit where. My knees had no interest in bearing my weight, so I rolled to the next mark just missing the three red shots that blew over my shoulder.

"Nice job, Beckett," Daniel called as he waited for me to come into view. "Let's see what else you got."

"What the fuck!" Moore screeched and leapt about six feet in the air. Mark shot him three times in the side then fell and laughed his head off.

"That!" Mark sputtered with laughter then rolled as someone fired off a shot at him. "Welcome to the house, Moore!"

"It fuckin' jumped at me," Moore cursed as he tossed a kid's toy as far as he could. Ah, yes, the famous Furby. I inched forward and nabbed the little shit, then tucked it inside my jacket. I wanted to be in on that game.

Mike let out a string of curse words as he stepped outside the training area covered in yellow paint.

"You're a big guy, Irons!" Frank called as looked at this phone screen.

"I'm like a frozen buffalo. I can't make myself be small!" he grunted over his shoulder and disappeared inside the house.

I waited for John to join me, and we both signaled

we'd fake left and go right. Of course, Daniel would be on to that, so instead I willed a higher power and we both raced backward. The red shots fired left as we expected, and just as we rounded the corner of the next barrier, red drops rained down on us, but none made contact.

"Nice," Daniel called and motioned for us to head inside. "Your job is done."

I toed off my boots at the door and headed for the stairs. Suddenly, a strange vibe went through me. I looked over my shoulder and saw Frank on the phone. He made eye contact with me, then he and Cole headed to his office. I hadn't noticed Cole leave the training area to come inside. Whatever it was it seemed important, though. The pins and needles in my legs made everything ache, and my muscles screamed at me to move, so I jogged down the hall and eyed Ivy's closed door. I'd lost track of her after I moved to the obstacle course. I listened to hear the coast was clear then hid the Furby in my drawer with a chuckle.

I heard a noise behind me as I turned on the water then dimmed the lights in the bathroom to nearly dusk. My senses told me I wouldn't be alone for long. I side-stepped into the closet and quickly peeled off my jacket, shirt, and socks, and that was when I saw her. I moved to the door and peaked through the crack. She tiptoed toward the glass of the shower and slowly opened the door. She'd changed into her classic silk blouse, and when a puff of steam found her plump breasts, the moisture outlined them as the fabric clung to her skin.

"Wait, what?" She huffed when she saw it was empty.

I came up behind her, wrapped my arms around her body, lifted her into the shower, and pressed her body against the tiles.

"Ty!" she yelped. "I'm in my clothes!"

"Mm, and I'm still in my pants."

I pulled her wet hair back and kissed her slender neck and up to the back of her ear. That was one of my favorite spots to kiss because of how her body always responded. She'd breathe heavily and grant me a tiny moan, almost as if it was unintentional.

"You think you can sneak up on me?" I grinned as I slid my hands around her front and undid her pants. My body fed off her warmth. "I felt you even before I heard you, baby." My fingers inched their way into her panties and slid inside her. She yelped, and I groaned and pressed my erection into her back.

"You're freezing, Ty," she half whimpered through her moan.

"Exactly. And I need you to warm me." I rubbed some feeling back into my fingers while I held her there with my body. "Take your blouse off," I ordered, and she did without hesitation. She also unclipped her bra from the front and tossed it aside.

Immediately, my hands moved to her plump breasts and gave them a gentle squeeze. My body hummed as heat flooded through my veins. Her desire built as her little moans and pants soon had my head spinning. Any memory of the cold was gone now, flushed out by her.

"Your body is my weakness," I confessed. "Seeing you on the dock, in your tight little jeans, got me through that training." I licked and sucked gently where her shoulder met her neck. "You should always be close to me."

I changed direction with my fingers, and she grinned with a chuckle.

"I love being close to you," she whispered. "Oh, Ty, that feels so good." She dropped her head back and reached to stroke my erection. "How can I want something so badly, even though I just had it this morning?" She opened her mouth and drew in a huff of air as I sucked and nipped her along her collarbone. "I want more!"

I tugged and kicked my pants off my slick body, and she did the same. Then in a fever we both found our way and I pressed into her in a rush of explosive heat. One arm wrapped around her waist and my hand went around her throat. I was careful not to press; I just held her in place.

"Are you okay like this?" I growled in her ear as I slowed for a moment, and she nodded rapidly.

"Yes!" she screamed, clawing at my arm for anything to hold on to. "Do what you want."

Her words sent me to a different head space. One I hadn't allowed myself to go yet because I didn't know if she was ready. I increased the speed, bit down on her shoulder, and showed her just how powerful my need for control was. She bucked and twisted with throaty moans and pleas to come. I nearly lost all sense of belonging as

I let my inner alpha show its needy head. She was incredible. She was sexy as hell. She was all mine. Up until now, I never understood why I never cared about having someone in my life. But now I knew it was because I'd never met her yet. I would kill anyone who stepped in our way. I'd already taken down one asshole who'd dared to threaten her, and I'd do it again to keep her mine.

I pinned her with my hips and held myself deep inside her as I panted against her neck then let out a hungry growl. I needed her to feel me, I wanted to leave my mark before we had to separate when we left this shower.

I thrusted again when she began to speak, hard and fast. I claimed her as mine over and over again.

"I can't, I can't." She started to thrash in my arms. "It's so intense!"

I tilted her head back, and with her eyes locked on mine, I took over her head along with her body. I slid my hand down between her legs and rubbed the pad of my thumb in circles. She instantly climaxed as I held her tight in my arms, then I fought for my own release with deeper thrusts that lifted her off her feet. I exploded into her with a cry. My heart pounded wildly, and prickles of electricity shot through my body as I gave her everything I had inside. She was putty as I rode out the last few spasms. I held her to me, just needing an anchor after such a release. Her arms wrapped around my neck as she let all her weight press into me.

"Are you okay?" I kissed her temple as I lowered her onto her feet. She leaned her forehead into my chest.

"I—" She went to speak but stopped herself. "Ahh, that was incredible." I wanted to ask what she really wanted to say, but when she smiled up at me, I could see there was nothing except satisfaction written all over her face.

"You made me lose my mind when you told me to do what I wanted." I slowly slipped out of her and felt the loss the moment I did. "You woke a side of me that I keep locked down."

She opened her mouth to say something but again held back and reached for the soap.

My phone caught my attention just then as it lit up on the counter. I rubbed the foggy door and saw Cole's name come up.

"Shit," I slid the door open and stepped out to read the message.

Cole: There's been an update. Living room 20 minutes everyone.

I filled Ivy in on the message, and she nodded without comment and grabbed a towel. She was quiet as she left the bathroom. I followed her as I considered what this was about. She walked toward the bedroom door and opened it a crack. Her towel was wrapped tightly around her as she peeked out the door to see if it was all clear. It wasn't often that anyone came up here, but now that Moore was two doors down, we had to be careful.

"Ivy?" I called to stop her from leaving. "Did I go too far?"

"No, not at all." She gave me a smile, but there was still something there just under the surface.

"Then what's wrong?" I pulled on my t-shirt. "Please don't go. I know there's something going on."

She closed the door and turned around. "Okay," she shook her head, "look, I know what I'm about to say is ridiculous, but regardless, I'm still a woman."

"All right," I closed the distance between us, "I'm listening."

"I don't do insecurity very well. I take pride in the fact that I can think rationally. So, the fact that I'm struggling—"

"Ivy," I lifted an eyebrow at her, "spit it out."

"You said you and Demi were strictly sex buddies." I tried hard to not react at the sound of her name. "How we had sex just now, is that how it was with her, every time?"

I shook my head, completely blindsided by her question.

"You know what? I'm sorry. I'm over it just by asking it." She stepped back, and I stepped forward. "I bet questions like that are why you avoid relationships in the first place." She gave a nervous laugh.

"My God, Ivy, I was so far from thinking of Demi," I blurted. "Sex with her was a release, nothing more, but sex with you is a connection, and one I crave more every day. Well, every time I look at you."

"Okay." She nodded. "I feel like a jerk for even asking that. It was incredibly unfair of me. I'm sorry."

"Hey," I ran my fingers down her cheek, "you're allowed to be human. Look how I handled it when your ex-fiancé was just talking to you. We're jealous at just the thought that someone else was where we are now. There's nothing wrong with that, but you need to tell me when you're questioning something."

"Now who's the psychologist?" She pushed up onto her toes and gently kissed my lips. "Thank you." Her arms wrapped around my neck and deepened the kiss. I knew I still had a few minutes before I had to be downstairs.

"Be careful," I chuckled and pressed hard against her stomach, "I've got more left in me."

"For the record," she pulled back and ran her hands up my chest, igniting everything inside of me again, "I've never come so hard before."

"Drop the towel." My head clouded.

"You need to go and..." She leaned in and licked from my collarbone to my earlobe where she gave a little nibble. "Suck it, sucker. You're it!" She hurried from the room with a throaty laugh.

"Seriously?" I called, and her laugh rang louder. My smile grew wider as I shook my head. She was good, so I knew payback would have to be epic.

Somehow, I got my head back on straight as I tugged on my clothes. I managed to make it downstairs with a few moments to spare. Ivy wasn't far behind. It amazed me she could get dressed and look normal so quickly. She made sure to keep her distance as she joined the wives on the far couch. She glanced at me with a sexy smirk. I crossed my arms and threw a warning glance at her. She was playful and flirty, my favorite kind of woman. She'd better be ready, because I was coming for her.

It wasn't lost on me that it was only Blackstone and the wives at this meeting. The staff were nowhere to be seen, and that made my senses perk up even more.

"I need everyone's attention." Frank stepped up to his usual spot by the stone fireplace and turned to us. "This involves everyone here in this room." The room instantly grew silent. "We have confirmation that Lexi's alive." Out of the corner of my eye, I saw Savannah grab Ivy's hand and look toward the kitchen where Keith stood with his shoulder against the doorframe. I knew Frank would have told him first. It was hopeful news, but I couldn't imagine how hard it was for him all the same.

"How credible is this intel?" John asked from behind me.

"Extremely." Frank held up an enlarged photo of Lexi. "My informant just let me know he was standing a mere ten feet away from her when this photo," he shook the photo, "was taken."

"Which was?"

"Forty-five minutes ago, in Rosarito."

"So, why aren't we on our way there now?" I stood as I asked the question. I could hear a few whispered comments around me.

"Hold on, hold on. We have to tread carefully here."

Frank handed the photo to Cole and held up his hands. "The informant warned me how precarious the situation is. If they think for even a minute we're on to them, she'll disappear into thin air again. From what I've been told, she's at this location to be auctioned off."

A few gasps could be heard around the room, and Savi put a hand to her mouth.

"We all know how valuable she'd be." Frank eyed everyone in the room to leave that impression on all of us. "Once it's done," he continued, "my informant will know the route they'll be taking when they leave the Castillo house. That's our best play."

"Martin Castillo has her?" Mark's mouth dropped as he thought. "Yeah, boys, we need to play this waaay careful. He's got more guys around him than the Pope."

"Right," Frank agreed. "There's zero way of getting in or out of that place without lives lost. Especially when someone like Castillo brought them there. He's totally unpredictable, and my informant warned me he doesn't trust him to stick to the plan and open the bidding until it happens. He's notorious for changing his mind like the wind. Castillo is paranoid. He'd kill anyone he suspected of anything without hesitation, including Lexi."

"He killed his own sister last year just for talking to the chef at her own wedding," John added to back up Frank. "If someone looks at him sideways, they're gone. They're right. We need to go into this extremely carefully."

"We have one chance at this." Frank cleared his throat. "Mike." He gave a look.

"I'll try again." Mike pulled out his phone and walked into the kitchen as he put it to his ear. We could hear him say, "Sorry for the calls, Morgan, but I really need your help." Mark whirled around to look at Frank when Mike mentioned Morgan's name.

Who's Morgan?

"When do we leave, Frank?" Cole pulled my focus from Mike.

"Pack what you need. The moment my phone rings, we're out." Frank stepped down and rushed out of the room while I stepped up to Cole.

"Cole, with all due respect, I can safely say I don't mind sitting in a ditch somewhere to wait for instructions if it speeds things up."

"I'm with you, but we have orders."

"Copy that." I stepped aside and looked for Ivy. She was next to Keith, talking quietly.

Savannah joined me. "Frank doesn't want you to ship out until Mike speaks with Trigger. And I bet good money you'll meet Trigger today."

"Logan!" Mike pointed to his phone, and both Cole and Keith rushed to his side.

"Who's Morgan?"

"One of Trigger's men."

"Okay, anything I should know?" I appreciated how candid she was with me.

"Trigger's terrifying, but he's a good person to know. He was dealt a hard life and does what he must to get by." She rubbed her neck. "His wife Tess is great, but don't be fooled. She's as tough as it comes and wouldn't think twice to gut someone if you threatened anyone around her." She grinned. "Don't ask too many questions, but answer all his."

"Anything else?" I dripped with sarcasm.

"Yeah," she turned to look at me dead on, "before you leave for Mexico, make sure you tell Ivy exactly how you feel." The way she held my gaze told me she wasn't kidding around. "You're not used to having someone, and she's never dated a soldier before. Your mind will be focused on your mission, while she'll be solely focused on your return. Leave her heart as full as you can."

"Copy that." I looked around for Ivy again, but she'd disappeared.

"Get the SUVs ready," Cole suddenly called. "We leave in ten."

"Mike!" Frank held up his phone, and they both whispered in the corner.

"Holy shit." Mike covered his mouth.

"Here we go." Savannah raced after Cole.

I found Ivy with Sloane in the entertainment room.

"Hey, Sloane." I gave a quick wave. "Ivy, we're heading out to meet up with someone. Keep your phone on you, okay? I wanna be able to get hold of you if we get the word to ship out."

"I will." She pulled it out of her pocket to show me she had it close.

"Good." I pulled her in and devoured her mouth for a moment. My hands slid up her bare back then over the curve of her bottom. Finally, I ripped away. "I'll be in touch."

I ran back upstairs, proud of myself for not leaving without speaking to her. We weren't exactly leaving for a mission yet, but the fact I said goodbye and sealed it with a kiss made me feel better. I had someone else to think about now, and I didn't want to screw it up.

Mike took lead on our way over. From the front seat, he gave the same advice as Savannah had.

"Don't ask questions, but answer all of his. Trigger trusts very few, so don't give him a reason to not like you. He's a good guy, but his life's been shit, and it's left him, let's just say, a bit edgy." Mike paused to think. "If he offers you a drink, take it. It's disrespectful not to."

"And you work with this guy?" Moore rubbed his head.

"Trigger and I go way back." Mike turned to look at us. "He's got a reputation for violence, but I trust him with my life. If that isn't enough for you, remember that Cole is in the SUV ahead of us. That should tell you something."

"Understood." I nodded to let Mike know we heard and respected what he was saying. "Anything else?"

"Yeah, treat his wife like you'd treat Trigger. Tess is Trigger's one weak spot. You look at her the wrong way, and Trigger will flip."

"Copy that." Moore shot me a glance, and I grinned. This should be interesting.

A short time later, I found myself in some dungeon-looking bar in the middle of nowhere across from some nasty looking bikers.

Trigger, Brick, Rail, and Morgan stared at me and Moore like we were something to eat. We'd been up against the Taliban before, but these guys were a whole lot of something else. We weren't totally intimidated, but a bit of healthy respect was needed. At least these guys were friends of Mike's and apparently had a history with Blackstone. I'd already filled Moore in on what I'd been told about the Devil's Reach from Mark.

One look at these guys and I knew trust wasn't something that came easy. That, I understood, because I was the same way. You could feel it as we walked into the bar. The overall vibe and smell were a mix of smoke, weed, and violence. One wrong look, and shit could go sideways.

"I'm sorry for what's happenin'," Trigger moved his gaze off me and over to Keith, "and that we're only hearin' about it now."

"You're here now, and I appreciate it." Keith's tone was unemotional.

"We been havin' some trouble at Min's club, and Grim's been off the grid." Mike nodded at Trigger to show he followed his drift. "As soon as Cooper got word to Morgan's cousin that you needed to reach me, we headed north." I wondered if Trigger knew the safehouse was in Montana. I doubted it, but what were the odds Trigger got here this fast? "Mike filled us in, and we already contacted Elio."

Finally, a name I recognized in the conversation.

"Vinni's good to go?"

"Yeah, he'll be in touch soon. Something will come up. I'll make sure of it." Trigger glanced at Morgan, who suddenly looked stressed at a call coming in then declined it. He caught Trigger's gaze and gave a tight nod before the two of them focused on me again. I couldn't help but wonder how dark their world actually ran. "So, you're the new team leader?"

"I am." I nodded.

"What's your team name?" I thought for a moment, as I hadn't shared it with the others yet. I wasn't sure I wanted now to be the time.

"Dark Water." I felt Moore look at me. I didn't need to explain my reasoning for it; he already knew. A team name had to mean something important. Dark water had saved our lives on countless occasions. If I was going to lead a team into a new kind of war, we were going to fight under that memory.

"Dark Water," he repeated. "Why that name?"

"Why Trigger?" I challenged, feeling raw on something as intimate as that name.

"Hm." He nodded while he thought. "Okay…" He waited a beat, and I thought he wanted me to say my name.

"Ty Beckett."

"I know who you are." He rubbed his lip.

"And you're the president of your club."

"I am." Mike glanced at Cole, but I didn't break my

gaze with Trigger. "You think you know me?" He stroked his beard.

"About as much as you know me."

Brick shook his head, and Morgan cleared his throat. All the while, Trigger and I stared at each other. His green eyes pierced through me. I was sure most would back down, but he was no match for my past. I'd stared down the barrel of a sawed-off shotgun held by a Taliban leader.

"Fuckin' good choice, Logan." Trigger looked at him.

"I know." Cole nodded, and I felt the tension ease at the table.

"The fuck?" Mike read something off his phone. "Holy shit, Trig. Guess who else Castillo has at his place."

"Who?" Cole leaned over.

"Rosa Coppola."

Trigger leaned over and whispered to Morgan. I took that opportunity to lean over to Cole and lowered my voice.

"How is it these guys got here so fast?"

"They knew ahead," he reassured me. "I told Mike to give this address to Morgan's cousin. Trigger knew where to meet once he got word. Mike knew they were on their way. We just didn't let Frank know." I had to remind myself that I wasn't in control right now. This was Cole's world. It was hard, but I also knew I had a lot to learn. I appreciated that Cole explained things. He could have just eyed me to back off and not question him.

Trigger signaled something to Brick, who immediately

shot up from his chair and left the table with his phone in his hand.

"Rail, call the VPs. Get the word out we need eyes in the northwest of Mexico." Trigger's men didn't miss a beat taking orders. I respected that. "Keith, I'll make some calls, man. See who else we can use. We're on it. Give me at most a day, and I'll check back in."

"Thanks." Keith nodded.

"We need whatever happens to play in our favor," Cole explained. "We have one chance to make our move, or she's gone." Keith's gaze dropped to the table hard.

"I get that." Trigger seemed genuine.

"Morgan, how is everything going?" Mike said cryptically across the table. I noticed Morgan rubbed his beard for a moment as he contemplated his answer.

"It's all good." He grinned, but everyone in the room could see the heaviness that rested behind his words.

"We'll figure it out," Trigger assured us. I wanted to offer some help, but something warned me to stay away from whatever it was.

"We've all got demons we're slayin'." Morgan indicated toward where Brick was. "Some for a lifetime, others come without warning."

"Let me know if…" Again, Mike said very little.

"Appreciate it, brother."

"Can you hear 'em?" Brick shoved Rail out of his way as he took his seat. "Mike, you just lit a fire under the mafia's ass. As we speak, the Capris are calling their pilots. Elio and his men are heading to the US to meet with us, and Vinni and Niccola are already on their way to Mexico."

"How much?" Mike asked, and the table went quiet. He pulled out a thick envelope, but Trigger shook his head.

"No fuckin fee." Trigger held up his glass and eyed the whiskey. "Castillo worked with my father. That's payment enough."

EIGHTEEN

Thirty minutes ago

ERIC

I watched from the back of the room as the vultures took turns checking out Lexi like the prize she was. A few threw slitty-eyed glances at each other to try to size up the competition. I wanted to step in and pull her away, but I knew if I did, I'd lose this deal. I had to leave it up to Chili. I needed to keep my face neutral. I could feel Castillo's eyes on me and tried hard not to make eye contact back. Each time I did, I could see him studying me, then he'd look over at Lexi. I could feel his interest grow, and I was afraid it would feed his paranoia.

Chili stayed put on the opposite side of the room. He was doing his best to get a feel for what the other buyers were thinking and how deep their pockets might be.

Though everyone knew Chili was my buyer, we kept some distance between us. I didn't want to make the others feel like they couldn't approach me and ask questions about the girl, and I didn't want them to think Chili had any information they didn't.

I'd worked hard to make a name for myself in this business, and everyone was always looking to get in good with a seller. And right now, with the reputation I had, I knew I was just as important as Castillo. Especially as they all knew I'd had the woman the past while and had spent the most time with her. A few had already approached me to ask a few questions. They wanted to understand what their potential purchase might bring them. It was another reason Castillo's hostility was building toward me. I needed to think of something fast or I might not survive this night.

I snagged a fork from the table behind me and briskly moved into the center of the room. I tapped the side of my glass and drew their attention to me. Castillo's face grew red, and I jumped right into it.

"Good evening, everyone." I smiled around the room and watched Lexi slowly slide a chair between her and one of the buyers when he looked toward me. He'd been fingering her hair, and if the size of his wallet was anywhere near the size of the bulge in his pants, he planned on her for dessert. "I think it's extremely impor- tant we acknowledge who brought us here tonight." I spun on my heel and waved an arm toward Castillo, who immediately lit up when the attention swung toward him.

"Over the years, Blackstone has played cat and mouse on our land, coming and going as they pleased. They've ruined countless sales and have escaped time and again when some of you tried to capture them. But now," I paused, "look what we have here." I turned to Lexi with my hand out dramatically. "We've taken one of their own, successfully plucked her from the streets. While Blackstone crept through our very streets to take her back, they went home emptyhanded like dogs with their tails between their legs." A few nods and laughter followed, and I gave a salesman smile as Castillo gave a bow. The room burst into applause at his accomplishment.

"She's here tonight, and one lucky man," I swept the room with my eyes, "will take her home because Martin Castillo did the unthinkable." I clapped again, and they followed. I watched as he lapped up the praise and fought to roll my eyes. "So, now I give you the man of the night, as I know he's got something special to blow your mind." I stepped out of the spotlight and let Castillo take over.

"Well, I wasn't expecting that." Castillo laughed and shrugged like he was modest. "Where to begin…"

I made my way to the back of the room and tuned out his words, mostly lies about how he played a part in her capture. He did shit but sit behind a desk and make a few phone calls. The reason I'd been doing all the work in this situation was because Castillo was lazy as sin and did as little as possible before he took the glory. He might find glory in this charade, but I'd get my own reward by selling her to Chili. I'd soon be on my way up through the Cartel world as a wealthy businessman not afraid to do the work to get me there. *Whatever*. I brushed off my frustration. There was only one part of the night I was waiting for, and it wasn't this.

"My, my, that was quite the show." Grim smirked like the demon he was as he oozed in next to me. He reeked like money, weed, and power, and the fact he was here with Talya made me burn from deep inside. "How'd Castillo ever fit that ego of his through the door?"

"When you want something bad enough…" I muttered. I hoped my conversation with Grim was noted by Castillo. I wanted to give him the impression I was mingling with one of his rivals to get information.

"I was flattered to get the invitation to attend the auction. I must say I was shocked at the merchandise. A Blackstone woman. Impressive." He spun the ice cubes around in the expensive crystal glass. "I guess he'll enlighten us as to how it all went down this evening?" He raised one of his curved eyebrows at me, and his nearly black eyes burrowed into mine as he placed a finger to the edge of his mouth.

Grim was tattooed from the chin down. His tailored suits often reflected his theatrical mannerisms. His head was shaved on the sides, but the front was styled in a nineteen fifties type hairdo. If he was anyone else but the infamous Grim Gates, I might have considered him an asset of sorts, one to cultivate. But knowing who he was and what he did for a living, I kept my distance. He personified the dark, seedy side of Vegas. I'd known people he'd done business with who I'd never seen again.

"I bet the hotshots up north are losing their minds." He grinned.

"That's the hope."

"Well," he unlocked the screen on his phone and glanced at me, "may the best man win." He strolled away with one hand in his pocket as he raised the phone to his ear.

Suddenly, I realized Castillo had stopped talking. I sensed a change in the atmosphere and looked toward him to see what he was up to.

"Yes, people, I have a surprise for you, a twist in the game." Castillo's excitement had caught the crowd as he signaled for his men to open a door, and a moment later, Rosa Coppola appeared. She pushed her walker and scowled angrily at the guests. "Everyone, meet the oldest member of the Coppola syndicate, Rosa Coppola." Her jet-black eyes scanned the room and then latched on to Lexi. Recognition came to Lexi's face. *Wait, what? She did know her?*

"Mikey?" Lexi blurted. "What the hell?" She took a step backward and bumped into Grim, who looked down at her with a dark grin. She jumped with a yelp and stepped out of his reach. "I don't understand. What's happening here?"

"Allow me to explain, my dear." Castillo moved toward her, and her gaze flew around the room and landed on me for help. I just shrugged; I had no idea.

"I'm sure you're all interested in how I came to take possession of this little gem." He patted Lexi on the back. "Well," he paused dramatically, "let me tell you a story. Lexi here once dated Antonio, the head of the Almas Perdidas gang in the States, for those of you who may not know, and being the greedy dirt bag Antonio is, he played *Mikey* here," he put extra emphasis on the Mikey as he pointed to Rosa, "at her own game." He shook his finger at Rosa. "Rosa was a very naughty woman, and Antonio made sure she lost a very large sum of money." Rosa glared at him.

Lexi's face twisted as she fought to catch up.

"But before Mikey could deal with Antonio, he and his gang were killed by your husband." He pointed at Lexi. "Mikey did me wrong, too, but when I got my hands on her, she offered to make a deal, one she knew I couldn't resist. She brought me you." He inclined his head at Lexi. "Tieri, her partner in crime, found you at a university in Canada, of all places." He chuckled.

The crowd hung on his every word; he was thoroughly enjoying this.

"None of this has anything to do with me!" Lexi screamed at him.

"It has everything to do with you, my dear." Castillo shook his head slowly. "We want to tear down Blackstone, and you're the first step to doing that."

"That's rich." She made my teeth clench at her bold behavior. "Well, the joke's on you because I'm no longer a Blackstone wife. They threw me out." Her eyes blazed as she screamed at everyone in the room. "Bid on that, assholes."

The room went silent, and Castillo looked at me in confusion. I shook my head to let him know it wasn't true.

Rosa hissed something in Italian and spat toward Lexi.

"You wanna say that again?" Lexi's temper flew again, and I wasn't sure what Castillo might do if things got out of hand any more than they were. I glanced at Chili, who stepped close and loomed above her.

"Think twice about where this could lead," he grunted at her, and she backed off but still looked completely unhinged.

"You can't say I didn't bring the entertainment." Castillo laughed loudly, and a trickle of half-hearted laughter could be heard at his lame attempt to smooth the situation.

When Lexi looked at me again, I shook my head and glared at her as a warning to calm the hell down. She flipped me off and folded her arms over her chest.

Castillo waved at one of his men to stand next to her in case she got out of control. "Oh, yes." He pressed his hands together as though to pray and then drew them down in a point toward Rosa. "You should know, Rosa, or Mikey, or whatever you call yourself, that I changed the terms of our deal."

"Excuse me?" Rosa's thick accent brushed over her thin, white lips.

"We let Teiri go free." A dark smile played across his

lips as her eyes widened. "You, it turns out, are much more valuable."

"We had a deal!"

"Deals can be broken. You taught me that." He waved at his men to have her removed. She held up her walker as a weapon, but they merely brushed it aside with a laugh and lifted her off her feet and dragged her away while she hurled profanities in Italian.

"Never a dull moment," I grunted into my glass.

"I think it's time we get down to business," Castillo called as he stepped up on a raised platform and stood behind a glass podium. I rolled my eyes again. Of course, he'd gotten a podium. "Bidders, get out your checkbooks because this little spitfire is up for grabs. Let's start the bidding, one million."

"One point five." Grim smirked down at Talya, who had suddenly materialized again and held tightly to his arm. Grim glanced down at his phone, probably waiting for his banker to call him. She glanced over at me and made a show to run her hand over his lapel. I looked away, unfazed. I had bigger shit to deal with.

The bids went up and up, and Chili stood back and waited. I pressed the prongs of the fork I still held against my thigh as I sat back and watched. Sweat soaked my collar, and I fought to keep my breath steady. This was a huge move, and it had to go just right.

"Five and a half million, going once, going twice—"

"Six," Chili called, and I felt my heart drop from where it was wedged in my throat.

"Six!" Castillo beamed with greed. "Do I have six and a half?" Chili stood like stone as the others eyed him, angry he'd jumped in and hadn't shown his hand until now. It was a bold move to wait until the very end. "Anyone?"

"I'll do six and a half," a buyer I didn't know very well said. I could feel Lexi's eyes burn through me. Grim tucked his phone away and shook his head at Talya. He wouldn't bid higher. That caught my attention. Normally, if Grim wanted something, he took it.

"Eight," Chili countered, and I got to my feet as the bidder looked at Lexi again, then hesitated as my heart pounded in my chest. Then he turned his nose up and looked away.

"Pass," he called. I let a little pressure off the fork.

I noticed Castillo glance at Roman, who eyed Lexi then shook his head, uninterested. That was impressive. Maybe her wild temper had turned him off.

Though that made me nervous that the other buyers were backing off, I wasn't sure Castillo wouldn't suddenly toss the whole bidding game aside and finish her off himself just to toss a curve ball.

"Eight, going once, going twice..." Castillo paused. "Sold!" He pointed at Chili, who merely nodded. I allowed myself to take a breath as he made his way over toward Castillo to seal the deal. Everyone began to disperse, some murmured together, and I caught a few angry glances and unhappy faces, but the deal was done.

Drinks clinked and music began to play, and a party atmosphere took over.

I snagged a drink as one of the staff members zipped by and downed the nasty liquid in one swallow. Lexi was thankfully quiet and had sunk down onto a chair.

I think that just took three years off me.

"I guess congratulations are in order?" Talya flipped her hair over her shoulder as she sucked away on a lemon from her drink. "She'd have been too high maintenance for Grim, anyway."

"And you're not?" I countered and fought hard to keep a bored expression.

"You never complained."

"Because I was in love with you," slipped through my lips before I could stop them. Her face fell, and I looked away.

"You love me?" Her sweet tone made me remember all the good times we'd had together in my room, but that was as far as it should have gone. The bar was a mistake, a relapse, an error. I'd strung her along, and that wasn't fair. I knew that then, and I knew it now. I looked at her sadly as I came to the realization that I needed to let go forever.

"Loved," I corrected her. "You're better off dating Grim."

"No one dates Grim. I mean, think of his nickname. He's like sleepin' with some dark force. Don't get me wrong, the man can fuck. Lord knows he can." Her mouth dropped open for a second as if remembering their time together. "But he's not someone to stay with for long."

That was something I didn't need to know. Her welfare no longer concerned me, I reminded myself.

"I'm not sure what that means." I noticed Grim hadn't even glanced at Talya when she left his side. Most likely, he didn't care. Grim turned heads. The darkness he carried made him intriguing and scary enough for chicks to want to dabble in their darkest desires. Why would he pin himself down with a girlfriend when he could party it up here in Mexico or Vegas with whoever he wanted?

"He's just a means to piss off my father and, well, you." She gave me a wry look.

"It didn't work." I shrugged through my lie. However, her comment about their sex life made it a little easier to push my feelings aside.

"That's too bad, because I would've gone all the way with you, Eric."

"Maybe in another life," I mumbled. Talya stood there just long enough for me to smell her perfume, and I started to cave. Just as the need to reach out and touch what I'd wanted so badly, she left with a sniff. The time had come to stop trying to hurt one another. Our time had passed.

"Eric," Chili was suddenly at my side, "the money will be wired by morning. Castillo said once it clears, she'll be delivered. I told him I wanted you to bring her to me."

"Of course," I shook his hand. "A pleasure doing business with you, as always. You had me sweatin' there for a bit."

"I wanted to see who I was up against before I made my move."

"Smart."

"I expect her at my place the day after tomorrow." He looked carefully over at Castillo. "I still don't trust him, so keep a close eye on her. I'll see you then." He left, and I allowed myself a moment to relax. This day had taken a toll on me.

Naturally, I wanted to watch Talya, but I found myself watching Chili as he headed toward Lexi. He held out his hand, and when she didn't take it, he whispered something in her ear. Slowly, her hand rose to meet his, and he smiled warmly as they shook. He spoke to her for a moment more then strolled away when Grim came to approach him.

"Another?" A waitress batted her ridiculously long lashes at me, and I tried to hide my cringe at her fake face. "Or I can get you something stronger? Or something else altogether." She ran a blue nail over her lip.

"No, thank you." I dropped my glass on her tray. "I'm just leaving."

"Well, if you change your mind." I nodded and stepped back as my phone rang and I pulled it from my pocket. It was Alejandro.

"Eric," he said before I spoke, "where's the girl?"

"She's..." I twisted and saw she wasn't in the chair anymore. "She was just here."

"Castillo's coming up behind you." The line went dead.

"Eric."

I turned to face him. "Castillo. Where's the girl?"

"There's been a slight change in plans." *Fuck.* "You'll both spend the night here. Just until the money clears, then I'll give her to you to deliver."

"Why is that?"

"Because I don't trust you."

NINETEEN

IVY

"Aren't you hungry this morning?" Abigail peered down at my untouched plate. I'd been so focused on something I found on Hill last night I hadn't even noticed she'd put my plate in front of me.

"I'm sorry." I pushed my laptop away and stuck my pen through my hair to secure the strands that hung from my messy bun. "You were so kind to make this." I smiled at her. "I'm just so close to something. It's right there, but I just can't get it. I guess I lost track of what I was supposed to be doing."

"Anything I can help with?" She topped off my coffee to warm it up a little as I bit into the warm avocado, bacon, and egg sandwich. The flavors smothered my tongue, and I nearly moaned at how yummy it tasted.

"Oh, my, this is delicious." I licked my lips, and she smiled. "Is there any chance you've been trained in entrapment?" I asked as I fought to get the stringy cheese in my mouth—very unladylike.

"Maybe," she winked, "but I'll tell you what, Savannah is pretty amazing at solving things, and she could sure use a distraction about now."

"Good to know." I nodded, wiped my mouth, and checked the time. "My friend Michelle should call at any minute. Can I ask you something personal?"

"Is this about your uncle?" She gave me a knowing eye.

"It is. Is it okay if we cross that line?"

"Of course."

"How is it after all these years I've never met you or even heard about you?" I stumbled with how that sounded. "I'm sorry that came off as rude, I just mean—"

"No, it doesn't," she assured me. "I know what you mean."

"Good." It still felt rude.

"I think we're just private people and have a very unique relationship." She unfolded and refolded a cloth napkin. "I also think there's a part of us that just isn't very good at the whole dating thing. If we brought other people into it, it might just spook what we have. Plus, I'm fiercely independent and don't want anything to change that."

"I understand being careful in a relationship." I really did, but there was a part of me that was hurt that Reid had never shared about Abigail. She was a great person and someone I would have loved getting to know. But I wondered if the situation with Ben hadn't arisen, if I would have ever met her at all. I pushed aside my discomfort on the topic and tried to relate.

"I was engaged years ago, and though it ended better than most, I still think there's a part of me that worries about any serious relationship." I decided to share a little. "I love my job and work damn hard at being the best I can at it. I won't let a man step in the way of that."

"Any man worth his salt wouldn't." She nodded. "Maybe that's why Reid and I work so well together. We both know exactly where the other stands when it comes to our passion for our work."

"That's good." I forced a smile. The sting still hurt that one of the closest people in my life hadn't fully let me in. It sat heavy in my heart. "Well, I should get going."

"For the record, Ivy, September fourth, the color silver, nutmeg creamer, five stitches to your right knee due to a snow mobile accident at fifteen. He may have kept me quiet, but I know a lot about you. He loves you like a daughter and shared countless stories about you." I couldn't help but be warmed by that.

"For the record, he loves you, too." I winked and gave a little wave then grabbed a coffee and headed toward my office. I felt a little better about Reid and Abigail. They weren't going to change who they were, so it was up to me to get to know her better.

"Morning, Ivy." My uncle fixed his collar using his

reflection in a picture as he headed toward the kitchen. I couldn't help but smile as I knew who he was going to go see. "How are you this morning?"

"Good. I just had a nice chat with Abigail."

"Oh?" He avoided eye contact.

"Despite being a bit sulky about finding out the way I did, I'll admit she's quite lovely. She's a lot like you, actually, but cooks a lot better." I chuckled.

"I cook perfectly fine." He lifted an eyebrow at my teasing. "I'm just limited at what I make."

"Yes, under-cooked and cooked pasta are two completely different things."

"Someone thinks they're funny today, don't they?" He gave me a pointed look. "I'm glad that I get to share her with you now. Abby's as important to me as you are."

"I know. I can see that. So," I changed the topic, "besides the kitchen, where are you off to today?"

"I'm on the hunt for Keith. I have a few things I'd like to discuss with him. Any sign of him?"

"Nope. I only heard Mark a few moments ago."

"That's not surprising." He smiled. "If you see him." I leaned in when he kissed my cheek.

"I'll send him your way," I reassured him.

"Thank you, dear." He held up his mug, and I rolled my eyes as he straightened and trotted off toward the kitchen and Abigail.

"Hey, have you seen Beckett?" Moore stopped me near the stairs. We seriously needed trackers for everyone. The house was huge, but the property was ridiculous.

"No, not since last night." The guys had decided to spend the night out by the firepit in an effort to distract Keith. I'd slept in my own room and had gone up a little early to give them all space.

"He's with Frank." Mark toed off his boots and switched them out for clean ones. "Abby!" he yelled, and I squinted at the sheer volume his voice took on. "Where was June last night? She didn't come home."

"It's none of your concern," Abigail called back.

"It's always my concern because I need to be in the know on everything." He grinned at me, and I gave him a look and shook my head at him. Mark was something extra at times.

Moore laughed. "He's a little like a Navy SEAL with a sprinkle of glitter and dash of pizazz."

"He needs that on a shirt," I huffed.

"He really does. Okay," he looked around then leaned in, "do you have any idea why Beckett is in with Frank?"

"No, I don't. Sorry."

"Would you tell if you did?" He eyed me playfully.

"No, I wouldn't. Sorry." I smiled at him.

"All good." He shrugged then looked down at me. "You know Ty must really be into you."

"Why do you say that?"

"Because when we were out by the fire last night, he looked up at your window at least a dozen times." He tapped his head and nodded to let me know he was on to us.

"Oh, yeah?" I tilted my head with a grin.

"Mmhumm." He matched my grin. "It got me thinking, we should spend some time together."

"Will you share stories on Ty?"

"Only the bad ones."

I laughed. "Then count me in."

"Let's get through this storm first, and we'll set a date." He checked his watch. "I gotta go! See you around, Ivy." I was pleased with Moore. He seemed to fit in perfectly here, and I even heard he had two sessions with Reid at his own request. That won brownie points in my book. The best part was how happy Ty was to have him here, and that scored big time.

I glanced at my phone. I was on pins and needles as I waited for my update with Michelle. I stopped short and almost spilled my coffee when I realized Cole waited on my couch. That was unexpected.

"I know I'm not on the schedule, but I'd like to talk if you have a few minutes." His haunted eyes showed the depth of his pain.

"Of course." I closed the door behind me, slid my belongings on the desk, and unplugged my iPad from the charger. I took the seat across from him, and right on cue, Scoot scampered out from behind my fern and plopped himself on the armrest. Apparently, this session needed his expertise as well.

"Where would you like to start?" I urged him to begin.

"I'm worried about what the outcome of this mission will be." I loved that he wasted zero time jumping into his problem. It was another sign that he had worked with my uncle for years.

"Understandable." I took note of his hunched shoulders and what must be a bad headache by the way he pressed his fingers against his temples, seeking relief. I got up and walked around my desk to grab him a bottle of pain reliever from my top drawer.

"I know you guys don't like taking pills, but when you can't think straight because your head pains, it doesn't do any of you any good. These work best for me and won't hurt if you've taken anything else."

"Thanks." He took two without water then set the bottle on the table and stared at it.

When he didn't speak again, I stepped in. "You've been locked in this dance with the Cartel for years." I wanted to give him time before we got to the personal stuff. "There are so many of them. They out number you by the thousands, so why, with such impossible odds, do you want to continue the fight?" I felt I knew the answer, but I wanted to encourage him to talk.

That pulled his attention.

"The police can't stop all the crimes that are committed right on our own streets every day, but they have to try."

"True." I waited.

"If not us, who else will?"

I shrugged, wanting more, and waited.

"It's about giving hope and—"

"No, I don't want the obvious answers, Cole. I want yours."

"I don't know." He struggled to find the words. "I do it because it matters." It hit me then that this session wasn't just about his fear for Keith. It was really about his own inner turmoil.

"Or is it because if it wasn't for the Cartel, you wouldn't have met your wife?" His gaze shot back, not liking that answer.

"You mean like I owe them something?" His face twisted as he looked hard at me.

"No, I'm merely showing you a different angle to look at the situation. This is more than just a war you're fighting. The Cartel are connected to you emotionally. And now with them having Lexi, the power's back in their hands."

"It's infuriating!" he snapped.

"Every case is important, but this one is a whole different level. This involves family. It's perfectly normal to feel like a loaded gun waiting to go off."

"Yeah." He started to roll up and down on the balls of his feet as if ready to push off and run.

"Cole, you're not just Blackstone's leader. You're a son, husband, father, friend, to a huge empire doing great things for your country." I leaned forward and softened my voice. "So, give yourself a minute and just sit here. Give yourself a free pass to let the scary stuff in. Then you can untangle it all and get your head back on straight.

Because the only way this," I waved my hand around, "keeps going is if you're okay."

A stillness fell between us as he mulled over my words. I suspected Cole didn't take a lot of time for himself and often put others ahead of himself. Which was a wonderful quality as long as he looked after himself too. I might plant a seed in Savi's head to get Cole to go out once this next mission was over. Lord knew the man deserved a night out with his wife.

His chin quivered slightly, and he leaned forward and covered his face with his hands. I stayed quiet so he could think. Scoot, for the first time, tuned in to someone other than himself. He pounced off the armrest and jumped onto the couch where he pressed himself under Cole's arm and onto his lap, then used his head and reached up and rubbed his face into Cole's neck. His loud purr could be heard across the room.

It was one of the sweetest acts of kindness I'd seen. I was astounded at the kitty's reaction to Cole. Cats were definitely underrated for therapy. I tucked that knowledge away. I found it extraordinary, especially for Scoot. I watched the two of them and soon realized they had history.

I blinked back my own tears as I watched this special ops, Green Beret, beast of a man seek help from a six-pound, moody, senior feline.

"We don't do what-ifs." He cleared his throat as he kept his head down to nuzzle Scoot. "But I admit, I'm scared as shit that if things don't go right here it could destroy a part of the house."

I thought about my words. I knew from experience that every family who lost someone got shortsighted because of the pain. The brain put them in a haze that could make the world seem distant and cold. But I also knew the need to fight inside was what eventually got us through it.

"I can't promise you things won't change *if* that happens, but I can promise you something." I leaned forward and gently squeezed his forearm, so he'd hear me. "You will get through it. All of you will."

"Can I ask you something else?" Cole's gaze found mine.

"That's what I'm here for." I smiled, happy that his tension had eased a bit.

"Are you going to stay here, at Shadows? I know things have been dealt with in Washington, but..." He didn't finish his sentence.

I loved my life back in Washington, but there was something about Shadows that called me. It was almost spiritual, and that drew me in. I felt like I belonged here, even before I met Ty.

"I guess that depends on you." I smiled.

"I'd like you to stay on full time, Ivy. I think we all need you in our lives." I couldn't help but feel my chest tighten at that. I knew I was appreciated back home, and I loved working with Eagle Eye and the other teams, but

I'd never felt the way I did here. A sense of family and belonging I hadn't realized I'd needed.

"Then I'd like that very much."

Cole kissed the furball and placed him gently on the floor then stood with a heavy breath. "I think I might go for a run."

"May I suggest something else too?" He looked back. "Call your kids and ask them about their day. You'd be surprised how much they can center you." His eyes lightened, and I could see he liked what I said. "They know something is up, no matter how much you think you shield them. A normal phone call could do a world of good."

"That sounds like a good idea." He nodded. "I'm glad we did this."

"My door is always open." With a lighter step, he left just as my phone lit up.

"Hey, Michelle, you have perfect timing." I flopped down on the couch.

"Girl, you owe me one, because that Rivera guy is more into himself than any man I've ever dated."

"I promise when I'm in town next we'll have drinks. My treat."

"Deal," she huffed. "I'm just going to jump right in because I don't have much time."

"Okay."

"It took about four rum and Cokes and a *coincidental* run-in with some of my sorority sisters to get him to start talking. And when he did, he wasn't holding back. I'm glad you gave me the names of the players beforehand, because it was a lot easier to keep up."

"Good!"

"Okay, so, apparently, Hill's been trying desperately to figure out where Ty's working. He knows it's somewhere in North Dakota but also knows he's at Camp Green sometimes. I know this personally because he strangely just happened to show up while I was there, and when he found out you and I were friends, he was relentless."

"Wait," I sat up, "Hill showed up?"

"Yeah, odd, hey? I'm telling you, Ivy, he's watching that place. I figure the fact that Ty just dropped off the radar is screwing with him more than anything."

"That would make sense. He can't watch over Ty or me, so he's keeping tabs on everyone else involved. I know he still hangs out at the bar that Philip's wife owns. I'm sure it's just to keep an eye on her and as a threat for her to keep her mouth shut."

"Exactly," she agreed. "To me, this is Hill unraveling."

"What about Rivera?"

"This is where it got interesting. I think he's nervous that Hill might snap. It seems Rivera testified on Hill's behalf on a whole other death, someone named Jack Lever. Does that name ring a bell?"

"No," I scribbled down his name, "it doesn't."

"Well, Rivera was trying to get Hill to go home, and Hill dropped that name to Rivera. He froze like a rat in a trap. Like, we're talkin' a stone cold, frozen in time reaction. Then Hill said something like, 'Remember, man, you put your hand on that Bible, so if I go, you go.' I took that as Rivera went to bat for him and lied."

"Wow." I circled the name a few times. "Anything else?"

"I don't think it's just Hill keeping an eye on the place, because I saw someone else who seemed way too interested in our conversation. He watched us the entire night but hardly drank more than one beer. But there's more. You *so* owe me, girlfriend. Later, after I left, I stopped for gas, and that guy approached me."

"You were followed?" I felt sick. "Oh, my God, Michelle are you okay?"

"I do Krav Maga three times a week. I could kick Hill's ass if I wanted to." She chuckled, but I was still worried about just what I might have involved her in. "Anyway, he turned out to be that Dustin guy you mentioned."

"Oh," I let out the air I was holding, "thank God. At least he's more decent than the others."

"He's actually really sweet." I heard her sip her drink. "He warned me that Rivera was trouble, and he told me it was in my best interest to stay away from him. And, ready for this?" I nodded like she could see me. "He said they, Hill and Rivera, were both under investigation and that things were getting ugly fast."

"Wait," I stood and paced a bit, "did he tell you why they were being investigated?"

"Of course." She laughed. "Like I'd leave that unasked. Brown's parents have decided to press charges."

"What?" *How did we not know this?*

"When I got home, I did some digging. I've got a friend down at the police station, and he said that the Browns were advised to file a report based on some evidence that was found."

"I'm pretty sure there wasn't any."

"Yeah, he said there wasn't, but what that does is put the spotlight on Hill and Rivera. Now they need to watch their backs for the next while."

"This is crazy. I can't believe you got so much information. I more than owe you drinks!"

"Yeah, you do. Dinner, drinks, and chocolate." She laughed as I opened the door to find Ty about to knock. "If I hear anything else, I'll call you."

"Thanks." I spotted Cole in the entryway as Savannah came in from outside. Before she could get her coat off, he wrapped her in a hug and tucked her head under his chin.

"I love you," he sighed, and she nuzzled in without asking what was going on. It was like she just knew.

"Not as much as I love you."

I held my phone to my heart as I watched the love that surrounded the two of them. They really were meant for each other.

"Hey." Ty came into view then looked at me funny. He followed my line of sight then smiled at me. "Did you have a part in that?"

"No," I felt warmth spread through me, "that's all Cole."

"So, ah, do you have an appointment, or can we talk?"

"Not at the moment." I stepped back inside my office. "I was actually on my way to come find you."

We both spoke at the same time. "I've something to tell you."

"You go first." He leaned against my desk and watched me as I plugged my phone into the power cord.

"Does the name Jack Lever mean anything to you?"

"Yeah, Jack joined the same year I did, but he only made it two years before he was—" He stopped himself. "Seriously?"

"Looks that way. I did a little digging on Hill." I saw his eyebrows pinch. "Thanks to my friend Michelle. Seems Hill's spiraling. I think it's because he can't find you, so he's in a panic." I spent the next ten minutes filling him in, and he just stared at the floor and listened. "Ty, they're getting closer to taking this guy down."

"I wonder how many others there are." I watched his face twist as he fought an internal battle. I figured he must be trying to let it all sink in. I couldn't imagine finding out that one of your fellow soldiers was killing off your own just because they could. The fact that there wasn't law and order in Afghanistan didn't make it okay. It was so backward and so wrong. They were supposedly there fighting as a unit for peace, not to kill off the very people who had their backs.

"I don't know. Hard to say, but I've got Michelle keeping her ear to the ground. She's got a friend who's helped her at the police station, and I'm thinking we should go visit him and then maybe Dustin. A little pressure, and maybe he'll talk." I tucked my hair behind my ear and snagged my empty coffee cup from my desk. "Sloane said the courts make deals all the time, so maybe we can get Dustin off if he talks. I really think Hill's time is coming to an end, Ty. We're close to something. I can feel it."

"Ivy," he took my hand, and I let myself tune into his mood, "we need to talk."

"That's never a good start." I tried to make light of the nerves that had a sudden grip on my stomach.

"Frank has offered me an opportunity to go back to Afghanistan." He saw my expression change and quickly added, "Just for forty-eight hours, to collect any kind of proof I can get against Hill."

"What?" His words echoed in my head.

"And I'm going."

Wow. "But, Ty, since you left there, that town's become infested with Taliban." I pulled out of his hold and took a step back while my body absorbed the shock.

"It has," he said calmly, "but I've spent years fighting the Taliban. I know how they work. They don't scare me."

"But they do scare me," I blurted and tried to shake the panic from my head. "But we've got so much more information to go on now. I mean, what do you think you're going to find there that could possibly help?"

"I don't know," he tilted his head, "but I need to try."

"No, you don't." Everything in me wanted to run,

which was not at all like me. I was a stable, rational thinker, but for whatever reason, I felt like I was falling and had nothing to hold on to.

"I don't expect you to understand this." He reached for my arm, but I took another step back. I needed room. I couldn't think.

"You're right, I don't. How can I understand you going back there to put yourself in such a dangerous situation, to find what? What could possibly be there now after all this time? Come on, Ty, think about what you're doing!" I felt my body heat. "You could be killed! For what?"

"I just need to try."

"Try here, stay here and work through it." My eyes glossed over, and I fought to find my center, but it was nowhere to be found. "We have leads, things to follow here. Why go back there where you'll be, like, a piece of meat in the middle of a pile of wild dogs? They'd like nothing more than to kill you." I knew I sounded dramatic, but I couldn't help it.

"Ivy—"

"How could I have been so blind?" Everything hit me then, like cold water down the back of my spine. "Jesus, it was right there in my face, but I thought maybe, just maybe, you'd forgotten it was there."

"What?"

"Old habits die hard, right?" I swiped at my cheek.

"What on Earth are you talking about?"

"When I went looking for my shoes the other day, I

saw it in your closet." He still wasn't following. "Your rucksack. It was packed and just waiting there for you to grab it and go. Because over there is your home, not here." My voice cracked on the last word.

"No, it's not like that anymore."

"Isn't it?" I folded my arms around myself. I felt like I might explode with all the emotion inside me.

"Hey," he stepped toward me, and I held up a hand, "Ivy." He pulled his chin in and looked surprised at my outburst.

"I'm sorry. I just can't."

"Can't what"

"Everything is spinning, and I-I can't. I need air."

"Are you having a panic attack?" He tried to take my hand, but again I stepped back. "Let me help you."

"You can't." I put a hand to my chest to try to stop the pain. It was like a sudden fracture to my heart. "I need to think." I ran out of my office, down the hall, and out the front door. The frigid air crystalized in my lungs and made it hurt to breathe. I nearly knocked over Frank when he came out of nowhere.

"Ivy," he took in my spiraling state, "are you okay?"

"No. Thanks to you," I muttered and left him staring after me as I headed for the helicopter hanger. Not even at the worst of times with my father or when my engagement ended had I felt this disconnected and confused. I needed to be alone. I didn't dare let anyone see me like this.

I blew through the hanger door and slammed it

behind me. As I raced toward the chopper, I felt my emotions shatter. What the hell was happening to me? This wasn't me. I climbed into the belly of the beast and curled up on one of the seats, happy to be alone. I finally let go of the sob I'd held back until now. It hurt my throat as it ripped from my core. I had never felt such intense emotion in my life.

"Ivy?" Keith's soft voice found me, and I wanted to die of embarrassment. I'd thought everyone was down at the house. I quickly glanced back where he knelt in the body of the chopper with a wrench in his hand. He didn't say another word, he just stood and shrugged off his coat and placed the warm jacket over my legs. He put the tool he'd been using back in the toolbox. "Misery loves company. I'd like to be there for you. I'd like to feel useful if you ever need an ear." With that, he walked briskly toward the door, leaving me to sob for both of us.

TWENTY

ERIC

Lexi was emotionally strung out. She'd been teary for the past few hours. I didn't blame her, but she'd be out of this hell soon, although maybe she'd find herself in a whole new kind of hell after. I kept my back to her. I didn't need to see her pain. I stood with my shoulder cocked against the doorframe of the patio with my hands jammed deep in my pockets as I wondered if the money had cleared yet. Rain poured down and steadily pounded against the stone railing. It made a soothing white noise.

I'd underestimated Castillo. Though he was stupid at times, he had a sixth sense when things were off. The truth was Chili and I weren't loyal to Castillo at all. There were a lot of moving parts in my attempt to be on top, and I only hoped he wouldn't realize I'd drop him like a rock, given the opportunity to improve my status here.

I tugged at the dress shirt and unbuttoned a few buttons, wishing I had a change of clothes. Jeans, t-shirt, and anything but fancy loafers would be nice right about now. I didn't think to pack a bag. I should have known to expect the unexpected.

I suspected the room was bugged when I was told I'd be rooming with the girl. So, I took a page from his book and did the same. I made sure I was connected to the correct online folder, hit record on my phone, and placed it face down on the dresser. I had a habit of recording things anyway, and this was one time I wasn't taking any chances. I must have broken her spell by moving because she cleared her throat.

"You know what hurts the most?" Lexi sniffed and blew her nose, and I finally looked at her. "Somehow you made me trust you."

Her eyes pooled with tears, and I had to look away. For the first time since I joined the Cartel, I felt a niggle of something like guilt. Her words bothered me. I'd made sure I never promised her that she'd be all right, but earlier in the evening, I'd done just that. I'd broken my promise that she'd go back to my place with me, and it stung. Slowly, I turned and studied her. She was curled in a ball on the floor, knees to her chest, her hair wild around her face.

"I don't expect you to believe me, but I'm genuinely sorry for tonight's outcome." I spoke carefully. "This isn't normally the way we run our operation. I've never been this involved. I made a promise to you that I couldn't keep, and for that I am sorry, but it was out of my control."

Something I said made her look up and study me, but before I could ask her what it was about, she shook it off.

"Can I ask you something?" She used the back of her hand to wipe her cheeks.

"You can."

"Tell me how I'm supposed to feel right now." She squeezed her puffy eyes shut as she swallowed back more tears. "You house the girls, hear their cries for help. Yet you, what, feel nothing? Then when they get sold off, doesn't it rip at some part of you?"

I remembered the first two women I had at my house, how scared they were, and how they begged for mercy as I lifted them into Chili's car. It never bothered me because I stood behind my life choices. They were necessary.

"It's a dog-eat-dog world out there, lady. Everyone has a role to play in it. Maybe you can't understand why I do what I do, or why I think what I do," I pointed to my head, "but I am who I am, and I'm just trying to survive like everyone else."

"I wonder what goes on in your head. Do you care about anything but yourself?"

"I'd never let anyone inside my head. Believe me, you'd never want to." I glanced at my watch and saw it was nearly two in the morning. "As for those women, they shut down and go numb if they know what's good for them, and when they get to their destination, they adapt."

"Spoken like a true monster."

"Perhaps some might see it that way." I pushed off the doorframe, done with the conversation. "Take the bed." I pulled back the covers and tossed the other pillow on the floor.

"Like I could sleep," she growled, and I caught a glimpse of the fire inside her. It percolated just below the surface, and I was glad it hadn't been extinguished. She was quite a woman, and in a different world—I shut that thought down fast.

"I only said it to calm your nerves. Didn't want you to think anything was going to happen between us tonight." I wanted her to know I wasn't totally the monster she thought I was.

She curled in an even tighter ball on the floor, so I yanked the blanket off the bed and draped it over her small frame.

"Things will—" I wanted to reassure her but couldn't find the right words. Then a knock at the door had me up straight again. Lexi's gaze shot to mine, and I put a finger to my lips. I opened the door to one of Castillo's men.

"Get the girl. We're leaving."

"Now?" What was going on? "I thought we weren't leaving until the money came through. The banks aren't even open yet."

"Castillo's orders. We leave in ten." He marched off, and I quickly checked my phone. Nothing from Chili.

I slipped the phone in my pocket and helped Lexi to her feet. I tried to ignore the alarm in her eyes. She held the blanket tight around her as we moved downstairs to where Castillo waited with at least forty armed men.

Alejandro caught my eye as he stood in the middle of the group. He looked at me, just as confused as I was. He moved his eyes, and I could see Filippo was there as well.

"Can you explain what's going on?" I called to Castillo as I tried to curb my frustration on not knowing the plan.

"I could," Castillo moved in close to me and drilled holes in my head as he attempted to read my mind, "but I don't have to. I'm the one in charge here."

"Yes, of course you are," I reassured him, but some kind of chatter had been put in his head, and the trust I'd spent years building with him seemed to have fizzled out.

My stomach sank. I wanted to warn Chili, but now wasn't the time to take a risk.

"Time to leave," Castillo ordered and signaled for his men to head outside to the line of vehicles.

"What happened?" Alejandro muttered when Castillo stepped outside. "Did the money come in already?"

"I have no idea. Just keep your head up."

"Boss, I don't have a weapon. Filippo either. They took our weapons last night."

"You'll do okay. You know how to knock someone

out, and we're surrounded by weapons. You'll figure it out." I urged Lexi forward. She walked outside like a zombie.

The rain soaked our clothes within a matter of seconds, and I scowled at the tiny slipper- things she had on. They barely covered her feet, and the strap looked like it would break off with barely any force. Why couldn't Filippo have gotten her sneakers or something that had a good sole, at least? They looked like they'd dissolve within a few steps. With a huff, I scooped her up and carried her the rest of the way to the car. Her bloodshot eyes found mine for a moment, then she checked out again. *Good. Stay in that mind space.*

"Boss?" Alejandro nodded at Filippo, who was being pushed into a car at the front of the line. I just nodded at him to go with it. Then Alejandro was directed to get into the car in front of us. We were being separated. I tapped my head to remind him to stay alert. Then one of Castillo's men pushed his shoulder to hurry him up, and he disappeared behind the tinted windows of the vehicle. I didn't like what was happening any more than he did, but I was helpless to do anything about it.

I got Lexi inside and slipped in next to her, only to be hauled back out and told to get in the front. Lexi realized I was being separated from her, and she reached for me in a panic. She managed to get a grip on my sleeve. I yanked my arm away from her and hopped into the front then immediately turned to reassure her I was in the same car. Castillo's guy grinned at me and put his hand on her leg.

"No," I snagged his hand and snapped one of his fingers back, "no touching." The man yelped, but when he went to take a swing at me, I blocked his arm and snapped another finger. "You've got eight more. You want to keep fighting?"

"American asshole," he grunted as the car began to move forward, but he backed off and didn't so much as look at Lexi after that. She kept her eyes locked on her tightly folded hands in her lap as I sat back in my seat and tried to assess the situation.

We drove out the gates, and soon hit the streets of Rosarito. I watched people going about their daily lives. Not many people looked up as the convoy of black tinted-out vehicles wound through the town. I knew it was in their best interest not to notice these things. Though it was pouring, it hadn't stopped the locals from opening their shops or food trucks. It didn't matter what time of day or night, these people lived for the hustle. Wavy tin roofing sheets were tugged out to provide some sort of protection from the rain for the customers as they ate their food.

I watched all this as we drove and wondered what they'd think if they knew that a mere six feet from where they stood there were SUVs full of savage Cartel members and one American worth eight million US dollars.

The creep that nursed his injured fingers stared out the window while his buddy behind me made sure I felt the tip of his rifle as it poked my shoulder. When we went by a streetlamp, I glanced in the mirror and noted his rifle was balanced just on the top of his shoulder. I knew if I was to jam the barrel of the gun backward it would smoke the side of his neck. I moved my attention to the driver. He had his eyes glued to the road as the rain poured harder now. The wipers fought to clear the steady stream that cascaded down the glass.

We slowed for a light. Some areas were totally flooded now. A bunch of drunk kids began to cross in front of us. The girls had on what looked like napkins for dresses, and a few of the guys had their shirts off. The driver made a disgusting comment about the girls' breasts as the kids took their time and danced along in the rain without a care in the world.

The radio in the driver's ear suddenly crackled, and I saw him glance back at Lexi then over at me. He turned his head away when he responded, and the sound of the rain made it so I couldn't hear him.

"You do that again, and I'll rip your balls off and shove them down your throat," Lexi hissed. I whirled around to both guys, who looked at her, confused. She latched eyes with me and motioned with them to look at the rooftops ahead of us. I had been so busy with the guys in the car that I hadn't paid attention to what was going on outside. I didn't look right away. I didn't want to be obvious, but when I chanced it, I strained to see any kind of movement. I suddenly caught a glimpse of what she had. We were being followed, but by who? I slowly gave a nod, so she knew I saw them.

"Crazy bitch," the guy behind me snarled to Lexi.

"You have no idea," she shot back. Christ, she had balls at the worst of times.

Boom!

A bright fireball lit up our car. The heat seared my skin, and for a split second sucked the air from my lungs.

I blinked and immediately assessed myself then spun around and checked out Lexi. The man behind me shoved his rifle in my face. I smacked my hand against the barrel and forced it toward the driver as he pulled the trigger. Blood sprayed from the driver's neck all over the windshield. Pandemonium broke loose as Lexi went for the mangled fingers of the man next to her, and he screamed as she squeezed with all her might. I shoved the butt of the rifle that just shot the driver back into the shooter's face with all my might. I knew how hard it was to aim a rifle inside a car. It was a stupid choice of a weapon.

"Ahh!" the man yelled from the pain in his hand as he tried to grab Lexi by the hair. I drilled my fist into his face, and he went limp.

Shots from the car ahead of us rang out. I knew Alejandro was in that car. We had to move fast. The rain had finally let up, and I was able to get another look at the movement ahead of us.

"Stay low," I yelled at Lexi, who tried to reach the door handle. Her knee was pressed into the unconscious guy's face.

"We need to get out of here!" She got the door open and dropped onto the street. I opened the driver's side door and shoved the guy out and dove over him onto the ground.

Zip! Zip! Zip!

Lexi screamed, and I threw myself on top of her. Bullets pinged around us as I lifted my head to try to figure out where the shots were coming from. A bullet hit the windshield but only cracked the bulletproof glass. I caught a glimpse of the shooter. He was on the right side above us on the roof top. The left side seemed to be clear, at least for the moment. I angled myself behind the door and lifted my weight off Lexi.

"Can you see the shooter? He's up there." I pointed, and she nodded and turned to reach for something. She'd snagged a gun from the floor of the SUV, and I eyed her nervously for a moment.

"Here, you take it." She handed it to me. "See if you can take him out."

I took careful aim and fired, the guy's head disappeared, and I didn't wait to see if I'd hit him. I snagged her hand, and we raced between two buildings.

Shots were being fired everywhere, and we ran blindly away from the vehicles.

"Follow them!" I heard Castillo scream after us.

Lexi's feet slipped in her ridiculous slippers as she tried to run on the uneven pavement of the alleyway. Luckily, I had practice running in loafers.

"What's happening?" she cried as I tugged her along. "Who are these people?"

"No fucking clue, but they want us dead." I nearly

picked her up as I dove down another street. Bullets nicked the plaster on the corner just as we flew around it. Lexi yelped and gripped my arm as she tried to keep up. There was an open door up ahead, and I raced us toward it. I didn't care what was inside and used my body as a shield as we burst through it. An old man was hunched down against a chair. He looked terrified, and his hands shot up in the air, but when he saw Lexi, he relaxed a little. I held my finger to my lips, and he bobbed his head, his eyes wide.

"You alone?" I whispered.

"*Sí.*"

"Back exit?"

"*Sí.*" He pointed toward the kitchen.

"*Gracias.*" I quickly dropped some money on the table for his silence, grabbed Lexi's hand again, and we moved through the house.

"What about a car?" she huffed behind me.

"We won't get ten feet in a car right now." I pulled the curtain back and scanned the rooftops. "On foot is best."

Yells from the front of the house made us move faster.

Zip! Zip! Bullets found us, and loud screams could be heard.

Shit.

"This way." I used the protection of the eaves as we fought our way around bikes, trash, toys, motorbikes, whatever people had lying around their back yards.

"Jesus!" Lexi screamed as more bullets flew over her shoulder. "Do you have any idea where you're going?"

"Nope," I tossed a wash bucket out of our way, "but I know we can't be here."

"Call me crazy, but I think they want me dead." She craned her neck to look back. "I thought I was worth a few million," she huffed sarcastically.

"You're worth even more now since we left the house."

"But you won't get paid if I'm dead." She tried to make sense of it all as I decided where to go next.

"It's me they want dead, not you." I motioned for her to stay put as I kept low and scanned the area. Empty. "Come on." I jerked my head at her to join me, and we raced across the exposed street and disappeared into the darkness on the other side.

"You think they saw us?" she asked as she tried to catch her breath.

"I don't think so." I leaned forward to look around but was careful not to out our location.

"We can't stay here for long. The moment the sun comes up, we're dead."

"Wait, why do they want you dead?"

"Because I made sure Chili won the bid."

"Why?"

"Because."

"Eric," she pulled at my shoulder so I'd look down at her, but it was too dark to see her face, "I've had friends who have been where I am now, but there's never been a guy like you in any of their stories. Who are you? Tell me the truth. Are you working for the feds?"

I grimaced, knowing she couldn't see my expression. "No, Lexi, I'm not a fed."

"Okay," I felt her move, and she pressed her hand against my chest, "then give me one good reason I shouldn't make a run for it. What makes you any different than them?"

"Because I'm your—" I pushed her back behind me when I heard footsteps. Her frozen hand latched on to my arm and squeezed.

"Search everywhere," one of Castillo's soldiers hollered.

Three men raced by us as we kept low in the shadows. One stopped and shone a light around but soon ran after the others. Lexi's grip grew tighter on my arm.

"We can't stay here," I whispered. "There's a side street just a few feet from here on our right." I pulled her hand off my arm and yanked her out into the street again. I cursed Filippo as her feet slid around on the wet stones. She tucked her head and put an arm over the back of her neck as she held on to my hand. I could smell her panic as I pulled her tight against a building. "Stay close," I warned then began to move again. Slowly, we inched our way ahead. I kept my eye on the dark area I aimed for. I had no idea what faced us there, but if we didn't keep moving, we were dead anyway.

I could see some light in the sky, and I knew we were going to run out of time. I glanced down the empty street then scanned the rooftops again. I spotted a food cart that had been parked for the night. I tapped Lexi and pointed toward it, and she nodded back. We tucked ourselves behind it just as bullets flew again. I couldn't see from where. We ran blindly then, as fast as we could. My heart beat in my ears and my mind constantly spun to think where to go next. Who the hell was after us? Castillo had his money. I could only figure that whoever else had lost the bid for her had decided to take her anyway. It could be any one of the players. My mind whirled but stopped instantly as more shots hit around us. I was suddenly jerked back as Lexi's hand flexed and pulled out of mine as she stopped.

"Eric?" Lexi sounded puzzled with her hands pressed to her stomach. I saw a dark stain spread across her top. She peeled her hands away and looked down at them.

"Lexi. Damn it!" I raced to her and swung her off her feet. "Who shot you?" I tried to think straight but couldn't pull myself together. I layed her down on the ground and pulled up her top to get a better look. She groaned as I rolled her over and felt around. The bullet was still inside.

Holy shit, this isn't happening.

"Who the hell shot you?" I pulled off my suit jacket and pressed it to her stomach as I tried to find a possible reason they'd shoot her.

"Does it matter?" Tears leaked down her cheeks. "It was only a matter of time, anyway."

"It's just a flesh wound," I lied. "You're not getting off that easy." I pulled out my phone and realized I'd left it on record. I swiped to open it, not caring at this point. The screen was smudged with her blood, and I tried to wipe it clean.

"Hey," she pulled my phone down so I'd look at her, "do something for me, please." Her color was fading fast, and I knew I had little time to make something happen. "Tell Keith I want him to find love." She paused and swallowed. "He deserves to be loved the right way. Our babies need a mother." She went quiet, and my tears broke loose. I squeezed my eyes shut and fought against the lies that guarded me from pain and death.

"Lexi," I brushed her hair back from her pale face as her eyes tried to focus on mine, "I need to tell you something." I leaned over and told her the truth.

Her voice was just a whisper as she answered, then the light faded from her beautiful eyes and I hugged her to me as pain filled my soul and I knew the world wanted to punish me for my sins.

Everything inside me snapped, an undoing of all I'd held together over the past several years. I couldn't do it anymore. I'd failed. I'd failed them all.

"No!" Fury took over and I shook her shoulders then pressed my ear to her chest. "Dammit, Lexi, breathe!" I started to do CPR, but with every push to her lifeless heart, more blood pooled from her stomach, making my jacket look sleek. "This can't be happening," I hissed. "How did this happen?"

More shots and voices from somewhere close by brought me back to reality, and I knew they would soon be here. I rocked back on my heels with my chest in a vise, and my heart fought for space. I knew the time had come. I had no choice left now because my death was almost upon me.

I used a code to access a different network on my phone and held it to my ear. When the call connected, I felt as if my mind had already left my body.

"Eagle Eye One … this is Fox One." A sound behind me made me jump up and whirl around. Alejandro's face was frozen in shock. He shook his head in disbelief, knowing the call signs, then turned and raced away.

Shit.

"Line is secure. Go ahead, Paul."

The End

ACKNOWLEDGMENTS

To my mother, my best friend.

To Elizabeth Clark and Jamie Johnson. Thank you for, well…you know what you did.

To my husband, for your "input" with some of these scenes.
To my betas and proofers, Kim Kelchner, Kasey Griffin, Veronica Nelson, Maggie Savarese, Rachel Womack, Jamie Johnson, and Elizabeth Clark.

My editor Lori for always making time to edit my books. To my husband Nathan, and my two girls, Tanyia Pfennighausen and Allison Cheshire, for the "2017 Great Debate" on how cookies should be packed.

I stand with Mark.

My street team, ARC team, my reader group, and my fact-finding group, thanks for providing me a safe place to go to hang out, ask questions, and laugh!

And of course, to my readers. I wouldn't be here if it wasn't for all of you.

Thank you.

TANGO
WHAT'S TO COME

ERIC

"Paul?" Frank repeated, and I squeezed my eyes shut and cursed. Everything was heading south so quickly I could barely keep up. "What's happening?"

"The subject…" the words were like a ball of acid in my throat that slowly dripped down into my chest and burned, "the subject is down—" A cry ripped through me. "Jesus, Frank," my voice quivered, "Lexi's dead."

Silence.

Frank made a sound then, and I knew it had hit him, then he cleared his throat and was back to business.

"Have you been compromised?" His normal voice commanded and helped ground me.

"Yes."

"Pull the pin, take nothing. Get out. You know where to go. And, Paul…"

"Yeah?"

"No man left behind. You'll be met. You do whatever's necessary to get both of you out."

"Roger that." The line went dead.

I glanced at my phone for a moment then shoved it back into my pocket as I desperately tried to clear my head. I needed a way out. I needed to blend in with the locals, and that wouldn't be easy with Lexi. I knew there would be police everywhere after the convoy was attacked.

I bent down and scooped Lexi's limp body into my arms and cradled her close to my chest. I raced down the street in the opposite direction from the one Alejandro had taken. Once I got to the end of the alleyway, I risked a quick look around the corner but quickly whirled back around, slamming my back to the wall. Two police cars crawled by with their lights flashing.

"Stay off the streets," one yelled in broken English over a speaker. "Go inside. It is not safe for you."

I inched forward, shifting Lexi in my arms, and saw a crowd of young people that looked like tourists, standing in front of a nightclub trying to catch a peek at what was going on. Clearly, the sound of bullets in the distance didn't get through their drunken revelry. Blood from Lexi's stomach wound made my hands slippery, and I fought to hold her against me. This wasn't going to work. If one person saw the blood, they'd scream. I sat her against a wall behind a trash bin and peeled off my bloody dress shirt, then whisked out into the busy street. A vendor was preparing to close, and I quickly caught the door as he went to shut it.

"Please," I said in Spanish, "I need a jacket, or a sweater, a shirt, just something. My friend got sick all over me and I need something clean." When the man shook his head, I fished out a bill. "This for anything you got." He turned to a shelf and tugged out a t-shirt and a ratty old blanket. He grabbed the bill and tossed me the stuff then yelled at me to get out. I was happy to oblige.

Keeping my head low as I pulled the shirt over my head, I hurried back to where I'd left Lexi and gently pulled her arms through the sleeves of my suit jacket and fumbled my way through the buttons. I pushed the ratty blanket inside the jacket to try to camouflage the blood.

"I'm so sorry, Lexi." I tucked her hair behind her ear and fought the nausea that wanted to come up. Suddenly, Keith's face flashed in front of me, and I heaved over to the side and purged what I had in my stomach. Mostly liquor. More sirens could be heard, and I knew I needed to move. The city wasn't that big.

Chatter from the crowd in the street made me gather up Lexi again. The group of partiers were loud and obviously had had a lot to drink, which would serve my purpose well. Some had their phones out, recording a patrol car that was stopped a few blocks down, others carried tequila or beer bottles as they milled about. The officers were placing barricades to block off a street. Fuck me, the entire city was going to be locked down. If I didn't get out of here soon, I'd be stuck.

I quickly darted across the pavement and joined the tequila-soaked crowd. Lexi's arm dangled, and I quickly tucked it up with a comment to a couple girls about my drunk woman.

"Any idea what's happening?" I stepped closer as I used their bodies to hide me from the police. I had to concentrate hard to fit in and not let my mind go dark.

"No," one girl looked at me, clearly half in the bag, "but there's police everywhere."

"Do you guys know where the blue hotel is?" I played dumb. "My girl's had way too much to drink."

"No, sorry, I don't." One girl quickly shut me down, but the other pulled out her phone.

"Do you remember the name of it? I could look it up for you."

"I feel like an ass, but no, I don't." I tried to look like a dumb tourist and shrugged with a sloppy smile. I hoped I looked like I'd had a few too many myself.

"Shit, bro, was that gunshots?" One tuned in, and I hoped to hell they didn't start to freak out or run.

Another police car came by and slowed as they went by us. I tilted Lexi's body like I was placing her down on her feet when one guy glared at me.

"Dude, she's too wasted to walk. Just carry her ass home." Then the guy turned and wrapped an arm around his girl's shoulders.

"That's what he's trying to do."

The girl shoved the guy's arm away.

I scanned the street ahead, and the guy must have caught my uneasiness.

"Take your problems somewhere else, dude." I didn't

like the look he gave me, and I backed off. His other friends seemed to be picking up on the uneasy vibe. Great, just what I needed right now, a scene. I swallowed hard as I felt Lexi's blood soaking into my t-shirt. I didn't dare look down and give them a reason to follow my gaze.

"I mean no harm. I'll ask a local for help." I stepped back. Just then, I spotted Filippo as he raced around a corner and more police lights lit up the building in front of us. They were closing in. It was now or never.

"Let's bolt. This shit is getting nuts," one guy called to his friends, and they all started to walk away.

Normally, I was more resourceful, but given that my head was stuck in a loop, and my brother's dead wife was in my arms, I found it impossible to get a clear thought.

I whirled around and ducked under an awning to get out of sight.

"Eric." I couldn't miss that smooth, whiskey, billionaire voice. "My friend, you look like you could use a hand." Damn, I wondered how long he'd been watching. "You look like shit," he added. Grim's eyes darted to Lexi in my arms then back up to me. The cross just below the corner of his eye twitched. It was obvious he knew shit was going down.

Shit…

J.L. Drake, born and raised in Nova Scotia, Canada, later moving to Southern California. Though she loves the weather in Cali, she would sell her left kidney for a good rainstorm. Jodi's love of the seasons back home in Canada definitely appear in her books.

When she's not writing, you can often find her sitting somewhere along the coast of Huntington Beach, reading, or at home curled up on a couch with her two children and husband, binge watching a good movie.

AUTHORJLDRAKE.COM

FOLLOW ME ON SOCIAL MEDIA

facebook.com/JLDrakeauthor

x.com/jodildrake_j

instagram.com/j.l.drake

tiktok.com/@authorjldrake

bookbub.com/profile/j-l-drake

BROKEN TRILOGY

Broken

Shattered

Mended

BLACKSTONE SERIES

Honor

Escape

Freedom

Courage

DEVIL'S REACH TRILOGY

Trigger

Demons

Unleashed

QUIET MAFIA SERIES

Quiet Wealth

Quiet Secrets

Quiet Power

Quiet Empire

DARK WATER SERIES

Shadows

Whiskey

Alpha

Tango

HAVOC OF SINS

Grim

Havoc

Sins

DARKNESS SERIES

Darkness Lurks

Darkness Follows

Darkness Falls

STANDALONE BOOKS

Behind My Words

Christmas At The Cabin

Omerta

For the suggested reading order, please scan the QR code: